THE WORLD WITHIN

Adriana Polito

ISBN-13: 9781724070418

DEDICATION

I dedicate this to book to my family,
and my fiancé, Tom.
Thank you for your unconditional love.
Thank you for supporting me and believing in this
crazy dreamer.
I promise to always watch out for you, in all
dimensions, for all time.
Love you all so much.

PREFACE

The story you are about to read is inspired by actual events. Hypnagogia is a real night-time phenomenon.

> ***HYPNAGOGIA, also referred to as "hypnagogic hallucinations", is the experience of the transitional state from wakefulness to sleep: the hypnagogic state of consciousness, during the onset of sleep.***
> *Definition from Wikipedia*

Our main character's journey starts with such an experience, in Rome, at the age of twenty-two. The author of this book had this very same experience whilst on a work trip, in Rome, at the age of twenty-two.

This single event was so powerful and transformative, it kicked-started an extraordinary series of night-time visions in the years to follow. Unable to logically explain these twilight apparitions, the author felt compelled to write this book in an attempt to express it in another form.

The World Within is a culmination of some actual life events and real dreams that followed that first hypnagogic experience, mixed with a heavy dose of fiction, science-fiction and pure imagination.

We hope you enjoy the ride. Happy travelling.

1

"Direct your eye sight inward, and you'll find
A thousand regions in your mind
Yet undiscovered. Travel them, and be
Expert in home-cosmography." -

Henry David Thoreau of Earth, Poet

UNKNOWN NARRATOR
23rd October 2002, evening, Rome, Italy, Earth
After about eight minutes, Aurora began to descend
into what you would call 'hypnagogia'; a trance-
like state in which the subject is neither fully
conscious nor fully unconscious, but somewhere in
the middle. Most people pass through this stage
with relative ease. It is quick and they don't even
notice it. It's a state that can be induced by
meditation or drugs. Aurora was not meditating.
She wasn't on drugs. She didn't know it yet, but in
the ninth minute, something would happen to
Aurora that would change her life. Something so

terrifying that it would make her question everything she ever thought she knew. Something that would isolate her from those she loved but ultimately unite her with something extraordinary. In the ninth minute, Aurora turned so that she could move from the foetal position into the more comfortable position of lying on her back. During this movement, her eyes opened, involuntarily. This is a common reflex movement connected with drifting into sleep. Humans believe that it's an evolutionary trait passed down through their ancestors so that they can keep a final eye on any potential predators that may be trying to sneak up on the apparently sleepy subject.

In this split second where the eyes open to make this final turn before falling into a fully unconscious sleep state, ninety-four per cent of the Earth's population sees nothing but dark. You may think that it's an entirely useless left-over gesture, like the appendix, but six per cent of your world's population would describe it as something else. They feel an electrical tug. They do see something. And that night, Aurora saw my nephew.

NARRATOR

Aurora Black never really thought about time. She didn't judge its effects or have much to say about it. She was just in a hurry to do things. Always in a hurry. Her parents never understood it; this desperate need to do everything and do it now, but they knew she was in a hurry to do *it*, whatever *it* was. They weren't surprised when she told them she was leaving their home town of Barnsley to move to London at age of twenty-two. They weren't surprised that she'd gained employment at The British Museum in London's Marylebone district just eight weeks after graduating from Sheffield University with a distinction in Archaeology and History. And they weren't surprised that she was now on her way to Rome, Italy, to represent the Museum's International Education Department on a work trip, only four weeks into the job. Aurora was in a hurry, of that they were sure. Just what she was racing against, well, of that they weren't as sure. They believed their daughter would figure that out for herself one day, all in good time.

AURORA
23rd October 2002, evening, Rome, Italy

This hotel room's nice. Yes, I could get used to this. Faux-gold tainted furniture, thick, heavy blood-red drapes, plush bed, marble floors *and* a set of French windows? Very fancy. Am I'm here! In Rome. The view's nothing to write home about, let's see...some rear-facing hotel room windows and a car park. Pretty standard. But hey, it's not like I'm going to be spending much time in here anyway.

Mmm, what to do first...I'll run a bath.

Ah, even the water looks luscious as it leaves the, what do the Italians call them again, 'rubinetti'? Yes, I think that's right. The Romans and their exquisite plumbing.

Still can't believe I'm here, representing the Museum. Hope I do a good job tomorrow. What's this blue liquid? Looks like bubble bath. I'll put some in and hope for the best.

Right, thinking cap on, what's first on the agenda for tomorrow? Where did I put those notes...ah, here they are.

8am: Get taxi to the National Museum of Rome, meet with Pasquale.

Objective: Try to secure at least eight more Italian visits for the programme.

10am: Get taxi to the Ministry of Education, meet with Secretary of State's private secretary.

Objective: Discuss benefits of the Art in Practice Programme, add lashings of charm. Did I actually write that? What a creep. In other words, remind yourself to big it up Aurora, strum up interest for future collaboration.

12 noon: Lunch with Pasquale and team.

2pm: Visit participating schools in the Rome district.

4pm: Meet some British teachers over on an art exchange visit.

6pm: Write report on outcomes.

Ok, day one should be relatively straight-forward.

Wish Johan was here. Sweet, gorgeous Johan. Can't believe it's our two week anniversary and I'm here in beautiful Roma without him. Might buy him a gift. Wait, don't want to seem too attached already. I could get him a pleasant, non-committal gift, like a jumper.

A jumper? Where did that come from? Doesn't that scream 'I'm dressing you now'? No, Aurora, can't buy him a jumper. Am I in love? Love is messing with my head, making me think about shopping for a jumper for a guy I've only just met.

Right, bath's ready. Let's stick a toe in....

...Aah. That, is, lovely.

NARRATOR

After her bath, Aurora dried herself down with a large, soft, marshmallow coloured bath towel. It felt as light as a feather duster on her tanned olive skin. She looked in the mirror. Her long dark brown hair was almost to her hips. She was pleased to see its auburn tints bounce from the reflection of light coming from the yellow marbled antique lamp in the corner of the room. Her meme, or grand-mére Lilian, had the same auburn slick in her hair. Aurora had always found it rather beautiful, as did her Grandpa Gethin.

Aurora had an athletic build, taken from her father's side. The Blacks from South Yorkshire came from a long line of coal miners. Grandpa Tom was the last of that generation to work the mines. Aurora's dad, Victor, got into accounting, but he had the same strong arms, legs and robust stature as all the Blacks before him.

Aurora's deep, deep brown eyes came from her mother's side. The Le Blancs had very dark eyes, almost pitch black. For eyes so black, it was amazing how much kindness radiated from those pooled abysses. Aurora's uncle Josh, her dad's younger brother, used to call her 'little bat' because of how dark her eyes were. When Aurora stayed over at uncle Josh and aunt Sarah's, her cousins Fred and Clare would request navigational help to get down the stairs and into the kitchen for midnight snacks. Aurora's night vision was so good, and she was so adept in the dark, that they called her 'Night Ninja'. Uncle Josh swore she had some kind of in-built sonar in her cranium.

23rd October 2002, evening, Rome, Italy

As Aurora slips into her Muse t-shirt, old netball shorts and Bettoja Hotel slippers, she feels a bead of sweat roll down her temple. The dense Roman humidity hugs her body as she walks towards the bathroom. She gives her face a brisk refreshing splash. Her naturally rosy cheeks react, bursting yet more fresh colour into her face. She brushes her teeth and licks her plump nectarine-coloured lips together to remove the last traces of chalky toothpaste. Aurora sighs, desperately craving one of Johan's tender kisses goodnight.

Preparing for bed, thoughts of Johan, work objectives and Johan's gift run through Aurora's head like a series of bullets firing from a gun. Eventually, at one a.m., tired, content and excited, she put down her notes, tucked herself in under the crisp cotton sheets and lay her head on the cloud-like pillow. Secure that her rehearsal for the next day's schedule was as thorough as it could be, Aurora turned off the light.

AURORA

It's not going to sleep in a different environment that's strange. I'm so tired right now, I could be anywhere. It's waking up somewhere new that's always confused me, those few moments of not knowing where you are. Your brain scanning every place its ever known in an attempt to match it with your current surroundings. Like a giant cerebral game of Snap. Yes, so sleepy, I'm sure I'll drop off really quickly tonight. Maybe I'll just think of Johan a little more before nodding off. Think about how he kisses my forehead when he thinks I'm asleep, or the way he smiles at me when I first wake up. Mmm. Actually, these thoughts are probably going to keep me awake and I need to be up in six hours. Right, come on Aurora. Settle down, *drop off, drop off, drop off.*

AURORA
What in hell was *that*?! Light on, light on, where's that light?!

UNKNOWN NARRATOR
Aurora's heart rate went through the roof. She went from a very relaxed state, to 160 beats per minute, not uncommon in night terror sufferers, most of whom are children. But this was no night terror. Nor was it sleep paralysis or any other kind of affiliated sleep disorder. Now I know what you're thinking. Aurora saw a ghost. I'm a ghost and my nephew is a ghost. Only we're not ghosts. We're real. We're just in a different dimension.

Aurora isn't the first person to see a third phase 'shadow person', as you call them. But we're always seen in the third phase for a reason. Humans have never been able to see us, shadow people, straight away. That was before the early hours of 24th of October 2002 Earth time, when Aurora Black became the first human on Earth to see a third phase shadow person without Feelers, Interceptors or any kind of testing. Aurora saw my nephew, and she wasn't the only one shaken up about it.

AURORA

What was that?! Calm down Aurora. It was just a dream, you were dreaming. *But I wasn't dreaming.* I actually saw a boy, with blonde golden curls. He was young, around five or six. He had a beautiful face, angelic almost, like a cherub. He flew right up to my face and smiled at me. He stared at me, in the dark, and when he looked into my eyes I saw.....what *am* I talking about? Aurora, you cannot lose your sanity at the age of twenty-two. Please, for God's sake, hold it together. You are tired. You are excitable. It's your first big trip overseas with work and your over-active imagination is *definitely* over acting. You're caught up in the heady romance of Rome, your first love, an exciting work venture. The ornate decor of your lovely room on Via Cavour is clouding your sleeping thoughts. So why is my heart still pounding? I've never experienced a night terror like that before. *Why did it feel so real?* I could see his image superimposed over the faint surroundings of this room. He appeared like an etched painting, the dark around my bed his canvass. What just happened to me?

***

"There has to be a revolution,
but it has to be a revolution of consciousness." –
Anon

24th October, dawnlight, Venezelu

Had the subject had an Interceptor Device, it really wouldn't have taken long for MEW5's scientists to acknowledge the event. News like that would have travelled really fast across the agency. At the helm that night was Professor Sykes, a tall, gingerly set type with clear blue eyes and reddish-blonde hair which flew in every direction. His black-rimmed round glasses sat with ease on his sturdy nose, under which sat a perfectly groomed short strawberry moustache. His face was long, wise and kind. With the agency for twenty years and counting, this smart and committed man was one of those who joined the Revolution in earnest. He was responsible for the remodelling of Feelers, making them less invasive to subjects' brains. He was assisted on the Feelers project by a relatively new recruit to MEW5, a Professor Zareb Fender who had previously worked in the Data Analysis department.

Zareb was robust, athletic and his greeny-grey eyes looked out from under a thick mop of bluey-black hair. His black skin had a beautiful crystal glow to it, only visible in the suruplight. In direct light it looked like fragmented stardust in a gorgeous night sky. He could have been a Zorb player in a past life, had all the skill to do it. Zareb always wore Revolution coloured tank tops, safe to wear in Ipa, not so safe anywhere else, and for that reason, they were reversible tank tops, with neutral colours on the inside, just in case he had to do a quick change. Zareb was previously responsible for

analysing footage that came back from phase two:
Inter-Dimensional Object Recognition in the
Sleeping Subject, or I.D.O.R.S.S. His progress in
this department caught Professor Sykes' attention,
and soon the two were busy working in the tower,
where all of the agency's new technologies are
developed. Professor Sykes received a call at
around dawnlight, asking him to meet the caller at
Jesomine's Taverna in an hour. Had it been anyone
other than his dear friend Zareb Fender, he never
would have left the tower that night and ventured
into Militia City. Sensing the panic in Zareb's
voice, the Professor picked up his coat and fled
without haste.

***

2nd, AS YET, UNKNOWN NARRATOR

Welcome. Yes, I'm talking to you. Thank you for
joining us. We have some matters to discuss. I'm
going to, as you Earthlings put it, cut to the chase.

Every living being, on all planets, in all
Universes, are restricted by their physical form –
but there is a way in which all living beings, on all
planets, in all Universes, *can* travel. Not all of them
know that they're doing this, which can make it
dangerous and humorous in equal proportion.

THE ENLIGHTENING

Universal enlightenment, as we sometimes call it,
actually gives you, in time, the ability to understand
how your own Universe works. It's the idea that
something very far away can give you answers to

something that's right in front of you, something *within* you even. It's the idea that this same thing that is so far away, has actually been accessible to you since the beginning of time itself. Understand that, and you have the key to understanding your own shape, size and movements. You'll also be able to comprehend what you can't see in your own Universe, as well as the secrets of how to send messages between your own galaxies. But the starting point, ironically, is always from within - a place not many humans dare venture, too distracted by the white noise of conscious, waking life.

HOW THE UNIVERSES INTERACT

According to some Earth scientists, your Universe is expanding, only it isn't expanding at all.

I need you to imagine an Earth soccer ball. Now imagine that all of the black hexagons on that soccer ball are Universes and that the white ones are just space. Now imagine these black hexagons moving around the surface of the ball in different ways. Sometimes they bump into other black hexagons, interacting with them.

When this happens, magic occurs. Only it's not real magic. It's what we call a pathway or a gateway. A dialling tone. An electrical short cut. In other words: inter-dimensional communication. The window doesn't stay open for long and it takes consciousness to undertake a conversation.

For now, imagine if you will, a neighbouring Universe that is passing *over* yours. We call that neighbour Universe 5 (that's *my* Universe). At present, the 'edge' of Universe 5 has come into contact with an 'edge' of your Universe, which we call Universe 6.

As time passes, as the glide continues, the surface area between our two Universes will expand. More gliding means more contact. More contact means more exposure to the other. More exposure means more patches of galaxy, on both sides, drawn towards each other in a gravitational pull. These are the boundary zones. This is where we interact. This is where the magic happens.

BUROV, Universe 6

Burov was so close to being the first planet in Universe 6, your Universe, to make contact with us. Unfortunately, Burovian fear, greed, pride and ignorance overtook its pioneering spirit. Certain Burovians never learnt from their mistakes. Eventually, they destroyed each other and their own planet.

Before that though, there was a letter. A letter from Dr. Jenny Rushton of Burov to her associate, Dr. Ken Masters.

The letter is about plate tectonics on Burov, which worked in a very similar fashion to the ones on Earth.

It's probably the best human analogy I can give to help understand:

1) how your Universe moves;

2) how it's moving right now, and;

3) why its current positioning is so important to us making contact.

It may not make much sense unless you're particularly into electromagnetism, and that's ok.

Bear with it, trust that your brain will understand the majority. And if you don't, that's ok too.

I won't read you the letter this time, Aurora. I think that's enough for today.

The others have said it's a total waste of time doing any of this, but I know you can hear me.

***

Aurora Black slept very little during the early hours of October 24nd 2002. In fact, she slept with the light on for most of the night. The next day, she got up, as usual, went down for breakfast and set off into her day. It was such a busy day, that the previous night's events had hardly entered her mind, even if she did feel a little different inside. Tired, elated and near exhaustion, she retired to her hotel room for the second night.

AURORA BLACK
24th October 2002, evening, Rome, Italy

What a day. I think it went pretty well, all things considered. Right, check list for tomorrow and then I really must get some sleep tonight. *I wonder if I'll see that boy again.* Ok, so 8am school visit to follow up on EU arts project funding, 10am meeting with Pasquale and a local archaeologist, 12 noon free time to catch up on reading and paperwork....perhaps I'll have lunch somewhere near the Spanish Steps...3pm visit Vatican and gather ideas on religious artefacts for educational seminar on Religious Symbolism. 7pm, get taxi to airport, 10.30pm home, to my own bed. Phone

Johan, arrange to meet as soon as possible and give him jumper. *I wonder if I'll see that boy again tonight.* Right Aurora, time to sleep, come on, drift off, drift off, drift off.....

***

Aurora Black had no visitors that night, and she slept a deep and peaceful sleep right through until dawn. And she certainly wouldn't have had another visit from Zareb Fender's nephew Marcux, for Marcux, at that very moment, was in a police cell awaiting questioning.

***

24th October, dawnlight, Venezelu

It was early, extremely early as Professor Sykes arrived outside Jesomine's Taverna in Ipa's Grassmarket district. As he stepped out his hover-carriage, he could see the morning dew glistening off the jade cobbled street beneath his feet. There was a low fog and the Taverna looked closed. Zareb had told him to come in through the side entrance and to be discreet. Of course he was going to be discreet, thought the Professor. He wasn't about to fly his way across town in the middle of the night to frequent a Taverna in the heart of Militia City without discretion. No MEW5 or CERN official in their right mind would be caught dead here at this early hour. Whatever it was Zareb had to tell Professor Sykes, he knew that it must be important, and possibly something that Professor Sykes may regret having knowledge of.

The side entrance was open and behind the door lay a spiral tunnel leading down into the cellar basement. *How sure can I be that it was Zareb I spoke to?*, thought the Professor. *Of course it was him, don't be foolish.* As he made his way down the tunnel, light from a chiandle started to give warmth to the cold, dark cellar walls. As he reached the bottom, Professor Sykes saw a very pale looking Marcux Grentil sitting at a table, shaded by the shadow of his uncle Zareb who was standing pensively by the fireplace.

"Zareb? What's going on?"

"Marcux found her."

"Found who?"

"The anomaly."

2

AURORA BLACK

I've been here before. The sandy beach looks
familiar. The medieval city behind me looks
familiar. Perhaps it's Sicily. Perhaps I'm dreaming
of Sicily. This feeling is intense. What is this
feeling? *Euphoria.* It's so intense it's burning my
insides. What happens now, I know this, I've been
here before. But there's something different. I find
myself on a roof top terrace, at a party taking place
at sunset. There's a man in front of me, he looks
happy and knowing. He has blonde hair and is
drinking a strange blue drink. He offers me some, I
drink it. I can hear music, chimes and panpipes.
"Wasn't I just on the beach a second ago?" I ask the
man. "You got the bus up here, don't you
remember?" And suddenly my mind is taking me to
a bus, I'm on the bus. This is weird. The bus is
packed full of people, all staring at me. They look
different, their eyes are a crystal green, their skin is

pale and shiny. I definitely know I'm dreaming now. That man was my subconscious, tricking me into filling in the gaps, making me doubt myself. These people, they don't look pleased to see me. I get off the bus. The town is on a slope, out to sea. At the top of the hill is a chapel. I must go to it. I climb the hill and on the way I stop off at a grocery shop. I go inside. I try to read the labels on the fruit and vegetables, but it all looks strange. In an attempt to fit in, and look inconspicuous, I approach the counter. "I'll have a quart of he-re-nagas, please." I say as I try to read the sign for the purple fruit. "Quart of herenagas, coming up." says the man. With him is another elderly man, sitting in his chair reading a paper. He slowly raises his head above his newspaper, looks over to his grocer friend and raises his eyebrows as high as the arches on his face will allow, pauses, then slowly nestles back into his paper.

"Where you headed?" asks the grocer.

"To the top of the hill." I reply.

"Why you going up there?" he asks.

"I'm not sure, but I feel like something's coming, something bad."

The elderly friend puts down his paper.

"Keep to the main road Miss," says the grocer, "stay away from the alleyways."

I grab the fruit which is in a brown paper bag. The grocer looks at me in utter astonishment.

"How can you…do that?"

"Renald," interrupts the other older gentleman, "no questions." Renald nods and steps away from me, looking scared now. I smile at both men and head out onto the main road. Almost instantly, I feel like someone is following me. I pick up pace, but the hill is steep and I'm running out of breath. Despite his warning, I take an alleyway to level out a second. I put down the bag of herenagas and hunch over to catch my breath.

"Well, well, well, what do we have here?" I turn to my right and see a man and woman walking up towards me from the depth of the alleyway. I turn to go back to the main road, but the mouth of the alleyway is blocked off by another two men.

"Who are you? What do you want?" I'm scared, I'm really scared.

The woman walks up to me, then pauses about a foot away. Her eyes are huge and a sharp piercing blue, a blue so clear, like no shade of blue I've ever seen before. "Why, we just want to say hello, don't we boys?"

I make my turn for the main road, but the two men are now right in front me, obscuring my escape. "Look at the glow on this one Carlos, she's a pretty little thing."

"Quite." says one of the men blocking the exit. I look behind him to the cobbled street. Every moment of this horrible situation seemed to be pushing me further away from being back on those cobbles.

The man standing next to the woman whispers something into her ear. She looks at him, perplexed, then motions to one of the men behind me, tapping her hip as if giving him some kind of secret instruction. The instruction was to Carlos.

I look straight at him, his stare injects something

into my soul, something terrifying, something dark. I don't like this at all. "Well, well," says the hulky oaf-like Carlos, sneering like a hyena, his strange eyes sparkling a little in the shards of light piercing the dark alleyway, like some kind of nasty disco. He pulls back his long heavy felt purple coat to show a kind of machete or samurai sword, speckled with sparkles even brighter than those hideous eyes. "Aren't you going to run?"

"I think we should leave her alone." says the man standing next to the woman. He has chin-length brown hair covered by stripey red and white sock hat, the kind a baby might wear. His sharp little goatee sits under a pair of kind yet tired-looking eyes, as though they are carrying the weight of the world.

"That's not how we roll, *Jasper*." says the woman.

"But her glow, it's…"

"All the more fun for us dear friend." says the woman, interrupting Jasper with a dismissive wave.

Carlos and the other man by the alleyway exit step aside, clearing a path towards the main road. "If I were you my bright little one," Carlos whispers, "I'd start running."

Next thing I know, I'm running. My legs feel heavy. Damn, why can't I run as fast I want to in these situations? I run downhill, thinking the momentum will help me, but the faster I go the slower I become. It doesn't feel right, the physics is all wrong in this place. I see the shore, the group aren't far behind me, shouting and trilling with their tongues - they're disgusting. They're all armed with knives, long, sharp knives, and those knives are meant for me, I know it. Goatee man stands away from them, his knife firmly in its holder. He's running, but not for me.

I reach the shore. This was a bad idea, there's hardly any cover here. Where shall I hide? The group is gaining on me, I'm running along the shore front, passing shops and houses I'm sure I've seen before. I start knocking doors, shouting for help, but no one answers. I see a beach hut and sprint towards it. I know they must see me, but what else can I do? I'm at the beach hut and there's a lock, I kick it off and scurry inside. As I go to close the door, struggling for solutions as to what to do next, I am faced with something even more terrifying than the armed bandits. An enormous tsunami, around a mile high is coming towards me. Well, that's it then, isn't it? Game over. I peer outside the beach hut to see if the bandits have noticed it. They have and they start to run in the opposite direction, all except one man, he's still running straight for me. I close the door, and scan my brain for solutions. How am I going to get out of this one? Surely I won't survive this? There's a bang on the door, I hold it tight, with every ounce of might left in me.

"Let me in, let me in!"

"No! Go, save yourself!"

"What is your name? Please, your name." This question surprises me a little. The man gains force over the door and stands in the doorway. It's goatee man. He looks down at me with a warm smile, which surprises me even more. The door is now wide open behind him and we have no cover.

"The door!" I scream. I can see the tsunami behind him. Its height is petrifying, but notice that it's moving really slowly. Unnaturally slowly. That doesn't seem right.

"Your name."

I look into the man's eyes properly, for the first time. They are sparkling green, and they show no fear.

"Where am I?" I ask the man.

"You're on Indigo. Now, please tell me your name. We don't have much time."

I look behind the man, the tsunami's coming, but it moves as though it's conscious, like a walking breathing person. I realise all at once something I'd forgotten along the way – *I am still dreaming*. The bandits must have distracted me from my lucidity.

"Aurora Black." I reply. "So what now?"

The man picks up the lock that I'd kicked off the door and laughs. "Incredible." he says, and takes off his stripey sock hat, unleashing a mass of beautiful brown hair, much more than I'd thought was under there. My gaze moves past his locks to something moving behind him.

"Watch out!" I shout. The tsunami has gained momentum and is moving really quickly now. It's only metres behind us. "Watch out!" My heart's racing, I grab the man close to my chest and feel his warm arms around me. I close my eyes. "Watch out."

27th October 2002, morning, London

"Arghhhhh!" The scream echoed in her head like a broken record.

"Aurora, what's wrong darling, are you ok?"

"I had this terrible dream Johan. I was on a beach, and there were these guys following me with knives, and..."

"Oh Aurora. You and your dreams. Must have been those prawns you had at the restaurant last night."

"I think I was lucid again. I mean, I felt like I knew I was dreaming, that's how I woke myself up."

"Wasn't it the fright that woke you?"

"Oh yeah, maybe. It's hard to tell. It was either the fright or knowing I could pull myself out of it."

"Well, you've awoken exactly 3 minutes before your alarm clock was about to go off, again, so that was good timing. Always in a hurry, Aurora." Johan kissed Aurora on the lips.

"Huh, I guess so. Well, suppose I should get up then." Aurora grumbled as she got out of bed.

"Only it's Sunday morning." said Johan, pulling her back into bed.

Sunday 27th October 2002, morning, London

Johan went to the local supermarket to pick up fresh orange juice, croissants and the Sunday papers whilst Aurora prepared sandwiches for their afternoon trip to Richmond. Their day out was perfect, even the weather was great. Richmond donned a scattering of autumnal reds and yellows on the park's grassy grounds. They eat their picnic at the top of a really high hill, granting them views across South London. They saw deer and foxes and young families, all out and doing their own thing.

Later, they enjoyed hot chocolate with cream at a local cafe back in Pimlico and spent the rest of the afternoon talking about their favourite Blackadder episode, the marmite question and Bill, the janitor at the Museum, whom Aurora suspected was actually an MI5 agent.

That night, they eat fajitas with all the trimmings, watched a couple of episodes of The West Wing, drank a few glasses of red wine and then retreated to Aurora's bedroom, where they talked by candlelight and hugged each other like it was their last night together, like someone was going to prise them apart if they didn't hang on. It was bliss, Aurora was happy. She looked at her clock. 10.30pm on a Sunday night and she was all snuggled up with Johan in her one bedroom apartment in Pimlico. The morning would bring with it the frantic beginnings of a new week, and all the excitement that entailed for them both. But for now it was 10.33pm, and time for sleep. Johan had dozed off about 15 minutes ago and Aurora had watched him for a while. He looked so beautiful at rest. His raven hair a sharp contrast against her ivory cotton bed pillows. Right, must sleep. Must sleep, must sleep...

***

3 Earth days prior, 24th October, daylight, Jesomine's Taverna in Ipa's Grassmarket district, Venezelu

"We need to get out of here." said Professor Sykes.

"Where shall we go?" said Zareb.

Professor Sykes looked at the boy with genuine concern. "Marcux can stay at a secure pod outside Ipa for a while, he'll be well looked after there. You need to inform his parents that he's going on a traveller's initiation training programme, important MEW5 business. "

"For how long?"

"Tell them you don't know exactly, perhaps a few months. It's safer for them if they don't know the truth."

Zareb gently pulled Professor Sykes into one corner of the room. "Is this going to work?"

"It has to. And we can't take any chances. This is the only way."

Zareb nodded reluctantly and then went for the chiandle. Before blowing it out he looked at Professor Sykes and Marcux and said, "Follow me."

The surup was low as the two men and young boy left the Taverna. A million thoughts were running through Zareb's head, but he tried to focus. Getting Marcux to the pod outside Ipa was going to be a difficult enough task, but more pressing was getting them out of Militia City, in broad daylight.

Professor Sykes thought the costumes Zareb had picked out for them were of relatively good taste. He wasn't sure why he had to get the ridiculously long curly moustache, his own short one being perfectly adequate for the job. Reading his thoughts, Zareb replied with, "We need to look different. You never know who might recognise us."

Zareb was dressed as an Apocalyptic, with a long jade green robe, the colour synonymous with that group. He carried a copy of the anti-book, a guide

no Apocalyptic would be seen without, as well as
two customary apocalyptic belt items: a hip flask
and a bottle of hallucinogens, both of which kept
Apocalyptics well away from awareness and in a
semi-constant state of merriment. Zareb completed
the look with a long wavy orange wig and full facial
beard. Marcus was dressed as a girl, with green
pantaloons and smock top as well as a short dark
bob. Professor Sykes was dressed as a Jeapordiser.
Their costumes mimicked those of CERN officials,
but were a washed-out navy blue. Jeopardisers
always had a black band on their upper arm. The
Professor fixed his weaponry belt around his waist,
the kind that Jeopardisers and Intolerants would
commonly be seen wearing, and which they, all too
often, tormented dreamers with.

It was morning rush hour in the Grassmarket
district, the main trading post in Militia City. Zareb
chose well, thought Professor Sykes. It's so busy
here on weekday mornings that they'd completely
disappear in the crowd.

Fish sellers were busy trading off-cuts at their
fish stands, desperate farmers were dragging their
cattle and goods across the shiny pebbled streets,
hoping to make a sale. The surup's rays were strong
this morning, but the air still held the coldness of
night. With the bustling bodies and animals and
stall carts making their way across the Grassmarket,
a warm and pungent steam rose from its pebbles,
another layer of disguise, thought Zareb. Walls
were plastered with rebel stickers and posters, as
well as vandalised pictures of General Quern. Most
had taken to his bald head, which was peppered

with crosses and the words 'TRAITOR'. His huge red eyebrows sit over a set of cold green eyes. His round peach smug face and pursed lips seemed a strange fit for the Revolution of good.

Out of nowhere, a loud piercing scream ripples through the market. Zareb and Professor Sykes each had one of Marcux's hands in theirs, and both felt him almost jump out of his skin upon hearing the sound. The scream turned into a wicked cackle, a laugh so disturbing that Marcux began to shake. It was coming from the East gate. The whole market was in a flurry of excitement. Professor Sykes could see the crowd beginning to part as something, something fast, was making its way into the centre of the crowd. Making its way right towards them. Both men held onto Marcux's hands a little tighter. Then, footsteps. Running footsteps scraping off the smooth jaded cobbles. *What is that?* As the crowds parted even further, eventually Zareb saw what was happening. An Izimite, in travel mode, an unawares, a dreamer, was being chased by a female Intolerant. The Intolerant was clad in heavy iron-top boots and a weapons belt almost larger than her frame. She couldn't have been more than 18 years old, thought Zareb. How could someone so young be so disengaged, so bitter, so disillusioned already? Had they been brainwashed?

The joy on the Intolerants' face as she chased and tormented the Izimite made Professor Sykes feel sick to his stomach. It made Zareb upset and Marcux looked just plain terrified. But it wasn't the Intolerant that terrified Marcux. He'd seen plenty of them in his young 5 years. It was the fact that an old man by the turnip stand was staring at him. The old man stood up and walked over to him. He knelt down and put his face close up to Marcux's, staring at him for what felt like an eternity.

"Out of all the worlds and all the places that Izimite could have visited, it ends up in Militia City on a Montag morning!" The old man erupts into laughter. A small crowd around them starts to laugh uncontrollably. Zareb and Professor Sykes look at Marcux, concerned that the poor boy is going to lose his nerve. To their surprise, and relief, Marcux starts to laugh, throwing in a bit of improvisation by tapping the old man on the shoulder and saying. "Dumb travellers."

"Come on *Maya*," interjects Zareb, "let's go."

As Zareb, Professor Sykes and Marcux make a swift and steady line for the East gate, the market bustles on behind them, unawares that the first domino piece in the Revolution had been tipped.

***

CERN knew that they couldn't cut off Militia City's main source of income, the Grassmarket trading post. Through their own self-awareness, they refused to use force against them knowing that the knock-on effect would impact trading families in the area. This upset a lot of people in Ipa's bustling metropolis. They wanted to protect visitors, and their own Government was letting Venezeluan residents undo all the good work they were doing. Many were concerned that the militia camp had grown in size since last year, and that the number of

Jeopardisers had increased. This is why the radio wave bar had been introduced. Not so much to stop CERN from picking up intelligence from Militia City, but to stop Jeopardisers picking up on Venezeluan intelligence and sharing it with their home planets. One of the costs of this communication cut off, was that it gave rebels more freedom to plan and plot without any interference from CERN. At one stage, CERN had developed an undercover troop to infiltrate Militia City, feeding back information to its headquarters. This initiative was launched by General Quern, then Head Operative in the Civil Law Department and now General of Venezelu, answerable only to the Supreme Court judges. But, after time, the initiative was over-ruled by the Venezeluan Supreme Court and the troop disbanded, on the grounds that it was costing too much zulan to run and that it was having a negative effect on the operatives involved. The operatives were purist Revolutionaries and over time, they found it difficult to keep tormenting visitors for shows sake. So, CERN put the undercover project on the back burner, but this did mean that the Revolutionaries' last link with Militia City had been severed, and they left themselves more open to attack.

***

24th October, midlight
It was nearing evelight as Zareb, Professor Sykes and Marcux arrived at the outpost in Zaatta, just outside Ipa. The trio could have flown there in

under an hour, but their operation had to be discreet and they wanted to conserve energy, so they went underground by oil cart.

As they travelled, they changed out of their militia disguises and into some regular dark attire, freeze drying and destroying their old clothes with a friz-gun.

The men and boy looked up at the midlight transition between surup and lunar. Midlight was always such a magical time of day, but tonight, its shadows and shades felt ominous.

"There's a forest around 30 minutes from here." said Professor Sykes. "Our pods are hidden there."

"Right," said Zareb. "Let's grab our things and get going."

"STOP!"

Zareb, Marcux and Professor Sykes froze on the spot.

"Don't move."

They had nowhere to move to even if they'd wanted to.

Behind them, to their right and left were buggy trucks, filled with people in pointy hats who were determined to close the trio in. "Dammit." said Professor Sykes.

A small dumpy man in a much larger pointy hat picked up his megaphone as the buggies finally came to a stop.

"Zaattan border police. Don't move, you're coming with us."

3

*"The clearest way into the Universe
is through a forest wilderness."*

John Muir of Earth, Explorer

25th October, dawnlight

Zareb, Professor Sykes and Marcux hadn't had
much time to talk in their small, grey rectangular
jail cell at Zaatta police station. They had a lot to
discuss too, but the small dumpy sheriff had planted
a tall lanky deputy with a small pointy hat right
outside their cell, all night. Marcux was fascinated
by the deputy's ability to just stare at them, without
expression or movement. The only possible
expression came from his right eye, which drooped
a bit, causing his right eyebrow to arch high which
made him look constantly surprised on the one side.
Marcux decided to try and 'stare him out', and he
was doing quite a good job too, until the small
dumpy sheriff barged into the holding area carrying

a bundle of papers, distracting them from their game.

"Right gentlemen, it seems that the info you gave us checks out. You're free to go. Felix, open the cell please."

Zareb and Professor Sykes looked at each other, trying to disguise the breath of relief they could feel rise up from their chest.

The tall lanky deputy stands and walks over to the cell to unlock it. For the first time since arriving at the station, he moves his lips into an awkward but heartfelt smile.

"Alright there, thanks for visiting Zaatta, we hope *not* to see you again soon. Uh hu."

"Thanks Felix." says Marcux, putting three fingers out for a celebratory high three. Felix hesitates, looks over at the sheriff and then gives Marcux a high three back.

Professor Sykes walks over to the sheriff. "Thanks sheriff. And our belongings?"

"You can get them on the way out. Will you be needing transportation to the Zaattan Mounties for your scientific expedition Dr. Bundle?"

"No, it's fine, we'll fly."

"Very well then. If you need anything, you know where to find us. And apologies, it's not every day we receive visitors from Ipa's Geological Society in the early hours of dawnlight. I hope we haven't delayed your investigation too much."

"It's our fault, we should have phoned ahead to make sure the permit had come through."

"Not a problem Dr. Bundle, just take care out there. Zaattan bears are not the friendliest of beasts."

"We'll stay alert. Thank you sheriff."

***

As Zareb, Professor Sykes and Marcux fly through the dawnlight sky, Marcux points to a dusty little diner deep in the Zaattan plane. "Guys, I'm starving. Any chance we can descend for a quick bite?"

Professor Sykes shakes his head. "I don't want to make any more stops buddy, we're almost there. If you can hang on for another 20 minutes then there's plenty to eat at the pod."

Marcux nods. His stomach grumbles. "Bet you I can make it in 15." Marcux jets off ahead, flying at top speed.

"Marcux!" shouts the Professor. "Just keep going straight! Honestly, he doesn't even know where he's going and yet off he flies."

Zareb laughs, "That's our Marcux. So, *Dr. Bundle*, we owe Lindar big this time, don't we?"

"We sure do. Can't believe I forgot to call her before leaving Ipa. I'll bring her up to speed tomorrow from our device at Stoffenlagen. Just as well she worked out our intentions when taking the call from the Zaattan police." The Professor pauses. "She misses you Zareb, you know that don't you?"

"I doubt that Professor. Besides she's so busy covering for you it's a wonder she gets time to miss anything." The Professor laughs.

Around 20 flight minutes later, Zareb and the Professor see Marcux grind to a halt ahead of them.

They are hovered above what looks like a sea of gently moving green leaves. "Are we here?" asks Marcux. The Professor nods.

The Professor takes the lead, descending into the trees. Zareb and Marcux follow close behind, hardly believing their eyes. "These trees," says Marcux, "they're so beautiful."

The section of forest at the foot of the Zaattan Mounties holds some of the tallest trees in all of Venezelu. Coming in at over a mile high, they provide the perfect cover for pods. The golden brown bark and branches are covered in dark green leaves, as thick as fern. The trees are scattered with awesome lights, like fibre optic glow worms painting the darkness with a warm glow of purples, blues, greens and gold. This forest, the Andanuan forest, feels warm, secure and safe, but Professor Sykes knows that it is home to some of the most dangerous living creatures in Zaatta, the biggest being Zaattan bears and the deadliest being Crosantian snakes.

"Keep descending, not far now." Professor Sykes shines a torch light beneath their feet. "Maybe just another 700 feet."

As the trio descend, the forest becomes darker and darker, the warm glowing lights become fewer and the early morning's suruplight now very much out of sight. Gone too was the silence of the tree peaks, the forest animals now making themselves heard, the cracking and rustling of branches and leaves growing stronger.

"50 feet...20 feet..." It's almost pitch black now. "10 feet..." Marcux and Zareb start to slow down.

"Stop!" The Professor hears the thud of footsteps hit against the thick mossy ground.

"Smells oaky." says Zareb.

"Hold on a second," says the Professor. Marcux and Zareb hear him get something out of his bag. Next thing they hear is a snapping sound, followed by a warm green light flooding the forest floor for as far as they can see. Zareb and Marcux stare with wonder at its beauty. Professor Sykes had activated a neon lightstick, which was now illuminating everything on the forest floor. Giant leaves dripped gold-tinted water onto the moss and rock surfaces reflected a shiny metallic purple sheen. Marcux could even see his face in them.

"Quick, just over here. We've got 20 seconds before the light goes out."

Professor Sykes walked over to the base of one of the trees. To Zareb, it just looked like the base of every other tree there, but the Professor knew this one was different. He stuck the torch in his mouth, highlighting the bark. Moving his hands over the bark, he found a crevice and with his thumb, cracked the bark open. Underneath the crevice was a scanner pad. The Professor placed his thumb in front of the pad. It scanned it instantaneously and made a small beeping noise. "Step back." said the Professor.

An entire front panel at the base of the tree split open, like a door, revealing a tunnel. "Quickly, let's go." said the Professor, and with that they were in.

The tunnel was long. It started off narrow but became wider and steeper as it continued. Zareb's eyes tried to adjust to the bright lighting coming from points all along the stone wall that curved and turned beneath his body.

"How much further underground is this pod?" asked Marcux.

"Not much further." replied the Professor. "It's designed for flying down, but I can show you a quicker way." The Professor takes out three small squares from his pocket.

"What are these?" asks Zareb.

"I call them," the Professor pauses, realising that he hadn't actually come up with a name for this latest invention, "sliding bags." He unfolds one of the squares, which turns into a shiny silver metallic sack, about the length of an average person. "You sit in them, and slide. Means you don't need to steer, gravity does all the work. Race you!"

And with that, Professor Sykes was off.

"Wait up!" shouts Marcux. Quickly jumping into his sliding bag, he too vanishes around the corner.

"Dammit!" Zareb was having difficulty unfolding his sliding bag, but eventually managed to get into it and get going. The ride down was incredible, the walls of the tunnel felt smooth beneath their bodies and the steepness of the tunnel allowed them to pick up lots of speed. "This is awesome!" shouts Marcux.

"See you at the bottom dear nephew!" shouts Zareb as he overtakes Marcus at a bend.

Zareb starts to see a pink glow, next thing he knows he's lying on what looks like a massive cushion. He sits up, feeling something very heavy land on his back immediately afterwards.

"Ouch!"

"Sorry, uncle! You ok?"

Zareb gives Marcux a playful hug. "I'm fine, you?" Marcux nods.

"Wow. When you mentioned a pod, I was imagining a small thing."

"Welcome friends!" It was the Professor, who had somehow managed to change into a lab coat and grab a drink in the time it took Zareb and Marcux to descend through the tunnel. "Other than myself, Lindar, eight trusted operatives and a large group of Zaattan monks you are the only other living beings who know about the existence of these pods."

"Pods?" asks Marcux.

"You brought Lindar Tahelso here?" enquires Zareb.

"Of course, she helped design it."

"I see."

"We started developing these pods long before you joined us in the tower. Their existence is on a need-to-know basis. Now it's time for you to know."

"Why monks?"

"The monks are known for their skills in construction, they're the best in their field. They know the Zaattan foothills well, have access to local materials and resources, worked like gods and, of course, could stay discreet. They're all for the cause."

"How many pods do you have?" asked Marcux.

"Four in total, they're spread out over the forest. Come, meet the team here at Pod 1."

Zareb and Marcux could hardly believe their eyes. The pod was large, larger than they'd both imagined. The giant cushion they'd landed on looked like a patchwork footstool, sewn together with lots of different coloured fabrics, soft and sturdy to the touch. They climbed out of their sliding bags and jumped off, landing on the steel floor with a thud.

As the Professor walked them through the pod, Zareb could see a mezzanine balcony above them, holding what looked like thousands of zulan's worth of MEW5 equipment. There were Feeler controllers, recording decks, inter-zol radios, stage 2 interceptors and equipads, to name just a few. At ground level he found a mish mash of old sofas, antique lamps and what looked like native Zaattan rugs.

"It's cosy. Are those Zaattan rugs?" commented Zareb.

"Of course, none other. The pods are full of them, but most of the budget went on technology."

"And by 'budget' you means courtesy of MEW5."

"I've self-funded a large chunk from my earnings, courtesy of MEW5, but yes, Lindar has been pivotal." Professor Sykes signals to Zareb and Marcux to keep walking towards the back of the pod, and up a set of stairs. "The rest has just been thrown together, whatever we could sneak out here in small loads or borrow from the monastery, but we like it."

Zareb takes the stairs, with Professor Sykes close behind him. As they reach the first floor they noticed that Marcux is already there, standing outside the door to an office with large windows and pretty curtain blinds.

"Sorry, I think stairs are a waste of time."

Professor Sykes laughs. "I know, why bother, right? We put them in just in case we ever have visitors someday. You know how confusing it is for non-Venezeluan's when they can't see any stairs. They freak out. Plus we can't always muster the energy required to fly after a long shift, the stairs help unwind our minds." Professor Sykes opens the door to the office.

"Come Marcux, meet your new friends."

Marcux glances up at his uncle Zareb. Zareb nods and signals him to go in.

"It's alright little man. I'm right here, on you go."

"Marcux, Zareb, meet Mikus B and Isobella."

Mikus B, a tall chap with dark brown eyes, glasses and head full of dark floppy hair rushes over to greet the group.

"Hi, call me Mikus."

Isobella stands up next, her smile as colourful as her long golden wavy hair, speckled with strands of blue, green and pink, just like the Andanuan trees.

"So nice to meet you both."

"Marcux, go with Mike, he'll get you something to eat and show you to your room. Zareb, come with Isobella and I to the main testing centre and we can start to prepare the Feeler's visit to the anomaly." Professor Sykes charges off, his excitement clear to see.

"Her name's Aurora, of Earth, by the way." Zareb tells Isobella as the two try to keep up behind the Professor.

"Lovely name." replies Isobella. Her smile is endearing, it distracts Zareb, making him blush before accidentally walking into a door.

"This way!" calls the Professor. "It would probably take us a couple of days to set up and test the equipment. We don't have that kind of time, but luckily Isobella's the best in her field."

The Professor was right. Zareb knew that time was against them. How glad he was for Professor Sykes, and Lindar, sweet Lindar.

That night Professor Sykes, Isobella and Zareb got to work in the testing centre. They started by retrieving every piece of equipment they thought they might need.

"Man, you have a lot of stuff here." said Zareb.

"It's taken years to bring it out here, we've had to do it in bits."

"You and Lindar?"

Professor Sykes pauses. "Yes, amongst others, you know, the other comrades within the pods."

Isobella interjects, "When do you need to be back at MEW5?"

"We'll stay another day." suggests the Professor. "Schedule a link-up meeting with the others for tomorrow morning. We'll spend the rest of the day on the Feeler, get some good rest and then leave at the crack of dawnlight the following morning. We need to make a presence at MEW5 before people start to notice our absence."

"Agreed." says Zareb.

***

"This is delicious!" says Marcux as he hungrily eats his way through a massive pile of tomaten soppen strudel.

"Glad you like it." replies Mikus B. "Do you know why you're here, Marcux?"

Marcux puts his forkette down and wipes his mouth. He takes a drink of water.

"Not really. I mean, I know what's going on with the anomaly and everything. I'm just not sure what part I have to play in it."

"You're going to be her contact, her very own shadow person. Once we've run all of the preliminary tests on the girl, we'll need a strong traveller for stage three download. First contact."

"First contact?"

"I don't know how much you know, or how much I should tell you. All I do know is that time is against us and it'll all become clear as we go. Tomorrow Isobella and I will give you the grand tour and start your training. The day after that we'll take you outside for a while. It's good to get out of here every couple of days."

"Cool."

"Want to see your room?"

"Sure."

Marcux's room was the only room in the pod that actually looked like a pod. It was oval and of a fair size, but the first thing that Marcux noticed was that it sparkled.

"Wow. Is this my room?"

"Yes. It's right under a stream just beyond our tree."

The room's walls were made of thick, transparent industrious plastics, thick enough to retain all the heat rising up from the heated floorboards.

"It's so cosy in here." said Marcux as he runs over to his dark blue bed in the centre of the room. Mikus B turns on the night light. Outside, Marcux can see all different kinds of fish and snakes in the dark green waters.

"What's sparkling, is it the water or the fish?"

"A bit of both. Zaatta is rich in minerals and the Andanuan forest is abundant in this kind of light."

Marcux marvels at the sparkles swimming past his bedroom ceiling.

"Can they see me?"

"No. The exterior to this room is disguised as a riverbed. It's a safety precaution. Want to see more of the pod?"

"Actually, do you mind if I have a nap? It's been a long day and I didn't get much sleep last night."

"No problem, we can carry on with the tour tomorrow. You get some rest, and happy travelling."

"Happy travelling." replies Marcux, before falling into a relaxed, deep slumber.

***

26th October, daylight, Zaattan Pod #1

Zareb, Professor Sykes, Isobella and Mikus B sit on pod chairs at a huge oval table in the centre of the conference room. The room is large and rectangular, with reflective metallic walls on the back and left-hand wall, interspersed with monitors and technical equipment. The other long wall on the right of the table is made of perspectine industrial self-replicating plastic, around a metre thick.

Despite its thickness, light from the riverbed and all of its creatures filters through, creating an aquarium effect and casting waves of colour across the oval tables and all those sat at it. A few old lampstands sit in the corners of the room, as well as a busted up two seater couch complete with quilts and throws, mostly used for catching a snooze on in between experiments. On the front wall, ahead of the table, sits a large hologrammed board, currently split into thirds, each third encompassing the other pod boardrooms. At each table sits two people.

"So we're on clear on the plan then?" asks Professor Sykes.

A series of replies come back from the hologrammed image.

"Yes."

"Understood."

"No problem boss."

"Defo."

"Great. So Zareb and I will head back to Ipa tomorrow daylight whilst Isobella and Mikus B carry on with their work here. Keep notes in the log as per, I'll be able to pick up a signal as soon as I reach the safety perimeter in Zaatta. Thanks guys, see you soon."

"Bye chief."

"Goodbye Professor."

"See ya."

"Thanks, bye."

"Zareb, I'll try to take you over to the pods after prelim contact. You need to meet these guys, they're phenomenal."

"They seem it."

"Mikus, Isobella, would you mind waking Marcux now and starting the day's programme?"

"No problem Professor, we're on it." smiles Isobella, leaving the room with Mikus B in tow.

"I noticed you left out a few details in that meeting, Professor."

"It's not the right time Zareb. I trust these guys with my life, but they've already sacrificed enough just being posted out here, I don't want to put them in any more danger."

"You'll need to tell at some point."

"I will, I will. Come, let me give you a quick tour before we start."

The day was a busy one. Professor Sykes and Zareb worked tirelessly in the testing centre whilst Isobella and Mikus B initiated Marcux to the training gym. Zareb had decided he would tell Marcux the full scale of what to expect only after the initial Feeler test had gone through. Marcux was the one of the best freelance travellers out there, so of course he believed him when he'd told him about the anomaly, but neither him nor the Professor had actually been to visit Aurora themselves, so they couldn't judge the scale of what Marcux had witnessed until they saw it with their own eyes. Marcux had Aurora's wavelengths imprinted into his channel readings now, so he could find her wherever she was on Earth. The temptation for Professor Sykes and Zareb to visit her in person via these coordinates had been tremendous ever since learning of her, but of course that would have been a risky move. All it would take is one of MEW5's Feelers to pick up their faces and the girl would be uncovered.

After a long and arduous day in the pod, everyone was more than keen for Mikus B's cooked Fraise Linguin with roasted potpots and caremalised brejins on the side. There was an excitement in the air, and the group laughed and joked as the enjoyed their well deserved meal. Professor Sykes, as was his habit, was scanning through programmes flashing from the huge televised set in the dining area, looking for old re-runs of 'The Goyan Show'. He stopped momentarily at a piece of Ipa metropolitan news footage. The newsreader was dressed in classic CERN blue.

"And news just in, an elderly man from Hydros passed away in the early hours of dawnlight after a group of rebels made him believe he was being thrown off a cliff. The rebels claimed immediate responsibility for the action."

Everyone stopped talking. Marcux put down his forkette.

"I remember that story."

"Yes, that was from a few months back." replied the Professor.

Everything on the televised set was pre-recorded. Despite the pod's depth, there were ways the team could have watched live televised networks, tapping into the Zaatta networks, but they wanted to keep the pods off grid as much as possible, and so every few months Lindar would bring out some new tapes.

The Professor started to fast-forward the tape. "Let's see if we can find something a bit more light-hearted, shall we?"

The Professor finds 'The Goyan Show'. He starts to laugh hysterically at the off-beat Venezeluan comedy. Isobella and Mikus B roll their eyes.

"He loves that show." said Mikus B to Zareb and Marcux, busily munching his way through a mouthful of crunchy potpots.

The rest of the evening was frantic, except for Marcux, who went to bed to read and look at the multi-coloured fish swim past his bedroom wall. Zareb, Professor Sykes, Isobella and Mikus B were in the testing centre all evening and stayed up as they late as they could, trying to make as much headway as possible on the testing equipment ahead of the next night's launch.

"Could you grab some E4 cables whilst you're in town?" asked Isobella, rubbing sweat from her brow as she concentrated on fusing some wires inside one of the Feeler's legs.

"Sure." replied the Professor.
The Professor starts to save his work on the computer and begins closing things down. "Ok folks, time we call it a night. See you in the morning."

***

27th October, dawnlight, Pod #1

Zareb was only half way through his toasted oat squares when he felt the Professor's hand tap his shoulder. "Hi. We need to go, before Lindar kicks our butts into orbit."

"Ok, I'll just go say bye to Marcux." said Zareb, quickly squeezing the rest of the oat square into his mouth.

"Of course. I'll meet you by the big cushion, you know, the one by the entrance."

"Why," asked Zareb, "is there another big cushion in this hideout I don't know about?" Zareb smirked, realising that his humour was lost on the Professor.

"No," replied the Professor, "we just have the one big cushion. Two of those things would simply be ridiculous."

Zareb smiled at that, and took a sip of his gingero tea.

***

"Can I come in?" Zareb slowly opens the door to Marcux's room.

"Hi uncle Zareb! Check this out, breakfast in bed! Isobella brought me it."

"That's nice Marcux."

"So, you going?"

"Yes, we need to have a presence at the tower today, but we'll head back tonight. You going to be ok?"

"Of course, I'm Marcux Grentil, son of Joshu Grentil and Harria Fender, nephew of Zareb Fender. I'll be fine."

Zareb laughs. "Great, see you later then. And Marcux, please do as you're told. Isobella and Mikus B are nice people."

Marcux rolls his eyes. "I'm not a rebel uncle Zareb."

"I know, just headstrong."

"These napcakes are delicious!"

"Bye Marcux, see you later."

***

27th October, daylight, Ipa, MEW5 tower

It's the start of daylight as Lindar sits transfixed by her computer monitor, typing away at ferocious speed. The day's suruplight tinges gold on her long, thick red wavy hair, casting a golden line down her back. Her dark purple-red eyes stand out against her hazelnut complexion. Only the freckles on her nose compete for the limelight against her piercing eyes. The phone on her desk rings, breaking her train of thought.

"Answer."

"Oh, hello Lindar, it's Griig, from Civil Law Department, can I come up?"

"Are you looking for the Professor, Griig?"

"Can I just come up please?"

"If you're looking for the Professor he's not back yet."

"Do you know when he *will* be back?"

Lindar hears a bang against the large floor-to-ceiling office window behind her. She turns to see Professor Sykes and Zareb waving at her from the outside.

"I'm not sure."

"Well do you have a *rough* idea?"

Lindar presses a button on her desk that opens up a window panel in the neighbouring office to her right, Professor Sykes' office.

"Can I take a message Officer Hawthorn?"

"Just tell Professor Sykes that Quern would like to

see him, as soon as possible."

"Ok, I will, thanks Griig. Good day." Lindar sighs. "Close."

She runs through to the Professor's office, her face red and her stomach in knots. As she flies through the door she sees Zareb lying on the couch and Professor Sykes in front of her with a metallic, shiny white parcel, wrapped up in green velvet ribbons.

"We bought you something." says the Professor as he offers her the gift. Lindar ignores it. "Have a nice time?"

"Lindar, I'm sorry, we should have....."

Lindar cuts the Professor off. "Justin, take a seat please."

Zareb sits up in shock. "*Justin?*"

Professor Sykes sits down next to Zareb, who stands up. "*Justin?* How does *she* know your name? You never tell anyone your name."

"Zareb, please," Lindar motions for him to sit back down. She puts her finger in front of her lips, motioning them to be quiet. She goes to Professor Sykes table, grabs a thinkpad and returns to the couch. She sits on the floor looks into the thinkpad, writing a message for them. Zareb and the Professor just look at each other. "*Justin?*" whispers Zareb. Lindar gives him a glare.

"Can I get you some tea, or kaffee?" asks Lindar.

"No thanks." says the Professor.

Zareb thinks on it for a second. "A tea please, thanks Lindar."

As Lindar finishes transferring her thoughts onto the pad, she lifts it and places it in front of them.

The pad reads:

'As you suspected, we have ears in here. No eyes found, have done a full scan, but there's an auditory bug somewhere and it's really well hidden. None of my equipment is picking it up. Quern intercepted your part of conversation when Zareb called your portable the other night.'

"Well, I'm going to have some tea too." Lindar stands up and flicks her finger, which makes the thinkpad turn onto the next page,

'....now he wants to see you....'

Zareb and the Professor look at each other, their worst fear now confirmed. Quern knows something is going on.

"I take lots of sugar, and milch." says Zareb.

"Yes, I remember." says Lindar.

Lindar looks into the pad again to relay the next part of the message.

'Contacted Ray for help in finding the bug....'

'....just received message from his wife saying he didn't come home last night. Hasn't been seen in last 24 hours......'

Lindar grabs some milch and sugar from the cabinet, she puts it into the cup.

'..Quern's people must have caught him trying to de-activate the malware on your devices here and at the tower. He's being treated as a potential whistleblower, a threat to Quern...'

....and talking of threats, if you ever leave Ipa without telling me exactly where you're going, I will kick your ass into orbit.....'

Professor Sykes mouths the word 'sorry'. Lindar turns the page again.

'...both of you.....'

Zareb nods in acknowledgement.

Lindar stirs the teas and hands one to Zareb.

"Thank you for the present. What is it?"

Zareb and the Professor smile for a moment. "It's a present, you need to open it to find out." adds Zareb.

"I appreciate the gesture, but I don't have time for surprises."

"It's a Glup Jock. Six months old. We picked him up from a street seller."

Lindar unwraps the gift and looks at the Glup Jock, a round, blue fluffy ball with no limbs or face but two protruding ears that looked like velvet triangles. She smiles, then shakes her head. "That's kind, but you must be kidding me. Take it back."

She points out the window towards Militia City, takes a sip of tea and quickly adds something to the think pad. The men stand up.

'Go show your faces at the tower, do some work, stay in restricted areas. I'll try and keep Quern's men at bay. Be at my place in 6 hours. We'll head to Militia City and discuss there before you head back to the pod tonight.'

Zareb nods and Professor Sykes grabs a bag and some documents from his table.

"I'm just off to the lab Lindar, if anyone calls please tell them I'll get back to them as soon as I can."

"Will do, boss."

As the men turn, they hear a small electrical buzz followed by a frazzling sound. They turn to notice that the thinkpad has self-destructed. "It's ridiculous how many of those we get through in a week." the Professor whispers to Zareb. And with that, the Professor and Zareb fly out of the Professor's window and head towards the tower.

***

6.5 hours later, Militia City

"Why am I always a Jeopardiser?" asks Professor Sykes as they turn the corner of Hassemburg and head towards Yana's Heaven.

"Because you suit the suit." replies Zareb, back in another Apocalyptic outfit. Lindar is dressed in her Intolerant disguise, complete with iron-capped boots and weapons belt. Her ragged skirt is torn and dirty. Her top, a torn and dirty re-assembled flag of Venezelu, sits tied in a knot over her right shoulder.

"Come on you two, and stay in character."

The Professor was frightened, but knew that Yana's Heaven in the middle of the day would be the last place anyone would expect Revolutionaries to hang out, especially top ranking officials of MEW5. As they approached the bouncers outside Yana's, Lindar grunted something towards one of them. The larger of the two bouncers bowed and let them past.

Zareb kept his head down as they entered. He could see the Professor's legs shaking. He hoped the bouncers hadn't noticed. It was dark inside Yana's Heaven, which was packed to the brim with rebels, and really tough ones at that. The music was loud and the wheat whisky flowing. Beautiful men and women in snake suits cruised the club, waiting tables, dealing cards and turning heads. Their skin was painted green and their hair dyed gold. These were Yana's staff, and not to be messed with. Zareb noticed how their dresses and suits glimmered against the chiandle light and how every rebel in there was powerless in their presence, like moths to the flame.

"This place makes me sick." said Lindar.

"Yeah, me too." said Zareb.

Professor Sykes just gulped.

"Come on, I know a place we can talk."

Lindar directs the men to a small stone booth with thick red drapes. The booth was one of hundreds carved into the West wall of the club. It looked like a giant stone honey-comb. No sooner had they flown up to it and taken a seat inside, a snake-suited woman approaches the booth.

"Drinkssss?" she hissed.

"Three wheat whiskies please." said Lindar.

"Water for me please." said Professor Sykes.

Lindar throws him a glare.

"Ignore my friend here, he's fairly new to Venezelu. Three wheat whiskies please."

The waitress nods and leaves, closing the thick red draped plumes behind her as she goes.

"Are you trying to get us killed?" asks Lindar, kicking the Professor under the table.

"What? I'm thirsty, besides, we have a lot of important work to do tonight. I don't want a fuzzy head."

"You don't need to drink the stuff Justin. You just need to fit in. No-one in here drinks water - ever."

"Right, ok, sorry."

"Ok," Lindar looks at her watch, "we're out of earshot from CERN's transmission waves - what are we going to do about Ray?" asks Lindar. Her face seems beyond concerned now. Zareb looks into her eyes and sees something else, something he's seen before. It wasn't fear, it was sadness.

"Do we have anyone else on the inside who can help find him, or the bug?" asks Zareb.

"Only Mia, who used to work in the Burovian block." replied the Professor.

"She's retired, isn't she?" asks Lindar.

"Yes," replies the Professor, "which is handy for us."

"Lindar, do you think you could contact Mia and start the search for Ray? If they have him, which I think they do, then I know he won't talk, but we need to get him back and we need to find out how much they know."

"Already on it Zareb, one of my contacts spoke to Mia today. What about Quern?"

"You said that Quern only heard the Professor's side of the conversation, right?"

"Yes, that's right."

"Well, in that case he would only have heard him receive a call in early dawnlight from someone asking him to meet him somewhere. The Professor didn't repeat the name of the Taverna or any of the details. I'm sure of it."

"I didn't, that's right." confirms the Professor.

"It's too late to find and deactivate the bug and I don't want to get Mia caught," says Lindar, "but we can maybe use this to our advantage in the future, throw him off."

"What about visuals in the office?" asks the Professor.

"I scanned, nothing," Lindar flicks a bit of hair out of her face, "visuals are too obvious, my fountain pen has the technology to fry any camera in sight. No, it's just an auditory bug that's left now. That and any reconnaissance bods Quern has allocated, though from the civil law security files there's nothing on record."

"Pah," laughs the Professor, "like Quern would make a note of that anyways."

Zareb hears the clinking of glasses approaching, it's the waitress. She rings the bell outside the curtain to ask permission to enter. Zareb pulls back the red drapes and lets her in.

"Three wheat whiskiesss. Three zulan pleasssse."

"Kraney, would you do the honours please." asks Zareb.

"Why yes, of course." Professor Sykes starts to look inside his bag for zulan. As he searches, the waitress looks at him with a puzzled expression on her face.

Zareb and Lindar take the whiskies off the tray and spread them out. There are some complimentary q-nuts, which pleases Zareb, they are delicious and you can't get them in the city. It's taking Professor Sykes a long time to find the zulan and so Lindar looks over at him to see what's taking so long. To her horror, she notices that the Professor's long curly moustache is steadily falling away from his face. Lindar nudges Zareb and then looks over at the waitress. The waitress stares at the Professor intently, her golden eyes glimmering in the soft light of the booth.

"I have it here somewhere," says the Professor, "sorry about this."

PLOP.

The sound of the Professor's moustache falling into the whisky wasn't a loud sound, but to the Professor, Zareb and Lindar, it was louder than the sound of their heartbeats, which were now pounding in their heads.

"Imposssters?" says the waitress, waiting for the words to actually sink in. "Revolutionariesss?"

"No, you're misunderstood. My friend here likes moustache fashion, and...."

The waitress cuts Lindar off, "Imposssssters! Revolutionariesss!" The waitress turns to run toward the drapes aiming to flee through the mouthhole of the booth, screaming at the top of her voice.

"We need to go...now!" Lindar flies from her seat and goes right for the waitress' legs, toppling her over. "Go, now!"

"Lindar, we're not leaving you!" shouts Zareb.

"Half of Militia City will be here in three seconds. Get out of here, I'll be fine!"

"She's right, come on Zareb." says the Professor, grabbing Zareb by the gown and dragging him out of the booth and into the club.

The waitress goes for the alarm tag on her ankle.

"Don't even think about it Missssy." says Lindar, pinning the waitress to the ground with ease. She gets her into a head lock and manages to smash the alarm with a whisky glass just in time. Lindar pulls a syringe from her weapons belt and injects the waitress, sending her into an instant sleep. Still on the ground, Lindar looks out under the red drapes and into the club. She can see Zareb and the Professor fly out of the East exit, unfollowed. She smiles. Moments later, she sees four sets of iron clad feet hovering on the other side of the red drapes. Lindar's smile disappears.

"We need to go back!" shouts Zareb. Professor Sykes descends into the oil cart by the dockside, dragging Zareb's gown and pulling him down with him.

"We *need* to get back to Zaatta. The Feeler needs to reach Aurora, tonight. Lindar will be fine."

"How can you be so sure?"

Professor Sykes hesitates a moment.

"Lindar's not who you think she is." The cart starts to move rapidly. The Professor starts changing out of his costume and goes into his rucksack for new clothes.

"What does that mean?"

"I thought she would have told you all this."

"All what? What's going on, *Justin*?"

"Lindar's an ex-CERN operative Zareb. She's CERN trained and was part of the covert, now disbanded initiative."

Zareb's head starts to spin. The velocity of the oil cart speeding across the rickety rail tracks beneath them isn't helping matters.

"Lindar was an operative?"

"She was one of General Quern's best."

Zareb sits down inside the cart.

"But I don't understand, wouldn't Quern know that..."

"She wasn't called Lindar back then. And she looked different too."

"What are you saying Professor?"

"I need to tell you this quickly as we'll be leaving Militia City's perimeter real soon…Lindar's real name is Shanna Delti. Shanna faked her own death three years ago at the end of a CERN mission in Militia City. She had a friend in Ria who specialised in facial reconstruction. She came to me saying that she knew something, something that was of crucial importance to the Revolution. Through my contacts I sorted her out some ID and gave her a job as my office manager."

Zareb sits motionless in the cart as it zooms round steep corners and descends into dark gorges.

"That explains a lot. I wish I'd known."

"She must have cared for you a lot Zareb. The kind of information she has on Quern, at a time when no one else knew, well, it was enough to cost her her life and endanger all those close to her. Heck, it still is.

"I didn't realise. I thought…"

"It's ok. Our priority right now is to get Quern off the trail, find Ray, send the Uni-drone to Miss Black and watch out for each other."

"Are you going to tell the others about Quern?"

"I think I have to, but I'm reluctant."

"Why?" asks Zareb.

"I trust those 8 individuals with my life. I would never have asked them onto this project if I didn't."

"But?" enquired Zareb.

"These guys are doing what they're doing because they know there's something corrupt going on inside CERN. They believe me because they'd all come to suspect it themselves. Data, information that didn't add up. Things that disappeared from their departments, important things that could have put Venezelu way ahead of the other planets."

"It's as though Quern doesn't want us to make contact with Universe 6."

"He doesn't," replied the Professor. "The minute that we make contact with Universe 6, is the day that all of Quern's dealings at CERN will become public property, transparent. It means he'll have to share all of his intel with the Supreme Court. He's purposefully doing his best to delay that. We suspect he's even selling intel to foreign pirates."

"From other planets?"

"Yes. We suspect that Indigo's been given intel. We also suspect that Quern is behind the bombings. He's targeting some of our most professional travellers."

"He really doesn't want us to make first contact, does he?"

Professor Sykes shakes his head. "It appears not."

"So what's your worry?" asks Zareb, "Haven't you been working from these pods for years?"

"Yes, but up until four months ago only Lindar and I knew it was definitely Quern at the source. Now we just need to find a way to prove it."

"Well I'm not going to tell the group if that's what you're worried about."

"No, it's not that. The groups' focus until now has been to carry on MEW5's work on our proximal tectonic plate planets' best cases, undetected from CERN, heck, undetected from MEW5."

"And why should that change?"

"If this girl is who we think she is, this is going to change everything. And it's going to be hard for us to keep her a secret. I trust my pod teams, but what if one of them is a double agent? Just waiting for us to fall upon someone like her? Just waiting to see if I knew who the mole was inside CERN so they can report back to Quern himself?"

"Professor Sykes, please, listen to yourself. Those guys have sacrificed everything. Their families, their lives back in Ozro. Don't you think if one of them was a double-agent that Quern would have made his move by now?"

"You're right. I just get so paranoid."

"If I learnt anything from the awakening, it's that the small parts make up the whole picture. No matter how small you make them, how much you jumble them up or distort them, their very essence is there."

"I know, I'm sorry, it's just there's so much at stake here."

"The small parts are there for a reason. Look at Marcux. Why him? Why did he find her, out of every being on every planet able to visit Universe 6, why did he find her? We're all part of a huge game Professor, and the dice has rolled in our favour right now. We need to make the most it."

***

27th October, early evelight, Pod #1, Zaatta

It was around 8.30pm Earth time when Zareb and the Professor eventually reached the pod.

Professor Sykes journeyed a further 60 kilometres North to a town called Stoffenlaggen where he'd set up an emergency portable device to make calls from. It was far enough away from Ipa and Ozro to remain undetected. The device was hidden in an empty tin of gingero tea which lay underneath a large rock in a small abandoned quarry. The device itself was composed of two parts; a small red clicker that worked like an Earth pager, sending a red flashing dot to everyone's watches (so that all scientists, Marcux, Lindar, Zareb and the Professor knew if someone was making a call out), and a linked ear and microphone loop, which is inserted into the ear and strapped to the cheek.

Upon receiving the flashing dot in Ipa or Ozro, said person would then go to a bug free safe point in or near Militia City (sometimes just standing near the wall would suffice) and use a similar phone loop to receive the call. The person in Zaatta would have to wait until their phone flashes red again to then make the call.

The only downside to the device was that those in Zaatta could alert those in Ipa to go to a secure spot to take a call, but those in Ipa had no way of getting messages to those in the pods. Militia City was free from interception and especially any incoming communication, but anything leaving Militia City could still be intercepted by rebel hackers, who, from time to time, could pick up any outgoing messages. Their resources were low and the chances of them actually picking up anything significant was slim, but it was a chance the team didn't want to take, so they only ever received calls from

Stoffenlaggen, never made them.

Of course, the other option for making contact with the pods would be to go to Stoffenlaggen (which was beyond Zaatta, so that would be a pointless exercise), or to just turn up to the pods in person.

The Professor made the dial for Lindar. Lindar, at the time not far from the Militia's East wall, found a seat by some old fruit carts and picked up the call. The Professor found out that she was met by some Intolerants in the booth. She'd told them that the waitress had gone crazy at her, accused her of flirting with her snake boyfriend, and that she'd had to knock her out as a result. The Intolerants, with their love of all things violent, approved of this move. Had Lindar been faced with some of Yana's people, things could have gone less favourably. Lindar even went for a drink with the Intolerants afterwards, knowing that the waitress, upon waking, would remember nothing. Her time as an undercover CERN operative meant she was well trained in the art of lying to rebels, but she didn't enjoy being in their company. Militia City haunted her with a thousand cruel memories. She told the Professor that she'd made some calls to Mia's contact, who reported back that Mia was already on the case and trying to find Ray. She hung around in Militia City a little longer, just long enough to pick up the Professor's call, then went back home, to the Metropolis, where she got ready for bed. Exhausted and knowing that the next waking day was going to be a testing one, Lindar quickly slipped into travel mode and dream travelled her way to a sandy beach on the warm and tropical island of Cancan on the planet Crystalis.

By 9.20pm Earth time Zareb and the Professor were sitting in the pod's testing centre. Isobella and Mikus B brought them something to eat and drink and gave them a brief overview of their work that day.

"How's Marcux?" asked Zareb.

"Sound asleep." replied Isobella. "Real smart kid. Mikus B did some stealth training with him today, to test his reactive agility. He took to it really well. In the afternoon, I took him up the Zaatta Mounties."

"You were discreet?" asked the Professor.

"Yes Professor, always. We stuck to the low grounds."

"That's fine, just, you know, the bears and things."

"We're always careful." smiles Isobella, flipping out a large flipknife.

"What is that?" says Zareb, nearly jumping out his seat.

"Precaution. The Mounties are great for exercise and fresh air, but you need to be careful, what with flying Zaattan bears."

"Sorry, they do what now?" Zareb looks over at the Professor.

"Nevermind that for now, let's focus on the Feeler. You guys have done great work on this. I think we're almost ready to launch."

Isobella leans over to Zareb. "Chloez from Pod #2 did most of the coding work on this one actually, just for fun, but if the Prof asks, you can tell him it was me."

Zareb laughs.

"Ok, folks. Feeler is in its cage and in travel mode." Mikus B is sitting with his headset and opti-eyeglass down, fully focused. "Downloading search software. Activating search programme."

Isobella takes a sip from her kaffee mug, "It should take Mikus no less than 20 minutes to find her," Zareb nods, impressed. Isobella takes another sip, "Let's hope she's not already asleep."

Zareb and the Professor share a glance. It was a good point. They really needed to set up the connector tonight. It was imperative that they could see through her dreamtime travelling eyes from now on. They had to be the only ones that knew about her.

At around 9.45pm Earth time the Feeler had traced Aurora to a house in Pimlico, London, England in the United Kingdom. It hung around her livingroom for a while, but got bored of watching human's watching a political drama on the televised set so it moved back into the bedroom. That was the thing about Uni-drones. They may have been elite machines, full of advanced programming, but they were also part genetically enhanced and so, over time, had developed high consciousness. A kind of artificial intelligence. It is always possible to over-ride them, but scientists found that in most cases it was better to just let them get on with it. The Feelers knew what their main objective was, and they were very good at getting results. It fact, it was Zareb Fender's paper 'How the treatment of Uni-drones and Sleeping Subjects affects the productivity of dream research.' that was responsible for many of the changes in stage one dream research across all three monitored planets. Zareb and Professor Sykes couldn't take their eyes off the large monitor in front of them. Isobella had gone to make more kaffee and Mikus B was monitoring the Feelers' strength levels and connectivity along its pathway. In essence, they were watching a machine's dream play out in real time right in front of them. Something they had all done a thousand times. But this time it was different. This time they had one chance to enter into the subject's brain through the optical opening. One chance to latch on before anyone else did. Luckily for the Professor and Zareb, this was Mikus B's speciality.

At around 10.15pm Aurora and her human partner brushed their teeth and went to bed. Her partner fell asleep at around 10.30pm. Luckily his hypnagogic susceptibility was in the minus range, meaning that his will against any such experience was strong. He didn't believe in anything that wasn't factual and never remembered his dreams. He certainly wasn't at risk of stealing the Feeler's attention away from Aurora.

"10.34pm Earth time and the subject has turned off the light and has closed their eyes." noted the Professor into the microphone.

At this point Isobella came back with the kaffee, making some noise as she went. Zareb could see that the Professor was annoyed at Isobella's untimely entry back into the room.

"Shh." he told Isobella, pointing to the monitor.

Around 2 minutes later, the most incredible thing happened. A white light, snapped and crackled on the screen. Its brightness blinded the scientists momentarily. The monitor's picture was fuzzy, loud crackling could be heard across the monitor. The picture then went back to normal.

"Wow." said Mikus B, unable to contain his excitement. Isobella couldn't stop smiling.

"Subject crossing over into hypnagogia, pre-connectivity tag. Very strong reaction." The Professor smiles over to Zareb. Zareb smiles back, unable to believe what he's witnessing. As the crackling sounds phase, they are replaced by a sonic pulse, followed by a large glowing green bar that appears directly over Aurora's head. The size and scale of the connectivity is clear for all of them to see. Isobella looks over at Zareb. He has tears in eyes, in fact so does the Professor. Mikus B just looks completely stunned. Isobella looks down at her lab coat and notices that tears are streaming down her face also.

"Subject..." Professor Sykes clears his throat. "Subject shows unprecedented elevated levels of connectivity in prelim stage. Feeler is in position, moving into descent."

This was it. As the Feeler started to make its descent from the ceiling down towards Aurora's face, it just needed a fraction of a second to reflect its electrical charge into her eyes. That she would see the Feeler, they were certain. Not since the beginning of the awakening had any one of them ever heard of or seen anything like what they were witnessing now. Marcux was right. She was wide open to connect with. Now all she had to do was open her eyes at just the right moment.

"In three..." the Professor, Zareb, Isobella and Mikus B watched as the Feeler descended.

"Two..." Zareb held his breath, this had to work, this needed to work.

"One..." And just at that, timed to perfection, their sleeping subject, Aurora Black of Earth, turned around, almost having sensed the Feeler's approach, and opened her eyes.

4

27th October 2002, London, 10.43pm
"Arghhh!!!!!!"

"What is it? What's wrong?" shouted Johan, jumping straight out of a light sleep.

"I saw something! A spider. It was huge Johan, and it was coming right down from the ceiling, all the way down to my face. It was huge and black and had piercing blue eyes."

"You had a nightmare, it's ok. Come back into bed."

Aurora had been so frightened by her hypnagogic vision that she had actually jumped out of bed, ran towards the door and put the main light on.

"Come back to bed Aurora. Come on, it's 10.45, we need to be up in less than seven hours."

It was true. A large shipment of indigenous art from three Columbian tribes was arriving at the museum at around 6.30am. Johan and Aurora were on schedule for a very early wake up call. Aurora put the main light off and returned to bed, putting the small bedside lamp on as she climbed back in under the covers.

"I'm sorry darling. It's just that it felt so real."

"You always say that. You have an over-active imagination."

"No, honey, I honestly saw the spider against the back-drop of the ceiling. Like it was super-imposed. My eyes were open, I would swear it."

"You're never like this at my place. Maybe we need to stay at mine more, or no more red wine for you before bed," said Johan, stroking her hair, "come on, rest that mind, tomorrow we have a busy day."

Johan held Aurora for a while. He could feel her heartbeat through her chest. He thought she was excited about hugging him. She knew it was her heart still calming down from seeing the spider. *It was real*, thought Aurora. She turned to switch off the bedside lamp. In the dark, Aurora hears Johan's voice.

"Do you remember how we met?"

"I forget." replied Aurora, her habitual response. Johan loved re-accounting their first encounter in the third person whenever Aurora was panicky or scared.

"Aurora met Johan on her first day at the Museum," whispers Johan. "He was a strapping, handsome young man, brilliant you might say," Aurora laughs. "Stunning Johan had started there just two months before the beautiful Aurora, and they were introduced by the Office Manager, boring Evelyn, who thought that their shared passion for

Ancient Egyptian deities was a sign that they should meet, and so that Evelyn would be left alone at the water cooler and spared a new fact about Ra or Ptah every Monday morning." Aurora giggles and snuggles into Johan's chest.

"How did it end up? For Johan and Aurora." whispers Aurora.

"They lived happily ever after." replied Johan.

"Goodnight Johan. I love you."

"You had to get in there first, didn't you? Always in a hurry, my Aurora. I love you too." said Johan.

It wasn't quite the scenario Aurora had envisaged for their first admission of loving each other, but it seemed apt enough. Aurora panicking and Johan calming her back down.

Johan continued to stroke her hair and the top of her shoulder until he could hear her breath deepen. "Sweet dreams, my love." and with that, she descended into slumber.

***

Uni-drones, or spiders, are electro-magnetic transponders that can cross universes using electricity as their conduit and consciousness as their 'on' switch.

After all, brains are just made up of electricity and neurotransmitters that send messages in the same way as mobile phones send messages to other mobile phones.

The laws of physics may vary from Universe to Universe, but what unites us is the potential stored within the components of all our Universes; its matter; its stuff. The raw materials are all the same, and so, when you eventually become enlightened enough to see the map, you'll realise where the pathways are, and that they have always been there.

After a Uni-drone implants an electro-recording device into your brain's hard wiring, it gives us a window. The process does not hurt, it just feels like an electrical buzzing in your brain for a short second, you may even feel a slight shock across the body.

Like dialing a number in a phone book, our scientists can find you. And once we Cosmi-tag you, we can always find you. The purpose of the Uni-drones, is to allow us visual access to see what you see whilst you're in the very delicate stage of hypnagogia and what happens whilst you journey through dreamtime.

Recording what you see and where you go is what allows us to evaluate whether or not your people and your planet are on their way to becoming consciously aware. We can also bring to trial anyone caught abusing your holographic travelling self.

Although you cannot be physically hurt, you can be emotionally traumatised, as most of the time, the dreamer believes wholeheartedly that what's happening to them is real. On a few occasions, that shock or trauma has been so significant, that it has permeated into the physical world, putting strain on the heart or aggravating an existing medical condition. That is why we take great measures to protect the more conscious travellers from unnecessary harm.

At present, on Earth, most people call this awareness a 'spiritual awakening'. It can be labelled or misdiagnosed as some kind of mental illness back in their real-time.

This is very common across galaxies similar in age to the Milky Way. It's just fear through ignorance of something that isn't empirically quantifiable. Religious people have faith and stories that defy all Earth logic, but talk about seeing people appearing in your bedroom and it's off to the psyche ward with you. We get it, we've seen it all before. Youth, naivety, ego. The need for answers, the necessity for facts and cold evidence. It brings reassurance. It brings peace.

Even here, on Venezelu, you'd think that we'd be enjoying peace, given our revolution of consciousness all those years ago. But you see, it wouldn't be a game if we had everlasting peace on Venezelu, or across the Galaxies for that matter.

Peace goes against the very nature of space and time. Moments are born and they die. Stars are born and they die. Comets burn bright and fade. Positive forces and negative forces: the one and only constant everywhere, and at all times, all at once.

Each variant dancing its little dance. They need each other, their tension, their sway towards one or the other. How it goes is completely unpredictable, because it is everything and nothing all at once. Have I lost you yet? Told you that it would be hard to comprehend.

The absurdity of time and space is also its beauty, and to be conscious of any of it, to be part of the game, win or lose – that is our gift. And so, we must carry on playing.

Building Uni-drones, trying to find the next 'conscious pioneer' that will link our Universes. But why does it even matter?

We may never have the physical capacity to see the bigger picture, to get to the end, to solve the enigma, but we have to trust that mentally, we already can. We know that it is *not* about rushing to the end for the big reveal, it is about taking stock of *how* we play the game, with others. *That* we play is crucial, *how* we play is life changing.

Let me tell you about phase two.

***

Phase Two is a series of tests carried out on the sleeping subject to build up their awareness levels so that they can fully engage in stage three – exposing shadow people.

Normally stage two tests will go on for some time, that's many Earth months to you, or sometimes even years.

The tests vary and are designed to assess different sensory responses. For example, the scientists will begin by giving the travelling tester a series of objects. The objects travel with the tester (through conscious awareness of the tester, they can bring any object they want with them into other realms) and then suspend the object above the sleeping subjects' head whilst they are in full hypnogogic state.

They move the objects slowly into the subject's line of vision whilst the scientists back home record how well the subject sees the object. They make note of the initial reaction and they observe for any signs of reaching out to touch the object.

These early tests are mostly playful and positive, inducing a relaxed and hypnotic reaction from the conscious observer. Chainmail blankets (closest Earth translation we could find) are foldable poster-like materials that testers bring with them into the dreamworld. They are metallic-filled foldable sheets that the traveller can hold out in front of the sleeper. They are pre-programmed fabrics that contain a series of coded messages from different planets, often coming across like a moving painting or very intricate etches to the human eye. Izomites have a very positive reaction to chainmail blankets (or as we translated for Izomites, Joskular Weaves). We think this may be attributed to their already quite trippy existence, which allows them to clearly identify our patterns and codes when they present themselves during hypnagogia.

The blankets, or weaves, can extend an Izomite's hypnagogic state by at least another 25 seconds. In Earthlings, the best we ever got was a hypnagogic state extension of about 12 seconds, after which, the subject becomes too excited by what they are seeing and regains full consciousness. As soon as the subject regains consciousness, our connection drops. As it starts to go, our connection freezes and 'buffering mode', as humans call it, ensues.

Aurora Black was about to beat the Izomite level, in fact, she was about to beat the galactic record too. But then Aurora Black was in a hurry to know more, and her subconscious wasn't about to let her conscious mind interrupt things.

5

AURORA BLACK
9th November
I'm in a cinema lobby, about to go and buy some
tickets for a film. I walk up to a group of people
who I feel an affinity with. Are these my friends?
The cinema auditorium has dark plum felt seating
and enormous large ceilings. It's packed to the
rafters with people sipping black drinks and eating
snacks. The place smells like sweet butter. I'm
sitting with this group of friends, though something
tells me I don't really know them.

I peer down into my bag to look for something,
not sure what, but I know it's in there. There's a
bronze pocket watch, with a pendulum on the back.
I turn the pocket watch around. The time says half
past six. When I look up, the entire auditorium is
empty. I'm a little scared. Where is everyone? They
were here just a second ago. I look back down into
my bag, I can feel my heartbeat in my chest. When I
look back up, the auditorium is full again, only I'm

sitting next to a guy with a green t-shirt on whom I've never seen before in my life, but who I know is Paul, and that he is my husband. I know that we married whilst we were drunk and that he's a comedian. I look at him intently. His caramel hair is soft and smells good. His pale green eyes are like rays of sunshine. He smiles, and his face lights up. My heart melts. This is home. He caresses my hands. His skin looks tanned and his hands hold mine tightly. I look up at him again. What is going on? It's Paul, but he's older, much older. He's hardly recognisable, but I know it's him and I know that I still love him. We watch the film. Every time I turn around to look at him he's at a different stage in his life. I'm scared to turn around in case I see a corpse or a baby in nappies, but it's just Paul, at different ages, in this cinema with his wife. Is that me?

A lot of flashing lights, like cameras, start flashing from the stage. Everyone in the crowd sits with anticipation. What are we waiting for? Has the film finished? Who's coming on now? The lights keep flashing and I feel a soaring feeling of fear and excitement all rolled into one. Paul squeezes my hand gently, and I can feel my heart rate come back down. Everything's going to be ok, I can do this. Wait, what can I do?

I'm back out in the lobby. People are walking frantically between auditoriums. I start to feel a little disorientated by all the movement. There's a guy dressed in blue by the drinks counter. I know he has a bomb on his person. He sees me looking at him. Without any conscious thought behind it, I mouth the words *'I know'* at him. In my hand is what looks like a camera-phone. I take a picture of him. I think this is what I was looking for in my bag earlier. I run into the nearest auditorium. He follows me in there. I take the fire exit out into the street, I can sense he's coming after me. At least the auditorium and everyone in it will be safe.

Outside, the streets follow a grid system. There's a park across the road and a bus terminal on an island in the road. A white car stops at the traffic lights in front of me. I jump into the back seat. Inside are three women. They all have beautiful golden brown skin with electric white hair. Their hair is styled in ways I've never seen before. One has yellow eyes, the other a mix of blue and purple. They seem startled to see me. The lady driving the car looks into her rear-view mirror. Her eyes are the sharpest of yellows, speckled with green. They may have been bizarre eyes, but I knew from them that she was concerned about something. The bomber. I turned around. He was following us in a hovering motorbike. One of the ladies in the back seat asks me if I want to play with a toy.

"What is it?" I ask her, looking at the gadget. It looks like a portable scanning device of some kind.

"It's fun, it can change your eye colour." she tells me. "Try it."

She holds the device up to my face and I look into its piercing blue light.......

***

Sunday 10th November 2002, London, 10am
Aurora woke from her dream in confusion. The

morning's sun was streaming through the French windows and right into her eyes. She'd forgotten to pull the shutter down last night. In fact, there were a lot of things she'd forgotten to do before going to bed.

"What am I wearing?" Aurora asked herself as she clumsily climbed out of bed. She was dressed in a pair of old football shorts and a Guns 'N' Roses t-shirt. A bandana sat across her forehead at an angle. Her hair was alive with chaos. Aurora stood up. Flashbacks of the previous evening rose with her, as did her desire to vomit. Last night's initial tequila shots were fine, but when Aurora's friend Sarah suggested following them up with flaming tequila shots, things got messy. The last thing Aurora remembered was Sarah singing Kriss Kross' "Jump" on her living room table dressed like a deranged rapper from the 90s.

At that, Aurora felt an all too familiar and unrequited feeling making its way up her oesophagus. "Bathroom." She sped off, just making it to the toilet in time. "Flaming tequilas. Never again."

Sarah had left Aurora's flat in a taxi at around 4am. She was booked on the 8.20am to Preston to visit her parents for a couple of days. Aurora didn't envy Sarah's rail trip on what must have been a similar dodgy tequila stomach. Johan was away on business this weekend, so Aurora was on her own. She'd decided to make the most of the weekend by planning lots of activities. As it stood, her hangover was taking precedence over any kind of activity, especially her plan to have an early Sunday morning run down by the Thames. After a long shower and an espresso, Aurora felt ready to head into town.

Aurora had never been to the British Film Institute down by the Royal Festival Hall on Embankment, so she decided to have a leisurely walk towards the Houses of Parliament, catch a film at the BFI, have lunch somewhere near Tower Bridge market and then head home via St Paul's Cathedral. Aurora loved walking her way around the capital. In fact, she walked everywhere. For someone who was always in a hurry to do things, it seemed surprising just how much Aurora liked to walk – she would have been quicker taking the tube. But Aurora knew that by taking the tube you miss out on the little things. Like the time she was on her way back from visiting a friend in Balham. She had stopped to make a phone call outside of Sainsbury's Supermarket. She spotted a small girl standing in the window display of a charity shop across the road. The girl was talking to someone - a large white stuffed bunny rabbit, about twice her size. The conversation looked lively and the little girl's smile lit up the entire shop window. But what really melted Aurora's heart wasn't just witnessing a unique moment in time, one that would never again be repeated, one that no one had noticed, not even the girl's mother who was busy looking at some clothes at the back of the shop. What melted Aurora's heart was what happened next. The girl stepped onto a toy box next to the bunny rabbit so that it brought her head height with it. She looked it right in the eyes, said something and then hugged it. But this was no ordinary hug. It was the best hug

Aurora had ever seen. Swaying on her tip toes, it looked like the little girl might disappear into the pile of books behind the display. But she didn't. She just held on tight and hugged the rabbit with all her might. When she was done, she stepped off the box, squeezed its foot goodbye, and disappeared off into the back of the shop.

Today's special walking moment happened as Aurora strolled through Westminster Cathedral Square by Victoria Street. She looked up and witnessed a musical and elegant display of bird migration. It was so beautiful it stopped her in her tracks. Observing it, she held on tight to her handbag, an unconscious reflex displayed by most stationery Londoners who have their attention diverted somehow. The birds, (were they swallows?) danced and swooped over and under each other with grace. So precise, so harmonious and so effortless. What a joy to be that harmonious with one another. There was probably a head cheerleader type, making decisions, gauging the wind factor, magnetic pulls and all the rest. Her heart swelled. She felt lucky to have witnessed this pixelated dance above her head in that very moment. So slick, so harmonious. Aurora was curious as to why not one bird thought to do its own thing. Such obedience, such loyalty. Was it survival instincts? Was it better to stick together then go off on one's own? Aurora decided she would call Johan after the movie and tell him about the birds.

As Aurora walked over Blackfriars's Bridge, she noticed the sun beginning to set on her left, casting an orangey-pink glow across the river's bend at

Waterloo Bridge. Beyond that, high rise buildings and office blocks etched black silhouettes across the creamy pastel sky. She felt warmth in her cheeks, despite the crisp and nippy November air. Aurora stopped on the bridge, dialled Johan's number, then quickly put on her gloves as his phone rang at the other end.

"Hello," said Johan.

"Move in with me." said Aurora, without missing a beat.

Johan laughs, his recognisable, adorable laugh. Aurora could feel the grin on her face spreading. She hoped she hadn't misjudged this gut decision.

"Are you sure? I mean we've only been seeing each other five weeks."

"Of course I'm sure."

"When?"

"As and when you're ready. Why don't I come meet you at Victoria station tomorrow and we can chat logistics then? There's this new Mexican cantina in Covent Garden. I've been looking for an excuse to go there."

"Ok then, I guess I'm moving in."

There was an awkward pause, Aurora wondered whether Johan had gone into shock over her impulsiveness. She decided to change the subject before he changed his mind.

"How's the land that brought us the Schwarzenegger?"

Johan was in Vienna at the Kunsthistorisches Museum on a professional development visit. The team in Austria had a fantastic system for cataloguing. Johan and a few others from the

Museum had gone over to learn a few of their techniques in exchange for an extra group of hands to help with the unloading of a massive cargo load arriving that weekend.

"It's fantastic, I'm bringing you back some Austrian chocolate, it's not too bad actually."

"Yummy. We can have that for desert tomorrow as we stroll home along the Thames."

"Sounds like a plan, ma'am."

"Great, see you at the station at 5.30 then."

"Look forward to hearing all about your weekend. Sleep well tonight my love, no nightmares now."

"No nightmares."

Aurora and Johan said their goodbyes. The sun was almost out of sight and the temperature had dropped considerably. Aurora decided to skip the St Paul's perimeter walk and go for a hot chocolate on Fleet Street instead.

Street lights started to flicker as Aurora walked past St Paul's Cathedral and made her way towards Fleet Street. The temperature now felt considerably warmer in the shelter of the narrow streets. The river's wind had left its chill on Aurora's face, but she knew a warm doorway was moments away.

Aurora spotted the warm dim lighting pouring out from her favourite coffee shop on Fleet Street. She wondered if Agatha was working tonight.

Agatha was a fine arts student. Aurora had met her at a Biodanza class taking place in a small first floor studio space down a darkly lit street near London Bridge. The vibe inside the class was warm and positive, even if the exterior wasn't. Aurora had only committed to a couple of classes. She enjoyed the experience, but decided it wasn't quite her thing. She was glad she tried it, and even more so for meeting the wonderful Agatha.

As it happened, Agatha wasn't working that night at the café, but Claude, the manager, recognised Aurora straight away. He offered her some complimentary marshmallows on her hot chocolate. Why not, thought Aurora. She thanked Claude and went to look for her favourite seat by the window, which was normally free at this time of night on a Sunday.

Aurora sipped her hot chocolate and pulled out her phone. She dialled her parent's landline number and gazed out the window in happy contentment.

"Aurori!" It was Aurora's mum. Josephine was half French and half Welsh. Aurora liked both accents pretty well, but was glad her mother had spent more time in France, thus holding on to her French accent more, with the odd interjection of Welsh.

"Hello mamman."
"How are you my darling?"
"I'm good thanks. You and dad?"
"We are good my sweet. Your dad's in the garage right now, he's looking for a saw he bought in 1992."

Aurora laughed. Her dad, Victor, had the biggest collection of DIY and power tools ever held by one person. But it made him happy, so the family humoured the ever-growing collection and quadruple thousand figure screw bits.

"How is Johan?"
"He's good thanks, just spoke with him actually,

he's having a good time. He's back tomorrow."

"Work is good?"

"Yes, busy, busy. How are things with you? You doing the Christmas Fayre at the club this year?"

"Oh yes, can't miss that. I'm making little tree ornaments to sell, as we speak in fact! That's why your dad is looking for the saw, for some wood I have here. You still coming home for Christmas?"

"Yes, of course, I can't wait." said Aurora.

"We are really looking forward to seeing you, as is your Grandpa Tom."

"Mamman…"

"Yes darling,"

"Would it be ok if I invited Johan to come stay over on Boxing Day?"

"Of course! We would love that!"

"I haven't asked him yet, but we're moving in together so…"

"Wait, what? That is wonderful! You wait 5 minutes to tell your mamman this? Ooh la la ma petite, c'mon now…"

Aurora starts laughing.

"We welcome Johan to the Black household anytime ma petite, mais oui. And he can sleep in your room with you. I will break that to your dad gently over a small whisky tonight."

"Mamman," Aurora blushed ruby red over the other end of the phone. She let go of her hot chocolate to try and cool off.

"Hahaha, it's ok my darling, we are all grown up now, non?"

"Thanks mamman. Tell dad I said hello, will you? Give him my love, and Grandpa Tom too."

"Ok then, I will. Where are you just now?"

"Indigo Coffee bar on Fleet Street."

"Oh, is that the place you took me and your dad that time?"

"Yes, that's the one."

"Oooh, how lovely. Ok then ma petite, you get yourself home safe, always walking everywhere like a little wanderer, eh? Be safe, ok?"

"I will mamman. Love you, speak to you in the week, ok?"

"Ok ma bebe, love you too, bye for now."

Aurora decided to catch the early evening New Talent night at The Covent Garden Comedy Club on her way home. She'd missed the first two acts but the four she did see had her in stitches. It was past 10pm by the time Aurora arrived home. She ran a hot bath with a few drops of lavender oil to help soothe her muscles and relax her mind. She was desperate for a good night's sleep. She felt that her dreams had been very strange of late. Aurora felt so present in them that by morning, it was as though she hadn't rested at all. Like she'd spent the entire night walking around observing things. Asleep, but awake.

Aurora stepped into the bath. Goose pimples slowly made their way across her body as her skin acclimatised to the warm water. There had been a chill on Blackfriars' Bridge, but Aurora hadn't felt it. Her body was full of warm excitement at this next chapter with Johan. Was she rushing in? Johan didn't seem as excited as she'd hoped. Perhaps she was over-thinking things again. She shook the thought away and replaced it with a feeling of love in her heart and bubbles in her hair. Aurora sunk her body down into the water, submerging her shoulders beneath the silky fragrant heat. Yes, she would sleep well tonight.

11.35pm

Aurora descended into sleep mode shortly after 11.34pm. In the first stages of hypnagogia, she felt a tug at her head. Not a physical one, but an electrical tug, like an instinctive impulse telling her something.

Open your eyes.

Aurora, half awake, half asleep, opened her eyes with absolutely no conscious thought behind it. She didn't send a signal to her brain telling it to open her eyes. They just opened as she turned before that final dropping off point.

But she wouldn't drop off. As Aurora looked up, there, suspended above her head, was a lightshow of greens and blues. Lines, circles and patterns flowed and danced like a Van Gough painting that had come to life, moving and twisting with elegance and grace.

What is this? Am I really seeing this right now? Aurora could see the light fixtures of her ceiling right above her head, she could see the pictures on her wall and the dressing table by the back wall. This mesmerising display of moving patterns was super imposed right over it, like a three dimensional holographic patchwork quilt of bizarre organisms she'd never seen before.

Aurora could feel her heart begin to race. Perhaps the bath had calmed her down too much. Normally, night terrors like this would leave her properly startled. But this was no night terror, thought Aurora. *This is….beautiful.*

Aurora started to focus hard on the full spectrum of moving images above her head. She noticed the colourful patchwork image picture fall towards her very suddenly. She jolted upright. She was now fully awake. Her eyes darted around in the darkness, trying to find any remnants of what she had just seen. It was too late. The dance was over, the images were gone. That wasn't unpleasant, thought Aurora. Not unpleasant at all.

Aurora laid her head back on her pillow and glanced over at the alarm clock. 11.49pm. But hadn't she only just put her head down on the pillow? Time felt distorted. So too would her head if she didn't get some sleep, thought Aurora. And with that, she dozed off, this time into a deep, peaceful sleep.

***

Venezelu, 10th November, Earth Time

"Dammit, I scared her!" Jessom, one of the scientists from Pod #4 lunged out of his travel chair and put the MagnaStrip down on the table with frustration in his eyes.

Professor Sykes, Isobella, Mikus B and Zareb were also in the testing room.

Professor Sykes put down his equipad, took off his glasses and rubbed his eyes. "It wasn't your fault."

"I'm sorry." said Jessom, taking a deep breath to

restore his composure. "Nerves got the better of me, I'm really disappointed with myself."

"It's ok," replied the Professor. "You're new to being on the other side, it's exhausting, we know."

"The MagnaStrip started slipping out of my hand, I couldn't find the float function on this new model, and her vibrations…I was taken aback by their strength, her receptivity…I guess my mind lost focus and before I knew it, the strip was falling towards her face."

"Listen," said Mikus B, "you've only done about what, four scientific travels? Two of them with Robertus? It's ok. We are entering unchartered territory here. Besides, you don't get to be the big man in all dimensions."

Jessom chuckled, knowing that Mikus was probably referring to his 7 foot stature, broad shoulders, and the fact that nothing made him nervous in his waking life. Jessom had won 6 gold medals in the Ipa games and 3 awards for bravery during the worst days of the Revolution. Jessom was a warrior on Venezelu, but a timid cadet in the travelling world. His specialism was monitoring sleeping subjects' vitals from the safety of his monitor, however his agility, strength of mind and body and his elevated fitness levels made him a prime candidate for travelling, able to withstand the physical pressures on the body that stays behind.

"A few more days and Marcux will be ready," says Isobella, "he can take over the missions from you."

"I don't think we have a few more days." interjected the Professor. "Here, watch this…"

The Professor grabs a small aquamarine chip device and enters it into a gel monitor. The group gathers around.

"In the last two weeks since inserting the Feeler chip, we've been able to record all of Aurora's travels. As you know, she is an expansive traveller, travelling far along our Universal boundary zones. She's even visited Zahow in Universe 3, barely making it back."

"What's the connection with these places," asks Isobella, "the ones she keeps re-visiting over and over?"

"I'm not sure Izzy. For some reason, she keeps going back to a volcanic location that we initially thought might have been Crystalis but which we then identified as another planet in our Universe, not hers."

Zareb draws a sketch. "The only other major volcanic planet is...Indigo?"

"Yes, Indigo." Professor Sykes takes a seat and puts his glasses back on.

"But that's..."

"I know Mikus, I know."

Mikus B stands and walks over to the gel monitor. "Exactly how far is this woman's reach?"

"We don't know," replies the Professor, "but she's drawn there for some reason, and locals are starting to pick up on it."

"That's pirate territory," says Isobella "if Indigans become aware of her, they may find her on Earth."

"That's true," replies the Professor, "but I'm not worried about the game. It's the Indigan rebels I'm worried about. They'll torment our anomaly until she loses her mind, visit her night after night, forcing themselves upon her night-time eyes until all hope for the Revolution disperses. They don't care about the rules. They know resources are sparse here at the moment, that CERN's got problems of its own, so they're less scared of authority than ever before. And that means obstacles in her real-time life. Should she return to Indigo once they've worked out who she *really* is, they'll make her dreams a living nightmare too. We must protect her."

Zareb tops up everyone's kaffee. "The Professor's right, she's incredibly susceptible right now."

"She does glow incredibly bright, someone's bound to put two and two together." says Isobella.

Mikus B takes a sip of kaffee. "She's quite obviously lucid. Pirates and Intolerants are so obsessed with tormenting travellers, here's hoping that all they see is someone they can toy with, whom they know will feel it profoundly."

Zareb gulps at the thought, then takes a breath.

"Worst case scenario, we hope."

"Let's not underestimate her," says Jessom, "she can handle herself well in any new city or dreamscape she enters."

Zareb nods, but knows that Mikus B is right. The pirates are relentless.

The Professors looks for his kaffee cup. "I think we're missing something that's right under our noses."

The group listen. "Indigo is a major competing planet, but any data they receive from Venezelu is most likely trade bits for other competing planets.

All they care about is violence and making zulan, not making contact."

The Professor finds his empty cup and goes to refill it. "Yes, if the pirates figure out Aurora's status," the Professor pauses and takes a sip of his kaffee, "then things are going to get tough."

Zareb sighs, understanding the full measure of what's now at play. Time was against them.

As if reading his mind, the Professor stands and goes over to the gel monitor. He taps the screen and drags a new timeline up to it. "Time is against us comrades, and there's something else, here on day zeb at 32:64 hours…."

Mikus B offers to take the Professor's cup of kaffee from him whilst the Professor scrolls through the recorded material. "Thanks…look, here it is."

There, on the gel monitor, is Aurora walking out of a large cinema and hitching a lift with a group of passers-by.

"She keeps seeing the rebel bombers, here on Venezelu. It's like she's trying to spook them out."

Zareb goes in for a closer look.

The Professor points at the screen. "She dreamt about yesterday's Auxenhall cinema bombing two hours before it happened. She wasn't there in real-time. Then, she was at the site of the Braxom Library bombing last week and the Nexus Mall bombing 10 days ago, always two hours before the actual event. She's purposefully going there, though she probably has no awareness of the fact."

"What? How is that possible?" Isobella takes a sip of kaffee, eyes glued to the screen.

"I have no idea. It looks like she is manipulating

the anomalies between our Universes, like she's aware of the different laws of physics and managing to alter timelines with one foot in both dimensions."

"But the bombings went ahead." states Mikus B. "Some of our best travellers were killed or injured."

"Sorry, when I said alter, I didn't mean alter the future. I think she has predominus abilities. The prophesy does say that the anomaly can posses predominus. Jimus Krakovia possessed it."

"What does that mean exactly Professor?"

"It means, Zareb, that she can see into the future, that she's naturally and instinctively attuned to things going on, across all worlds, across both Universes. She'll probably start experiencing predominus in her own world."

The team's expression is blank. The Professor elaborates.

"In downtime dreaming, the part where the brain just plays about with the day to day data, that's where it'll start to happen. She'll be able to see events from her tomorrows, small things at first, then larger narrative sequences. Given how awake she is when she's asleep, it could be quite disturbing when it happens, but she'll put it down to 'déjà vu'."

"What's 'déjà vu?" asks Isobella.

"It's Earth talk, means 'already seen'. Most unenlightened species put predominus down to strange phenomena, a weird glitch in their brains."

"Not our gal," says Mikus B, "she'll make the connection."

"Let's hope so." says Zareb.

"It's part of her that is currently underdeveloped," says the Professor, "but it will get stronger. And there might be something in it, some message for our attention. We need to stay vigilant for patterns, clues, anything at all."

"We need Marcux," says Zareb, "set him up, get him ready."

"What about the remaining phase two tests?" asks Isobella.

"There's no time left for that," replies the Professor, "Aurora's ready, we start phase three tomorrow night."

***

11th November, pre-dawnlight, Zaattan Forest, Pod#1

It's before dawn and the main conference room in Pod#1 is bustling. All eights scientists from the four pods are present, and not one of them is sitting down. Papers and equipads are being exchanged around the room, pots of kaffee are steadily being poured and chatter is frantic and excited.

The Professor, Zareb and Marcux walk into the conference room.

"Welcome, team!" says the Professor as he ushers Marcux in with encouragement.

The whole room starts to clap, the excitement on the scientists' faces is clear to see. Just then, Marcux understands the magnitude of the task ahead.

I'm here to make first contact with Aurora of Earth. He gulps, suddenly aware of the fact. Marcux feels his uncle Zareb's hand on his shoulder. He looks up at him and smiles. *It's going to be ok, I can do this.*

"Right folks, lots to do, lots to do," the Professor pulls out pod chairs for Marcux and Zareb, "please, all, take a seat and I'll introduce you to our newest team members."

The Professor looks around the table.

"These guys each have their specialist area of expertise. The reason they are here, is not only because they are excellent at what they do, but because they are exceptional all-rounders. Should, Kilos forbid, something happen to any one of us, each operative is qualified enough in all areas of dreamwork to cover all bases. We all suspected that something underfoot is happening within CERN. Battling against the daily threats from the Rebels is one thing, but discovering that important data was going missing and possibly being sold to other planets in some kind of self-attack, well, turns out that was just the tip of the ice-berg. When we started to pick up on patterns and signs indicating the beginnings of the prophecy, we knew it was time to branch off, create a secure unit where we could carry on MEW5's work, undetected and secure from insurgents."

Professor Sykes looks around the room adoringly at his crew.

"The biggest hurdle wasn't finding you guys, some of you plucked straight from University or through the grid, but getting you out here, unbeknown and asking you to leave it all behind, in the name of truth. For a shot at the game."

Professor Sykes pours himself some more kaffee.

"Ok, so, you already know Mikus and Isobella quite well, but let me tell you a bit about their professional background."

The Professor stands behind Isobella.

"Isobella is a Stage 1 operative, specialising in Feeler engineering, programming, construction and maintenance. A Feeler mechanic of sorts, the best there is. Her numbers man is Mikus B, data engineer from the Feeler program back at MEW5. Mikus has the best ocular-insertion precision this side of Universe 5. We literally had to fake his death to remove suspicion of his absence from MEW5."

"Thank you Lindar." Mikus B brings a salute up to his head.

The Professor moves around the room.

"From Pod #2, we have Chloez and Higgins. Chloez is a Stage 2 specialist, responsible for designing, building, programming and maintaining our inter-dimensional sensory equipment, our Magnastrips and the like. She then analyses data responses and writes up lots of lovely reports on her findings."

Chloez smiles, her short red bob and freckles reflect off her golden turtleneck top. She has sparking hazel eyes and a small scar on her left cheek, caused by a faulty three dimensional rigger bobble that exploded on her one Aprilz afternoon.

Professor Sykes points over to Higgins. "Higgins is an expert in alien biology, chemistry and psychology. He monitors and analyses the sleeping subjects' responses from an holistic alien perspective. He looks at Chloez' data and together, they sign off on whether the subject is ready for

Stage 3."

Higgins waves to the group. He's a small man with a big warm smile. His greyish-brown hair is split neatly into a side parting, he has thick-rimmed glasses and a polka-dot tie.

"In Pod#3, we have Robertus and Gisella. Robertus is a Stage 3 specialist, responsible for finding, training and monitoring travellers. Given that this operation is so covert, Robertus hasn't been doing much in the way of recruitment. Pulling any of our registered, top grade travellers from the program at MEW5 is far too risky, as much as we'd love to save them from the current attacks against them, orchestrated by Quern's bandits. So, Robertus has been operating as our main traveller. He's been working with Jessom from Pod#4 most recently, and together they manage the workload."

Robertus nods to the group. His long, dark wavy hair sits down to his shoulders. And those shoulders are broad. In fact, most of Robertus' features are defined. His jaw, his brow, his piercing black eyes. His skin has a translucent glow, its reflection highly noticeable by night-time eyes. He blinks, and his eyes change colour, first to emerald green then to a deep sprinkled red and gold. Perfect photon-reactive eyes, most distinguishable to the sleeping subject. The Professor moves around the table and puts his hands on a woman's shoulders.

"Gisella, ah our dear Gisella," the whole groups laughs.

"Gisella was one of my students back when I taught at M.U.C." The professor turns towards Marcux, "she's the joker of the group."

Gisella winks at Marcux, who giggles. Zareb looks on, confused.

"You know, being out here, isolated, far from family and friends, working long hours, it gets tough, mentally. We all know why we're here and we're committed to what we are doing, but even with our connectivity to the enlightened source, we are still just Venezeluan flesh and bonas at the end of the day. And so, our non-sleeping time is often filled with hilarity from this wonderful healer. Gisella has two jobs. She is our Stage 3 whisperer, our auditory, or hypnopompic specialist. She puts words into our shadow people's mouths. It's a very selective skill, one which stood out during her University years, and it's a complex job. As most of you already know, seeing and hearing are not exclusively available to all sleeping subjects. Some can only do one or the other, few can do both. Very advanced subjects will try and talk to shadow people when they see them, but this is incredibly hard for them. They need to tightrope walk the line between consciousness and unconsciousness in order to do this. Formulating words and sentences is something that most species can only really do in conscious thought. It's different from sleep talking, a sleep talker is just a subject who is dreaming and not consciously or coherently able to respond to any other conversations going on in their realworld. A conversation with a shadow person, or even a Stage 2 object, yes, it has been known, but it's very difficult to do. Not only that, but having the subject keep calm enough to acknowledge any kind of communicative response, well, that's even harder.

"And Gisella's other job?" asks Marcux.

She's a naturally gifted creative, an artist, a healer. She keeps us sane, and sometimes, she lets us keep her sane too."

Gisella smiles and bows her head. Her long poker straight blue hair tumbles onto the table. She brings her head up, her green-tinted skin and emerald eyes sparkle like the room's underwater reflections.

"Last, but not least, Pod#4." The Professor motions over to the last two people at the table.

"In Pod#4 we have the ever wonderful Kara and Jessom."

Kara waves, her brown-grey skin looks like liquid metal, her kind pink eyes are large and radiant. She has short, spikey black hair, with strands of blue poking out. Jessom is a large muscular looking man, with a tight top and training shorts on under his lab coat. He has pale yellow skin, blonde curls and deep, purple eyes. He gives the group a thumbs up.

"Both are trained medics, Kara's specialty is psychiatry and consciousness studies, with focus on the academic side of what we do, journaling and recording everything that goes on so that we have records for future covert operatives. Jessom is our health guru, he keeps us fit and healthy through a specialised nutrition and exercise programme. He also specialises in monitoring a sleeping subject's health during stage 3, things like their heart rate and vibrationary motions. He's just recently started training with Robertus as a traveller to take some of the work load off him, but, if Aurora is who we think she is, we can pull our focus on to just one subject, using Marcux as our primary traveller."

The Professor stands and walks behind Marcux. "Marcux has been travelling since he was a baby. He is a born traveller, and will be delivering the download sequence to Aurora. He is an important part of the prophecy, just as you all are. We all have jobs to do, and we can only do our best. Everything is a game, everything is a test. Let's give it all we have. Now, down to business..."

The Professor sits down and the conference room lights dim. Schematics and graphs appear on the holographic board. The group gets to work.

A few hours later, and the conference room is bustling with chatter and energy. The scientists are laughing and talking, testing out technical equipment and Gisella is giving Robertus a shoulder massage.

Robertus rolls his neck and takes a deep breath. On his exhale, the pod's internal alarm system goes off. The holographic image switches to the main tunnel's camera.

"It's ok," says the Professor, "it's just Lindar back from Ipa."

Lindar gives the group a wave from the tunnel and slips into her sack.

"Take a lunch break folks, see you back here in 40 minutes. Jessom, could you take Marcux out to the woods for some fresh air? It's going to be a long night, I think some exercise will be beneficial."

"Copy that boss." Jessom and Marcux stand to leave.

The Professor turns to Zareb, "Zareb, come with me."

Pod #1, Professor Sykes Office, Andanuan Forest

Professor Sykes' office is tall and circular in shape, with a cone-like opening at the top made from thick plastic. Riverbed light beams make their way into the ceiling, creating dancing lights along the top of the cone-shaped walls. The room is sparsely furnished; one armchair, a few lamps, a rug, a tea-making facility and lots of books and ancient Venezeluan artefacts. Some of the Professor's clothing and personal belongings are strewn on the floor. Lindar's on the couch with Zareb. The Professor walks over to Lindar with a cup of gingero leaf tea, Lindar accepts and the Professor takes a seat on the floor, stretching out his legs across a hand-made Zaattan rug, courtesy of the Zaattan monks.

There's silence for a few moments.

"Do you want the good news or the bad news?" asks Lindar.

Zareb looks over at the Professor who has his head in his hands. "We'll take the good news first."

"Mia found Ray."

"That's great," says the Professor, sitting up with elation. "Is he alright?"

"He's shaken up. Mia traced him to a jail in the Curzon district, a dingy out of town heap market. Poor Ray, he'd been beaten and was dehydrated when they found him, but he's been re-located and is lying low with his family."

"Glad he's out of harm's way," replies the Professor.

"His services as de-bugger are totally out of service," says Lindar, "for a start, Quern will have had everything down to your toothbrushes bugged whilst you've been out of town. Plus, it's too risky to bring him back in, he's red hot at the moment."

"As long as he's ok," says Zareb. The Professor nods. Lindar smiles at Zareb, a smile that Zareb felt lasted a little longer than any of Lindar's other smiles of late. Maybe he'd imagined it.

Zareb breaks eye contact, aware that he's beginning to blush.

The Professor takes a deep breath. "How bad is it?"

Lindar takes a sip of the gingero tea, hesitating, but clearly enjoying the warmth and balming properties of the nectary refreshment after the long flight from Ipa.
"I'm going to lay it out straight," says Lindar, "you've been suspended Justin."

"Suspended?" asks Zareb, "For what? Can he do that?"

"It's a rouse, a trap" replies the Professor. Lindar nods in agreement.

"We're lucky that Justin wasn't framed for Ray's disappearance, it's their style. But they've gone simpler. By suspending him, on account of missing too many regulated sessions at MEW5, a technicality within the legal framework, Quern can attach some reconnaissance agents to Justin, follow him, see where he's going in his free time. Quern and Griig are on to us. They know nothing of the pods, of that I'm sure, but they know that something is going on."

"What about Aurora, has anything about her come up on the system's databases?"

"Nothing yet. But as part of your suspension, Quern wants you to hand in all of your access privileges. That doesn't matter much, I can get you anything you want, but you will need to be very vigilant."

The Professor takes a deep breath. "How long is the suspension?"

Lindar looks down into her steaming cup of gingero tea. "Three months."

"Three months!!" The Professor leaps up from the rug, struts about for a second, pauses, then goes over to bang his desk.

Zareb walks over to the Professor. "Professor, Justin...there are ways around this, there must be."

"I don't think so Zareb. Presumably I'll need to return to Ipa to sign my suspension papers, after which, Quern will have eyes all over me to see if I return to wherever it is he suspects I am."

Zareb sits next to Lindar again. "Lindar, do you know anyone who can create a distraction, a decent cover story?"

"I do. It's a risky one, but might just be enough to get you back to the pods in a couple of weeks time."

The Professor nods.

Lindar takes another sip of steaming warm tea. "You need to be boring for the next week. Go home, watch re-runs of The Goyar Show, eat musenli bran." The Professor's eyebrows scrunch into a frown. "That's exactly what I *do* do in my downtime."

"Good." replies Lindar.

"What about Phase 3? Can the Professor leave after tonight's experiment?" asks Zareb.

"We all know the answer to that," says Lindar. She stands. "You need to leave immediately. I've secured cover for re-entry to Ipa. One of our allies, a comrade of Ray's, will cause a distraction by the city gates, no one will see you re-enter."

"The city gates?" asks Zareb, "isn't that dangerous? The place is crawling with Quern's guys."

"All the more reason to go back in that way."

"Lindar's right," says the Professor, "it's the best way back in. Once I'm past the walls, I'll just head straight home. Wait, then what?"

"After a week, they'll probably reduce the number of eyes on you, but you'll still be monitored. This is where we can lead Quern off the track."

Lindar pulls out a map. "I want you to go into Militia City, draped in grey robes and a prominent bundle of documents in hand. You will be followed, but that's ok. You're going to take these guys on a very long goose hunt."

The Professor sits up, "I'm listening."

"There's a woman who lives in the Grassmarket, her name is Maggie, she's a psychic from Fraz County."

The Professor looks taken aback. "Not sure where this is going, but ok."

"I want you to go meet Maggie," Lindar draws a circle on the map, "around here."

Zareb and the Professor inspect the map. "You want me to march into apocalyptic grounds with a shamanic woman from Fraz?"

"The shamans are our friends, they live for the prophecy, but we can't disclose anything to them.

The gap feels like it's closing and we can't do anything to compromise Aurora."

"Of course." says the Professor.

"Head to this tavern, it's a well-known gossiping hole. Punters may be confused as to why you *leave* with Maggie, but Quern's people and the rebels will trail you from here, word will spread."

"Great," says the Professor, less than enthusiastically.

Lindar continues, "From here, you and Maggie need to head to the Jeopardisers' camp up on the hill."

"What? What exactly is the point of all this Lindar?"

Zareb turns to look at Lindar, curious of her plan.

Lindar sighs, "Would I waste any of our time when it's time that is so precious?"

The Professor shakes his head.

"The plan is, that we want as many eyes on you as possible, both from Quern and the rebels. If a known high level CERN operative is visibly seen carrying a bundle of documents into Jeopardisers' territory, it looks like a hand-off." Lindar smiles.

"Are you trying to get me killed? Or worse still, arrested?"

"Of course not Professor." Lindar takes a breath, "By the time you get to the camp, the heat on you and Maggie will be strong. Griig, if he does his job right, will notify Quern and take him to the situation room to monitor proceedings. That gives me the opportunity to break into Quern's office and steal his data."

Zareb interjects, "What data?"

"Hopefully, remnants of conversations with whichever pirates Quern has been dealing with. We all know he's been selling Venezeluan data, but we don't know why, to whom and, well, we don't have any evidence. It's impossible to get past Quern's security whilst he's in the building, but with him in the situation room, I'll find a way to break in and get those recordings."

Zareb scratches his head, "Surely the head of CERN won't have recordings just lying around his office of underhand deals with other planets from competing jurisdictions?"

"He won't," agrees Lindar, "he'll have deleted them. But I know someone who can de-code the material and recover the original files."

"Impressive plan Lindar, but what do I do once I reach the camp?"

"That's simple, you just head to the old tree of enlightenment with Maggie and take a seat."

"Take a seat?"

"Yes. The authorities will jump you there and take you back to CERN for questioning, but you'll be well within your rights to be there. They'll take the documents and see that they're just run of the mill revolutionary manuscripts and chants. You tell them you wanted to go worship, but were worried about your safety given that the Jeopardisers have set up camp near the Holy Tree, or what's left of it. You brought Maggie for protection, to raise alarm of any impending beatings. At worst you'll be in a questioning room for a couple of hours until they work it out."

"That is genius Lindar!" Zareb squeezes Lindar's

knee. "Every Venezeluan has the right to worship by the Holy Tree of enlightenment, it's a constitutional right." Lindar smiles with surprise.

"And so's a beating if any of the Intolerants get to me first!" says the Professor.

Lindar sighs. "Do you have a better plan?"

"Fine, if I need to be bait, I'll be bait. Beats posing as a Jeapordisier I guess."

"No moustache." laughs Zareb.

"No moustache." says Lindar. "Quern is hiding something, he has a secret. His levels of paranoia have reached an all time high. I'm convinced he thinks you two *know* his secret, we need him to continue thinking that we do. He wouldn't compromise Venezeluan intel, all of our dreamwork and research since the enlightenment, unless it was something big, something damaging to him and his seat of power at CERN."

"Lindar," Zareb clears his throat, "the girl, she has predominus. We can use her."

"She's showing signs of predominus? Already?"

Zareb and the Professor nod.

"Making first contact with her is still our main goal," Lindar stands and places her empty cup on the Professor's desk. "If we can connect Universe 5 with Universe 6 through Aurora Black, then we can move on. The game is won and we can focus on getting Quern out of power, shaming him in front of Venuzuelans and getting on with our lives, until the next cosmic drama."

Zareb laughs. "Have you ever wondered what will happen once Universe 6 makes contact with Universe 7?"

"What the shamans in Fraz County call the Final Chapter?"

Lindar shrugs. "I've heard some of their prophecies. What they call the big re-calibration. All that is comes together with a smash, and all starts again."

"We'll be long gone by then," says the Professor, "but we still have a game to win – here and now."

"We can't see what's right in front of us," says Zareb, looking at Lindar, "but can connect with something we can't even see."

"The sooner Aurora gets it, the sooner we can save Venezelu." says the Professor.

"Connecting 5 with 6 is our duty, our purpose here as revolutionaries. It's why we fight this fight. Getting rid of Quern, that's our little bit of happiness, our glimmer of peace in a restless Cosmos. It's our chance to return the moral arc towards justice, and away from hate and fear." says Lindar.

Zareb garbs Lindar's hand and squeezes it. Professor Sykes sees this and shifts. "Right, I better get going if I'm going to make the sentencing. I'll grab some stuff."

"I'm sorry Justin," interjects Lindar "but you need to go now. Our set up at the gates is time sensitive." The Professor nods and walks towards the door. "Thank you Lindar, as always, you have my back. Good luck Zareb, you're holding the fort now. Lindar will be here when she can, but we need you to push everything ahead for first contact tonight."

The Professor turns to go then runs back again, "Obviously I can't take any calls for a while, but just go to the portable device in Stoffenlaggen if you need to contact Lindar." Zareb nods.

"Bye guys, good luck."

Zareb looks on, his heart filled with trepidation, "Bye Justin."

As Lindar and Zareb walk down the dark corridor outside the Professor's office, Zareb gently pushes Lindar against the wall. "Zareb, what's gotten into you?"

"Please be safe."

"I will."

"I know, Lindar. About your past."

Lindar shrugs out of Zareb's grip. "How long?"

"Just a couple of weeks, the Professor…" Zareb corrects himself, "Justin, he told me."

"She's dead Zareb, you must never utter her name outside these walls. It could blow everything for us. We're so close now to unveiling Quern for who he really is."

"You know I'd never disclose that. I just wanted you to know that I knew, and…."

Lindar cuts Zareb off by kissing him forcefully on the lips. Zareb is stunned to begin with but then kisses Lindar back, holding her tightly in a passionate embrace. Lindar feels the yearning on his lips, like he's been waiting an eternity to kiss her again.

Their deep embrace is interrupted by the sound of running footsteps down the corridor.

"Zareb! Zareb!" It's Isobella, she's crying.

Lindar and Zareb release their grip and turn to notice the tears running down Isobella's face.

"It's Marcux. He's been attacked."

6

Flying Zaattan bears are dangerous. Zaattan border police started a petition to kill the bears, but local Zaattan's didn't oblige. Sure, they were just as petrified as the next person, but if they learnt anything from the enlightenment it was that murder was unacceptable. Death through self-defence was forgivable, but pre-meditated murder? Not for them. They'd take their chances on Koli's green planet.

Koli means energy, by the way. The unifying source of all things, the big guns. You call them Gods or Deities. Enlightened ones call it Koli.

Back to Zaattan bears. They come in at five and half Earth metres in height, are about two metres in width, with thick, black matted coats, completely covered in multi-coloured strands. Like Earth fibre optics. The coats are deep and are incredibly pungent. Luckily, the bears smell of, well, the closest smell to a human plant would be Lavender.

Their arms are webbed, like bats. They only need to take a few short running steps and they can take off at a remarkable speed. You can hear them running to take off, the forest trembles every time it happens, and a delayed sonar echo booms between the bark of the Andanuan trees.

Their faces are small, in comparison to their heads. They have small black eyes, a relatively small pouty snout, multi-coloured bear whiskers, oh, and a huge mouth.

They are vegetarian, or pescatarian, believe it or not, surviving on the lush green vegetation, sweet berries and logar fish that are abundant in the Andanuan forest.

This means they have small, flat teeth, good for grinding berries, leaves and fish bones. They have an incredibly bad temper, serious anger management issues. Definitely not enlightened, which is a shame, as most other animals, mammals and birds on Venezelu were already ahead of the Venezeluan's when it came to living in harmony, still are in a lot of ways.

We may have had a conscious shift, a spiritual and internal awakening, but the soul being as it is, with infinite freedom to decided its own destiny, well, some were swayed towards a different path, a rebellious path.

For whatever reason, the poor Zaattan bears got left out of the awakening altogether. Perhaps it's their positioning in the remote Andanuan forests that kept them out the loop, never having to interact with other species, other than their forest friends.

It doesn't take much to anger a Zaattan bear, especially if you are a Venezeluan. They'll use any excuse to have a swing at you with those impressively long, sharp bear claws. Claws that can extend out of their paws at a distance of up to 45 Earth centimetres.

You probably don't need to know all this. I'm not sure how relevant it is, but am glad you know. I'll be back later.

7

11th November, Earth Time, dawnlight, Quern's Office, CERN Headquarters, Ipa

Quern walks into his office, a large gold trimmed pentagonal room with brown and gold covered furniture and solid wood chairs. His large heavy hands smooth over his bald head. Sweat is rolling down his brow, clinging over the edge of his fury red eyebrows for dear life. His green eyes look sad, or empty. His round face glows a pasty-peach.

Quern locks his office door and points at his interior windows. The panes slowly darken with the wave of his hand. He points towards the external windows, and they do the same. Lines of surplight turn opaque, from top to bottom, with velocity and synchronicity, like scales moving about on an elaborate fish.

Quern walks over to his desk. He puts his hand underneath the desk and presses a black button which is hidden underneath. As he does this, an infra-red web-like net consumes the office, covering

its every crevice like a neatly wrapped parcel.
Behind his desk is a large rectangular cupboard. He
presses a dark gold button on his desk which opens
the cupboard, the doors splitting off to the left and
right. A gel monitor appears.

Quern looks at his watch and clears his throat,
"Indigo."

The screen looks like a molten pot of metallic
liquid, Quern hears a beeping sound which is soon
followed by a visual.

In the gel monitor, Quern sees a group of Indigan
rebels sitting around a small wooden table in what
looks like an underground cellar. Just one of them is
standing, a female pirate at the back of the room,
her back slightly turned towards the door. She's
wearing a long dark purple hooded gown, with the
hood up, and can be seen peeling a juicy purple
herenaga with a long, sharp knife.
The group are made up of Indigan pirates,
Intolerants and Jeopardisers.

"I don't have much time," says Quern. He studies
the group. "Where's Jasper?"

A man with a long green beard replies, "He's not
feeling well."

Quern's eyes suddenly replace emptiness with
pure anger.

"Is the zulan on its way?"

"Yes, sir. Frayaraz here is going to do the
transaction herself, once we receive the data."

"What news from your client?" says Quern, a
slight quiver in his voice.

The female pirate, Frayaraz, bites a slice of her
herenaga and slowly moves forward from the back

of the cellar. She flings her knife onto the wooden table, startling the others. Quern doesn't flinch.

Frayaraz moves right up to the camera and takes down her hood. She has long pink hair which is speckled with green. Her eyes are huge and blue like the Indigan cliffs. She takes a bite this time, her eyes looking sternly forwards, like hot pokers trying to infiltrate through Quern.

"You won't get us to talk about that, not whilst we're on camera. We're here as a multi-planetary group representing our client."

Quern looks unimpressed. "This room has been fort-proofed from interception, not even our best spies could hear what's going on in here. As for the recordings, you know I fry them."

Now it's Frayaraz who looks unimpressed.

"Need we remind you, Quern, that you're lucky you're getting any zulan at all. After all, it's not *us* captured on feeler intel tormenting the daughter of Hydros' highest ranking officer whilst she retires to her bedchamber at night, not to mention the countless other women you've spied on across the cosmos." Frayaraz laughs, a dirty, gritty hearty laugh. The group joins in, one man laughs so hard that he falls off of his chair.

"Enough!" shouts Quern, "the transaction goes ahead at 3-00 daylight hours."

"Have you prepared everything for the bombing?" asks Frayaraz without hesitation.

"Yes," replies Quern. "I have my best operatives on it."

"It takes a sick kind of individual to destroy his own dream centre," says Frayaraz, spitting to the ground. "..but I guess that a connection with Universe 6 means more light on you from the Supreme Court, and we wouldn't want them finding out what you've been up to, would we?"

Quern's brow is now dripping with sweat, his eyes in a frown and his face cast in shadow from the office's dim light.

"We blow up MEW5 in 3 days time." says Quern, without a flinch on his stony face.

Frayaraz nods, waving the purple fleshy herenaga in Quern's virtual face. "And we get our data to sell to competitors. See, isn't it fun doing business together? You're such a great business man."

Quern scowls at Frayaraz. "You better have our backs covered on this one Quern, it could all so easily come right back at you."

"The blame will go on Venezeluan rebels, when you enter Militia City, we'll organise a distraction."

"You know us rebels love a good fight, and we'll just keep on fighting if we need to. Good playing with ya." She cuts the transmission.

Quern bangs his desk, "Damn you Kilos!"

There's a knock at his office door.

Quern goes to the door and touches it, a small section becomes transparent on the inside. It's Griig. Quern opens the door. The infra-web grid disperses almost immediately, evaporating like ice in hot water. Quern flashes his arms towards the windows with two brisk hand moves, surupbeams come flashing in like a barrel tipping with liquid gold.

"General, I came to see if…"

"Close the door."

"Yes General." Officer Griig Hawthorne was a six-foot-seven soldier and ex-combatant; one of the scariest guys in the civil law department. That he had the biggest dimples and softest baby-face features was an inconvenience to his public image, but his eyes were hard and knowing. They were dark, murky stone-grey eyes that looked as old as the pebbled ruins of Jorkey beneath the Roko ocean.

"I need that meeting at 3-00 hours to go ahead, you know the one."

Griig nods, he knows exactly which meeting Quern is referring to.

"Yes General, not a problem."

***

11th November Earth Time, just after dawnlight, Beachfront, Indigo

The Rebel Indigan group from the cellar are all sitting about on carts and boxes left over from the abandoned funfair on Vulcanus beach.

Some are smoking juniper-grass, others are drinking sola soda, all are becoming quite merry.

The surup has just come up. It looks like it's dangling above the oceanic horizon.

About twenty Indigan yards away from the group sits Jasper, hunched over on an old fruit cart, staring out to sea.

The woman with the hood is the group's leader, Frayaraz, an intolerant rebel from Sikamey.
Frayaraz is sitting with the old green bearded man.
She looks over at Jasper. "What's gotten into him?"

The old man shrugs his shoulders.

Frayaraz rolls her eyes and continues carving out the letter 'I' into her wooden cart. "He's probably still spooked from almost being engulfed by that tsunami." She cackles an insensitive laugh. "Lucky that it disappeared at the same time as that glower freak." The old man laughs, scratching his long green beard. His laugh is cut short as he spots something in the distance, along the beachline.

He whistles a shrill-like whistle, alerting the group to an oncoming stranger.

It's a cloaked figure, walking down the beach towards them. Jasper looks up, he's closest to the figure, but doesn't move. Frayaraz drops her pen knife into the sand and stands up.

"What we got here then." She straightens out and puffs out her chest, almost exhilarated by the potential of a fight.

The bearded man puts his hand on his knife belt. "Looks like a visitor."

"They're no visitor Patró, this one's a Venezuelan, I can smell it," Frayaraz sniffs the air, "She smells like Venezeluan Gojine plants and sea salt." Indigans have a very keen sense of smell, better than any Earth animal.

The cloaked figure removes their hood, revealing a woman with long wavy golden-orange locks, locks that roll out and down to beyond her thighs. Her eyes are chocolate brown and her face has a glittery shine to it. She opens her white robe to display an array of colours underneath, which come right down to her knee high army boots. She opens out her arms in a surrendering motion. Suruplight bounces off her white fingerless gloves in every

117

direction.

"What's a girl got to do to become a pirate around here?"

Jasper looks up, then looks over at Frayaraz who is scowling at this uninvited guest.

"What's your name stranger?"

"I'm Hispanica, from Militia City on Venezelu. Word is there's a storm brewing soon, and I want in on it."

"We don't know what you're talking about." says Patró

"Rebel lies are transparent to other rebels, I don't know why you bother." replies Hispanica, taking off her gloves.

"What's in it for us?" says Frayaraz, kicking up her knife from the sand and seamlessly sliding it into her belt.

The wry smile on Hispanica's face disappears. Her eyes go deadly serious. "I have intel, but no band to work with."

"Why us?" asks Jasper, now standing next to his crew.

Hispanica looks at Jasper and smiles. "This is too big for one chica to handle. I need a crew, and I heard you guys are top of your game."

Jasper looks over at Frayaraz. He nods and sits down. Frayaraz looks over to the rest of the pirates and rebels and they nod too. She steps out in front of Hispanica and extends three fingers.

"Let's talk."

Hispanica smiles and the group go back to drinking sola soda, laughing, singing and general merriment as Frayaraz and Hispanica go over to a large rock to discuss Hispanica's intel.

Patró wanders up to Jasper and takes a seat next to him on the sand.

"You'll never find that girl again Jasper, she could be from anywhere."

Jasper doesn't respond. He puts his hand through his thick brown hair, revealing a scar on his upper right temple. Beneath it, green eyes shimmer like scalom leaves on a sunny afternoon. Jasper strokes his trim brown goatee.

Jasper looks away from the horizon and turns his head towards Patró. He hesitates, then says, "She looked human to me."

Patró looks taken aback. "Human? But there's no way. You sure she wasn't from Kalestio? They're a bit funny looking on that planet too."

"I'm telling you, she wasn't from our Universe. I checked out some pictures. She definitely looks human."

"But she was wide open."

"I know." Jasper looks back out to sea, his eyes darting the waves as though he'd somehow find Aurora in its surf. "Do you think she'll ever come back?"

Now it's Patró who hesitates. He'd never seen a pirate openly show such sadness before, such emotion. He didn't want to hurt him further, but couldn't hold back the question at the forefront of his mind. "Even if she could, why would she?"

**

11th November Earth Time, just after dawnlight,

Pod #4,

"Marcux!" Zareb came flying through the doors of the medical room annex, closely followed by Lindar.

Kara and Higgins were in the medical room adjacent, operating on Jessom who was fighting for his life. Zareb didn't even notice that Jessom was in the next room being operated on, he just ran straight to Marcux' bedside, a single bed in a room filled with medical supplies and other equipment. Zareb crouches down next to Marcux wiping the tears from his eyes. "Marcux, Marcux, wake up."

Marcux opens his eyes. He coughs, a groggy, dry cough.

"Oh thank Kilos he's conscious." Just at that Isobella runs into the room and makes her way over to Zareb, Lindar and Marcux.

Isobella told Zareb and Lindar what had unfolded. Marcux and Jessom were looking at some logar fish in the stream, when a large male Zaattan bear got territorial, thinking that Marcux and Jessom were there to poach fish from him. Seeing the Zaattan bear head straight for Marcux, Jessom flew into him to push him out of the bear's way. Marcux was knocked unconscious by a nearby tree, fracturing a couple of ribs and bumping his head. Jessom, unfortunately, got the full blow of the angry bear's weight, which crushed him to the ground, slashing his calves on the way down.

Micro-seconds before the attack, Jessom managed to sound his ankle alarm, alerting the pods. Kara and Higgins jumped into a hover pod and went straight to their location, taking them back to Pod

#4 which had the more advanced medical equipment.

Zareb looked into the operating theatre. Jessom had tubes coming out of his mouth. Kara and Higgins worked with ferocious precision around him. "Thank you Jessom." he whispered under his breath. At that, Zareb felt a hand grasp him tightly on the shoulder. The person's touch sent a warm tingle up his arm. It was Lindar.

***

11th November Earth Time, daylight, Pod #4
It had been 4 hours since Jessom had gone into surgery. Kara exited the operating theatre first. Her clothes were covered in blood and her face tired but resilient.

"It was a bad attack," she takes off her surgical gloves, "but he's going to be ok." Higgins comes out of the theatre, his face drained of colour and looking exhausted. He remains silent.

"Should we contact the Professor once he arrives in Ipa?" asks Isobella, already knowing the answer to her own question. Lindar shakes her head. "I'm afraid not. If Marcux is up to it, we stay on course for tonight. If not, Robertum goes in."

Zareb interjects, "He's far too weak."

Lindar gives Zareb a stern stare. He'd definitely seen *that* look before.

"It's ok," spluttered Marcux. "Lindar is right, we go ahead, tonight. I'll be fine."

Zareb was concerned for his nephew's health, but deep down he knew it was the right thing to do.

Time was running out. Quern and Griig were gaining advantage on them and their activities. Aurora seemed to be able to jet about the multi-verses as easily as dashing around the shops of an Earth mall.

Zareb nodded in agreement, then looked fondly on at his nephew. "The moment Marcux's vitals show anything resembling under par, we pull him out."

"Of course," replied Lindar, with a reassuring smile. Zareb had seen that smile before too. It looked convincing, and Lindar could be convincing.

"I'm going to head back to Ipa now, I should have left by now. Only contact me if things *don't* go to plan."

"Ok Lindar." replied Zareb. "Take care won't you."

"And you Zareb."

8

Monday 11th November, 9.30pm Earth Time

"Oh Johan, it's lovely!" said Aurora, gently and gingerly folding up the piece of crisp green dotted crêpe paper that had enveloped the finely decorated and dainty silver pocket-watch pendant Johan had brought her back from Vienna.

Johan and Aurora were already in their pyjamas, sitting on the couch in Aurora's front room. They sat cross-legged, inches away from each other in the centre of the, already slightly drooping, couch. The night's delicious Mexican meal was also sitting comfortably in their bellies.

"To help you keep a track of time, all the more." Johan took the pendant from Aurora's hands and moved in, raising his arms over her shoulders to put the pendant on her. He peered over her shoulder with a stretch of the neck, checking to see if he'd attached the latch correctly. "Done." He sat back, admiring how the pendant sat on Aurora's neckline and how niftily the clock sat between her bosom.

He leaned forward and kissed her head. Aurora smiled. She kissed Johan back on the brow. Johan laughed, he liked this game. Next it was his turn to kiss Aurora on the nose, then she on his lips. But Johan was feeling cheeky this evening and snuck in straight for the lips. The two embraced so tightly that Johan could feel the tiny pocket-watch dig into his chest bone.

"Thank you for moving in." said Aurora.

"Thank you for asking." replied Johan. "Shall we watch one more episode of Columbo and then to bed?"

"Make it two and you have a deal." replied Aurora.

"Two more and then to bed." smiled Johan.

"And then to bed." said Aurora.

Johan pulled Aurora in towards him as they turned to face the TV. He gave her a tickle to the ribs. Aurora was incredibly tickly, and Johan knew it. She let out a rippling roar, "Ah, stop it," she laughed, "press play already."

Johan obliged, and they resumed their position, Aurora buried her head deep into Johan's chest, her arms squeezed around his midriff, his heart beating in her ear.

***

The night of 11th November, Earth Time, was a disaster. An unmitigated one.

Contact with Aurora Black failed. Marcux made his presence known, but he was still very weak. As Aurora's brainwave frequency reverberated at the perfect levels, right between Alpha and Tetha frequencies, Marcux jumped onto the line.

But he wasn't strong enough to manipulate the photons that night. Aurora's photoreceptors were highly receptive and the anomaly to her visual cortex made it possible for her to have excellent inter-dimensional vision. However even if you can stay at optimum frequency for prolonged periods of time, like Aurora could, if a traveller's light isn't strong enough to begin with, then there's no way for a subject to translate and spread those electrical signals to the brain. Aurora could see something, but it was too faint to make out.

Marcux's vitals sky-rocketed, his heart rate increasing the harder he tried to stay on Earth. Zareb commanded that he be pulled out and Robertum sent in. Aurora's brain frequency was so powerful at the Alpha-Theta border 8Hz that it overwhelmed Marcux. Aurora lingered in Alpha-Theta for a long time in Universe 5's dimension, but just minutes in her own dimension. Higgins pulled Marcux out just as Aurora moved over to Theta-Delta.

They'd missed their chance. Next stop for Aurora was Delta waves and the dreamland superhighway.

Aurora Black did go back to Indigo that night. Unbeknown to the team back at the pods, Marcux's presence did awaken something in her. Her frequency at Delta-Gamma that night was off the charts.

***

THE ALPHA STATE

In order to understand what is happening to you, Aurora Black, it is perhaps wise to start with Beta and Alpha states.

Humans have 'a dialling tone', a perfect state of Megahertz electro-connectivity needed in order to 'communicate'.

There's much confusion on Earth between what dreams are, what lucid dreams are, what out of body experiences are and all the 'phenomena' therein.

I come from a place where these experiences are not 'phenomena', they are an intrinsic part of our reality. When we woke up, we were able to use the full potential of our brains and internal dynamics to comprehend something much larger than we could see. We knew we were intrinsically connected to this energy. As connected as a herengana is to a herenga tree, until the fruit ripens and falls that is.

Earlier I told you about how our dimensions interact. At this moment in time, your Universe is moving underneath Marcux's Universe. This movement gives us a perfect window within which to try and communicate with one another. A gateway is opened, allowing inter-dimensional contact, via electrical impulses, to communicate with one another – in exactly the same way as electrical messages move around the bodies of living things. But you already know all this.

Resting state is negative, but when the surge begins, gates open, allowing negative charges to move in amongst positive charges, and vice versa.

Alpha waves are oscillations in the frequency range of 7.5–12.5 Hz which come from electrical activity from the thalamic pacemaker cells in humans.

Electroencephalography (EEG) or magnetoencephalography (MEG) can detect Alpha waves and come from the occipital lobe of the human brain, mostly during relaxation and with the eyes closed.

They say that the strongest EEG brain signals in humans happens when the eyes are closed. We know this as the frequency which helps facilitate what humans might feel as a 'tug' to their consciousness as they settle for sleep. That 'tug' isn't a bio-mechanical reflex – what they feel are our Uni-drones, what they sense in their bedrooms are our Feelers.

***

THETA STATE AND THETA BRAINWAVES

There are five main frequency brain waves in humans: Beta, Alpha, Theta, Delta, and Gamma. These waves are always moving.

We use these frequencies for different activities. For example, Beta state is when humans are alert and awake.

The Alpha state is one of initial relaxation. That place where humans daydream or meditate. It also contains the bridge between the subconscious and the conscious mind.

Theta state is a place of very deep relaxation. It's most commonly known for its uses in hypnosis and REM Sleep. The brain waves are considerably slowed to a low frequency.

Some people work very hard to reach this state through continuous meditation, in search of the 'bridge'. Aurora Black's brain chemistry and biology is such that she has a quick circuit to this place. She doesn't need to meditate, she doesn't need hallucinogens. All Aurora Black has to do to go to this place is close her eyes and relax. Within minutes, Aurora bypasses the initial Alpha state and enters the Alpha-Theta bridge. It's a powerful, all encompassing place, and the best frequency for us to reach you on. Aurora's dial up to 8Hz is incredibly quick, and she can stay there for some time before she swaps over to Delta frequency. Delta state is when you're in a very deep sleep. This is the frequency you use to travel on, your private jet to the multi-verse.

Gamma waves are related to interaction within deep sleep. Those who are very connected within their dreamland use Gamma frequencies to read signs, talk to other living beings and basically take notes on their travels. Again, Aurora, you are very good at this.

In fact, there is already a bit of heat surrounding you, young Miss Black, due to an incredible visit where you started going around asking other living beings questions about their planet. You seem to do this a lot. Lately, you've even been memorising street names and trying desperately to manipulate and interact with your surroundings, all of which you have become quite skilled at. The Revolution encourages this behaviour and thinks it is a crucial part of human Gamma development. I'll be honest, some people just find it nosey, or that it's another human taking advantage of their hospitality, but you'd be wise to ignore them.

***

HOW ELECTRICTY WORKS

Electrical charges jump from one cell to the next until they reach their destination. Human minds are no different. This is exactly how they travel in dreamland and between Universes.

Electrical signals are fast, they allow for almost instant responses. Again, the brains of most living things work in the same way.

Almost all cells in all living beings in our Universe are capable of generating electricity.

When cells in a living body, or entity, aren't actively sending messages, those cells are slightly negatively charged.

It's the same for Universal contact. When our 'hexagons' are in floating mode, they are slightly more negatively charged. When they crash, slide or interact with another Universe – where there is action or charge – then it allows for positivity to enter.

When things get really bad, as they do on all planets from time to time, we crave positivity to enter – but for this to happen we need an active gateway, we need to *allow* positivity to enter, and allow negativity to exit.

This is what the Revolution is all about. Craving the interaction between Universes so that this exchange can happen. So that the positive charge can be drawn in.

But this is also where respect is given to the Duality Pendulum, for without the negative charge there would be no darkness for the light to be attracted to, and vice versa.

Negativity is the natural resting state of most living cells. In humans, for example, it's related to an imbalance between potassium and sodium ions inside and outside the cell, creating a platform for your electrical abilities.

Human cell membranes practice something called the sodium-potassium gate. For Burovians, it was the kalipo-frotonar gate, but it all ultimately works in the same way.

When the body needs to send a message from one point to another, it opens the gate. When the membrane gate opens in humans, sodium and potassium ions move freely into and out of the cell. Negatively charged potassium ions leave the cell, attracted to the positivity outside the membrane, and positively charged sodium ions enter it, moving toward the negative charge.

This change between the positive and negative generates an electrical impulse which can then move from one gate to another.

But, like all electrical processes, sometimes the motherboard can trip, or become overcharged. In Universal terms, we align this with the big re-set. In Delta waves travelling terms, we attribute it to any kind of electrical override or brain damage experienced by the living being in their own dimension, or if they are unfortunate enough to get caught in some kind of electrical storm in a Universe far, far away. This would be bad for the dreamer – very bad – and could fry all of their hardwiring. Thankfully we've not had many cases of this within our monitored planets. Except Burovians, they experienced all sorts of misfortune. An override of negative charge, complete electrical breakdown - but that's another story.

9

"The light which puts out our eyes is darkness to us.
Only that day dawns to which we are awake.
There is more day to dawn. The sun is but a morning star."

Henry David Thoreau of Earth

11th November, Earth Time, dusk, Indigo
It's getting dark, I can see the bruised purple pink clouds stretched out over the sea. I can hear music, sounds like a pan pipe or a whistle tinkling a merry tune. I follow it.

I'm now down an alleyway. I don't like this. I've been here before and something horrible happened. I can't remember what, but I know I've been here. There's candlelight shining out onto the wet alleyway from one of the open holes in the building on my left side. I can smell seaweed or fish in the air, it's so pungent. I look down at the puddles of water on the ground. Is that blood? Or wine? I can't tell.

I hear voices. There are people inside a stone room to my left, where the light is coming from. I decide to stand quietly out of sight.

"The transaction went through this afternoon, so this is our official 'Operation Go' meeting ladies and gents." It's a woman's voice, she has determination in her voice, a voice that sounds all too familiar somehow.

"Some of our rebels in Militia City went to MEW5 this afternoon where our contact Griig gave them access to the Lower Boiler Room on level -3. It's an annex of the main engineering room and very rarely visited. They dressed as Quern operatives and hid the explosives. We have the remote detonation device which we'll release on Quern's orders. There's enough powder in them to take out half of Ipa."

I *know* that voice. I must take a look…

As I turn my head and look into the room, I notice around fifteen or so people all sitting around a small hexagonal table. There's candlelight in all corners of the room, people are smoking pipes and carving fruit with short sharp knives. There are large bits of paper laid out on the floor and on the walls, there's a sack with objects in sitting on the table's edge. I feel like I've met these people before. I get a queasy feeling in my stomach. It's a very uncomfortable and edgy feeling. I feel unsafe.

I feel a change. I look towards the right hand corner of the room. A woman with long golden curls and brown eyes is staring right at me. No one else seems to have noticed me, but she has. Her eyes look different from the others, kinder. She stares at me for what seems like an eternity. I'm not sure if she's going to alert the others of my presence. Eventually, she smiles, I can see glitter glistening off her face in the candlelight. I suddenly get the feeling back in my body and quickly dart behind the safety of the wall again. *She saw me*, and yet said nothing.

I go to look back into the room, only I'm not on that alley way anymore. *Where am I?*

It's cold. I'm looking into a large, cold, ice-blue room. It looks metallic and container-like, but I can tell I'm inside a building, what feels like a very large building. My feet are cold. I look down and see that all I'm wearing is my old Britney Spears t-shirt and a pair of cotton red polka dot knickers. No wonder I'm cold! This is what I went to bed in.

I hear an echoey metallic clang coming from the opposite end of the room. I start to walk towards it. As I make my way through all the different pipes, vents and bits of machinery on the floor, I notice that pipes, vents and fans are also making their way out of the walls and ceiling. Am I in an engine room of sorts? It smells like burnt orange and old running socks. The clang goes again, I can hear whispers.

I make it to the other end of the room and see a doorway into a corridor. There's no light down it, but I know I must follow it. I outstretch my hands so they reach the walls either side of me, as a guide. I can feel the corridor twist to the right, and then to the left, before straightening out again.

There's a speck of light coming from around a

corner, about 5 metres away.

"Jasper, what *are* you doing? You'll blow us to smithereens!"

"Relax Jesse, I just need to cut this little…"

I can't help myself, I turn the corner, desperate to see who's there.

"Hello?"

Two men jump back so far I could swear they momentarily jumped out of their skins.

"I'm sorry, I heard voices and wondered.."

One of the men has a stripey beanie hat on, which fell off as he jumped back, revealing a bundle of bouncy brown hair.

"Kilos above!" he shouts, going for his sword.

"Please, please don't hurt me." Though somehow, I already know he won't.

The man picks up his hat and moves the candle forward, scanning my face. The other man is still in the corner of the room clutching his chest and breathing heavily. "How…how did you get past Hispanica…?"

Get past *who*? What is this scared little man talking about?

"I'm sorry to have startled you. I've no idea where I am, a minute ago I was in a fishy smelling alleyway and now I'm here. Not sure what's possessing me to ask this, but I must know, what day is it please?"

The man with the beany hat clears his throat and grabs a pad from his pocket. He types in some numbers. "It's the 14th of November on Earth. You're in the low level grounds of MEW5, on the planet Venezelu."

"Oh, ok", I say, not really registering this new information, but deciding that I really must try and remember what he just said when I become conscious. When I become conscious? Am I not conscious? No, I'm not. In fact, I don't even feel like I'm dreaming. This feels…different.

"Please leave Aurora, it's too dangerous for you here, someone might see you and then, well, you're in the worst possible location you could imagine right now."

The man walks up to me and brings me into his arms. "Go back Aurora, go back, go back…" His green eyes are streaming with tears.

"But how do you know my…"

***

12th November 2002, wee small hours, London

"…name."

It's pitch black. I can see someone sitting up in bed with a bright light coming from their hand. My mind catches up with everything - it's Johan, he's on his phone and tonight was Steve's bachelor party. "Hey darling, how was Steve's party?"

Johan jumps, clearly unawares that I'd woken up. "Hey babe! Did I wake you coming in?"

"No, not at all, I was dreaming and…"

"I know," he chuckles, "I was listening."

"Listening?"

I think you said "14th of November," Johan starts laughing. "That's two days away, babe. Are we time travelling now as well?"

"Oh," I scratch my head, which hurts like hell. "I don't know Johan, can't remember. I do have a blinding headache though. My head feels like play dough."

"Well, why don't you let me get you some painkillers and a glass of water, it's the least I can do for waking you at 3 in the morning – and to answer your question, it was hilarious. At one point we had Steve running across The Heath in a Gingerbread man outfit. There's video footage."

"I'd love to see that, or maybe I don't!"

"Caroline would find it funny, am sure you'll get to see it after we post her the aftermath footage."

"She's getting to see that? Oh dear, call the wedding off."

"I might get myself some paracetamol too, take the edge off this hangover before it begins. To be honest, we eat so much Indian that I doubt the 5 or 6 pints have even sunk into my bloodstream yet."

"Oh Johan, such a part-time drinker."

"Well, it is a school night."

"So it is. Ok, you're off the hook, lightweight."

Johan laughs and stumbles out of bed, still fully clothed and heads towards the kitchen.

"Be right back, night mumbler." Aurora smiles at that, and curls back up into bed.

***

12th November Earth Time, Lower level, MEW5 Engineering Room, Ipa, Venezelu

I've been here. I know where I am. Think Aurora, think… *low level grounds of MEW5, on the planet*

Venezelu – I'm in the worst possible location I could imagine right now.

There's a small emergency-green looking light causing a sickly haze over the small rectangular shaped room in front of me. I see some tools and yellow cardboard-looking boxes scattered by my feet. I stick my head out into the long, dark corridor. A cold draft whizzes past my ears. I step back into the room and, for no good reason, my instinct tells me to start looking into and around the boxes. Nothing of note. I'm drawn to the corner of the room, I see a large sheet of blue cotton-like tarpaulin. *Go to it.*

I pull the tarpaulin back, almost not surprised at what lies underneath. It's like part of me already knew I'd uncover a massive load of explosives. *I knew about this - how?*

I decide that the *how* isn't as important as the right *now*. Why is this dangerous? What day is it? What time? Why did I come here? Who did I meet here before? Think, Aurora, think!

"Who's there?"

If I wasn't lucid before, I am now. Who was that?

"Who's there? Respond operative."

Operative? What do I do? I want to fit in, but doubt my Britney Spears t-shirt will achieve that.

A tall man with blue skin appears in the doorway. He's dressed in a very official looking blue uniform and has a pilot style hat on. "Identify yourself please. This is authorised personal area only."

The man turns the green emergency lights off and a yellow-orange light appears instead.

"I, erm, I'm…" I pull my t-shirt down, feeling

quite self-conscious and intimidated by this Nazi looking geezer.

"Wow." he says.

Is it my hair? Is my bed head so bad that I've actually scared the living day lights out of the unknown 'operative' stood before me? "I'm sorry, I'm asleep right now and I know I shouldn't be here. I won't ask you any questions, so no need to get upset. I'll just be on my way."

"You…" he pulls out a pistol from his holster. "You're glowing, you're glowing green, a lot."

This man makes no sense, but I can tell I've perturbed him if he feels the need to get his pistol out.

"I'll be on my way."

"No, you're coming with me." He grabs me, and to my surprise, his grip can hold me. How is this so? I didn't think I could be gripped? Why do I think that?

He seems a little surprised himself. He quickly presses a button on his watch. "Attention control room, intruder alert at MEW5, subject looks alien, yet to scan identify. I repeat, subject looks alien. Glowing like a mint rock, awareness levels high, unprecedented."

Just at that, an alarm goes off and the man in the uniform is moving a scanning device up and down across my body. "Excuse me, what are you doing? Unhand me!" I manage to get out of his grip, and realised that I only believed he had a grip on me because he tried to grip me. He never actually did. Did he? I was standing there because I forgot I was lucid, Ah, funny old brain.

Wait, I'm lucid? So I can escape this nightmare? *But it's more than a nightmare, stop denying what's going on Aurora, you know it's bigger than that.*

The alarm sound is getting louder and louder, the blue hat guy continues to scan me. Let's go Aurora, let's get out of here…let's go, just close your eyes and all this will disappear.

I close my eyes and can feel an electrical charge spark across my body, the alarm sound is getting louder and louder.

"Got it!" shouts the man. "I've got your ID details now…." He looks down at his scanner. "Wait a minute, there's no record of you…how can that be?" The man takes a picture of Aurora, flashing his watch in her face.

"Ow, that was really bright." I tell him.

"What's that pile behind you?" He asks, pushing past me, but almost walking through me.

"It's explosives."

"Wait, what? You know about this? You're in big trouble, and this has all been recorded on my devices in any case. We'll find you, fugitive. No one burns as bright as you and slips through the net." He tries to scan me again.

That's it, I'm tired of being prodded and poked, I'm outta here.

Indigo, 12ᵗʰ November, Earth Time

Really? I want to wake up, and here I am, standing on a hexagonal table in an empty cave room. I'm back at that stupid alleyway again, and it smells of pee. Great.

All I need now are those blooming Pirates of the

Caribbean to re-appear, start waving their swords
and hurtling herenagas at me.

Wait, no, this is Indigo - and I need to find Jasper.
Yes, I remember. I jump off the table and make a
dash out into the alley.

It must be early, I can see what resembles dawn
light piercing up from the distant horizon. A woman
with long blondey-orangey curls is sleeping against
the wall outside the cavern. She has her hood up,
but I know her, I recognise her. Her skin is a
glowing bliss of glittery sparkles. She looks so
peaceful, I daren't wake her.
I run towards the end of the alleyway, desperate to
leave this place and reassemble with the other local
weirdoes on this totally weirdo island, or country or
whatever it is.

I'm seconds from the main road and I hear the
blonde woman shout out after me. "Aurora, no!
Stop!"

Not another one that's after me. I keep running
and run right out into the main cobbled street. It is
bustling like I've never seen it before. There must
be hundreds of people with carts, animals I've never
seen before, produce, boxes and bicycles. Is it
market day?

I turn my run into a walk. I'm ok, I'm amongst
others, I'm safe.

I hear the woman shout again, it echoes down the
alleyway, "Aurora, no!!"

Feels like it's echoing on forever now, because
everyone else has fallen silent. I hadn't realised it,
but villagers, adults, children, even the animals are
all looking at me. You could hear a pin drop on this

hilly terrain.

I look over to the woman with golden-orange hair, and it's at this moment that I understand how beautiful she is. She's not evil. She doesn't want to hurt me, she never has. She stands there now, silent, her eyes full of tears. Her glittery face seems a sad reflection of the smiling woman I saw earlier. She drops her head into her hands.

I look back at my surroundings and out of nowhere, every villager, child and old person has, what looks like, a mobile phone pointed at me. They're just gawping and clicking and flashing. What is the deal here? Why do people keep taking pictures of me?

And then I saw it. A photographed image captured on a child's tablet-like camera. I see myself, and I am positively brimming with bright emerald green colour, you can barely see my outline because of it, but you can see my face. At the bottom of the picture there's a box. In it, says, 'Scanning ID: Earth, London, ID unknown.'

I see Jasper, the man with the stripey hat, run up the street. But when he sees me in the middle of Indigo's morning market, surrounded by all the budding clickers he just stops in his tracks.

"I'm so sorry Aurora," he mouths, " I'm so sorry."

***

NARRATOR

Aurora had just waltzed through the streets of Indigo with a green glow that could have caught the attention of Grezorbs in the deepest caverns of the

Hydros mountains.

Jasper had wanted to protect her, but he didn't know how. As the rebels started to chase Aurora down the street, everyone in town saw how brightly she glowed. She was wide open. Aurora of Earth, live and on the move. To use an Earth analogy, Aurora had just inadvertently given out her IP address to every living creature this side of the dimensional plate.

Jasper's heart sank as he saw people's cable devices flash and flicker with the spreading news. It would only be a matter of time before it got back to Quern. And then, whoever had been harbouring this dream fugitive, this connected one who was clearly off grid at MEW5, well, Kilos help them.

10

Three Months Later, Supreme Court, Venezelu, 19th February 2003 Earth Time
19/02 Last Hearing of the Day

Defendant:
It began about 40 minutes before the subject fell asleep on 11th November Earth time. The drone had picked up on some human activity in the bed chambers and left again, as the subject was not quite ready for sleep. The drone returned around 5 minutes before the subject fell asleep and just waited to ride onto the connection.

Connection made, the traveller descended, making themselves visible to the subject for the second time in the subject's perceptive experience.

Although the subject's vitals were not as elevated as we imagined they would have been upon first seeing the traveller, back in Rome, Earth, her vitals were high and vibratious. Add to that that our main traveller was not at his peak fitness at the time, we were unable to establish any kind of meaningful connection between subject and traveller. We decided to bring Marcux back and just send Robertum the following night, give Marcux a chance to rest.

It wasn't until we saw the subject's dream footage the following day, that we realised we'd been compromised. It was already too late.

I'm not going to lie to you in the Supreme Court. Yes, we knew about Aurora Black of Earth. But now the Indigans knew about her, as would the entire Universe, as did Quern himself. In addition, it was Quern who had planted those bombs there. Quern and his men.

Prosecutor:
Objection, without evidence this is an allegation your Honour, not a statement of fact.

Supreme Judge: That goes without saying, overruled.

Defendant:
We'd seen the footage your Honour, yes, we can't evidence it, but that night, on November 11th, the anomaly went to Indigo, intercepted a meeting that was planning to blow up MEW5, and then she went to the source of the bomb site, just after the bombs had been placed there, and as such inadvertently alerted Quern that he had been compromised. So the bombing never took place, but in his attempt to shut us down, destroy us and the anomaly, he ultimately created enough rope to hang himself with.

Prosecutor:
Objection!

Supreme Judge:
Denied, please finish.

Defendant:
The point is, we had all been compromised. Our main concern at this point was to try and keep the anomaly safe. With her sudden overnight fame would come pain, and it did… it still does.

It was only a matter of time, and torture, before the pods were compromised, and we knew we wouldn't have the resources to protect her how we wanted to. That's why we agreed to come to you with this appeal, despite all of Quern's underhanded fake evidence against us. Yes, we were working covert, but knowing what we did about Quern, can you blame us?

Supreme Judge:
Thank you Mr Fender. The Prosecution may proceed.

11

*"Look at it well; it is wholly real and it will be so.
You cannot doubt it."*

C.G. Jung of Earth, Psychoanalyst

**Three months after compromise on Indigo, 20th
February 2003,
Yorkshire Psychotherapy Unit, Barnsley, Earth**
Aurora despised these sessions with a vengeance,
but promised her mum and dad that she'd attend
them at least once a week.

Amy, her psychotherapist, was a lovely and
qualified enough person, but she was ill informed
on what Aurora knew and what she'd been
experiencing.

"Aurora, you've been coming here for around 6
weeks now, yes?"

"Yes." Aurora watched as the petite therapist
scratched her dark blonde ponytail with her biro. If
she were an animal she's be a gerbil. A cute,
inquisitive gerbil.

"And we still haven't gotten any closer to what
might be causing this insomnia."

"I told you," said Aurora, sighing with despair.
"Nothing has *caused* this. It's part of an ongoing

thing, something that's always been in me, but that has just...well..."

"Manifested itself?"

"Please stop putting words in my mouth."

"I'm sorry, do continue."

Aurora pauses for a minute, watching Amy's tiny frame hunched over her notes. Her green armchair engulfs her. Why couldn't she have an armchair too? Why did she have to sit on this uncomfortable chez long?

"Well, yes, it is a form of manifestation," says Aurora. The therapist looks on, rather smug with herself, Aurora rolls her eyes and continues, "but it's just the intensity of the visits and my dreams that's putting me off kilter in my waking life, I can't seem to escape it."

"You know, often it is that which is buried deep within one's self that is the hardest and most challenging thing to face. To face inwards, to look into ourselves, it's hard."

"Please spare me Amy, you *know* I know all this. This is not a psychotic nor schizophrenic manifestation of an underlying problem. This is real, and I know it sounds mad, like, totally mad, but what I'm witnessing as I fall asleep, and beyond that as I sleep and dream - it's real, it's already in motion, I'm not processing it out of my imagination. I'm merely a witness."

"Right," Amy looks down at her notes and starts sucking on the top of her pen. "Tell me more about these visitors that come to see you before you go to bed."

"No, that's not right Amy."

Aurora sees Amy writing something down and suspects it reads, '*Patient in denial, hallucinations worsening.*'

"It's not *before* I go to bed, it's whilst I'm *in* bed, on the brink of sleep. If I saw that stuff whilst I was at the supermarket or in the toilet, then yes, I'd recommend further tests."

"So you never see these 'visitors' at any other time."

"No, never. Just upon falling asleep. The conditions have to be pretty much the same too; dark room, state of pure relaxation, transitioning between consciousness and unconsciousness and not on any drugs or alcohol."

Lately that hadn't been entirely true. Aurora had been experiencing 'sensations' and seeing flickers of movement from the corner of her eye when she had been conscious, but those experiences were of an altogether different nature. Aurora had always been relaxed when picking up on these 'movements', but she only ever saw them from her peripheral, never square on, not when she was fully conscious anyway.

"So this is why you've been sleeping with the lights on, music blaring and drinking a bottle of wine a night?"

Aurora is slightly taken aback by this, and sits up fully, bringing her legs up onto the chez long and crossing them defensively. Her normally long bouncy auburn brown hair is now cut short into a bob. It's much duller than it was, but so too is her complexion. Her previous olive skin now looks pasty white and her beautiful dark eyes which were once midnight pools of endless softness look sullen, with bags and a darkness that didn't radiate hope at all. But how could it, with all they had seen these last few months.

"Excuse me, I never said anything about drinking a bottle of wine a night."

"Your father mentioned that you'd been drinking heavily."

"I have one, maybe two large glasses before going to bed, it helps stunt my brain somewhat, it shuts them out."

"What about drugs?"

"What about them?"

"Are you using any?"

"No. Believe me, I've been tempted to smoke all the weed available in Barnsley, but once you go down that path, well, I just didn't want to get addicted to anything like that. Stunting my active unconscious sleeping brain is one thing, but…"

Aurora pauses, taking a deep breath as she realises the raw honesty of her response, "I need my facets in this reality, it's about all I've got at the moment, well, barely even that."

"What do you mean?"

"This *will* sound crazy…I'm seeing things, before they happen."

"Ok, tell me more."

"Just silly things, like I'll dream about meeting someone, someone I know, only they're behaving differently. We'll have a conversation about something very specific, and then, the next day, in real life, I'll bump into them. And I already know what they're going to bring up, what will be said, because it's already happened."

"Does this happen a lot?"

"Yes and no. I sometimes see symbols or pictures that often come up in my waking life. A few nights ago I saw the ticket booth for a comedy club I used to visit in London. The next day, I received two free tickets to any show, valid for a year."

"That was nice." Amy is scribbling frantically in her book, barely keeping her glasses on as she hunches over her notes. "Have you had any further contact with your ex-boyfriend, what was his name..?" Amy looks down at her notes.

Aurora helps her out. "Johan."

"Ah yes, Johan."

"No, no I haven't."

"Would you like to? Don't you need a friend?"

"I have a friend, her name is Sam. We go back as far as Primary School. She's been very supportive."

Sam was a dance nut. Her and Aurora were at Jump Primary School together in the 1980s. Upon returning to Barnsley, Aurora randomly bumped into Sam on the main high street. Within minutes, she realised that Sam hadn't changed all. She was still fun and ditzy, exactly the sort of influence Aurora needed in her life right now.

"Forgive my assessment," it's Amy who shifts in her chair now, "but from what I know, you've been through some massive changes in the last few months. Severe lack of sleep, restlessness, interrupted sleep, nightmares. Your boyfriend breaks up with you, you're put on extended leave from work due to stress, you leave London and move back in with your parents."

"How much are my parents paying you to make me feel better again?"

"The point is, your brain would struggle to process what's happened to you recently even if it was running on 8 hours sleep."

"Amy, what's happened to me recently is exactly because I've not been able to sleep!"

"And why is that Aurora?"

"Because they won't leave me alone! So many of them...and the taunting.." Aurora bursts out crying. The therapist had pushed her client to breaking point, but in a way, Aurora was thankful of the release.

"Let it out Aurora. You're trying so hard to stay strong and still operate, but you're not operating well, are you? We clearly have some issues to iron out. Whenever you're ready. I'm listening, I'm not here to judge or question your sanity. I'm here to help you get through this."

The therapist extends a box of tissues, Aurora grabs one and blows her nose. "Thank you."

"Whenever you're ready."

Aurora lies down on her back and takes a deep breath.

12

12ᵗʰ November, 3:20am Earth Time, Quern's Office, CERN Headquarters, Ipa, Venezelu
Griig's soft baby face had never been this shade of red before. But then Griig had never had to run through CERN headquarters at this pace. Beads of sweat fell down his round plump cheeks, his stony eyes fierce and focused. Arriving outside Quern's office, Griig stops, composes himself, squares up his navy uniform, wipes his brow and knocks on the door.

Quern answers, with a heavy-set glass of Jorkey whisky in hand, looking perturbed, as though he'd been interrupted doing something malevolent. "What is it, Officer Hawthorne?"

Griig grabs a breath, "Sir, in the basement."

Quern's face turns ice white. He drops his glass, smashing it into a thousand liquidy pieces.

***

12ᵗʰ November, 3:32am Earth Time, Professor Sykes Office, MEW5 tower, Ipa, Venezelu
Lindar is sitting in the Professor's tatty thinking chair by the tall glass windows. It looks out of place in the modern set up, but she's compelled to sit in it,

seeking a little comfort from the familiar ties to her revolutionary roots. As she stares out the window, her phone starts to buzz. She pulls it out to reveal news reels flashing like angry fireworks from the screen. 'BREAKING NEWS'.

Lindar looks up at the large televised screen in Professor Sykes' office. The picture shows Aurora, standing in the middle of a market square in Indigo. The news reel reads 'NEWS FLASH! – unidentified awakened Earthling found on Indigo." Lindar drops her phone to the floor.

***

12th November, 3:32am Earth Time, Professor Sykes Apartment, Ipa, Venezelu

The Professor hadn't slept since returning home from the pods the day before. All had gone well at the gates in Militia City. As promised, Lindar's contact had caused a big enough distraction to entice the violent-thirsty rebels' attention away from the Professor's re-entry into Ipa.

The Professor's apartment was modest for someone of his ranking at CERN, but then he was a modest man. Most of his income had gone towards constructing and maintaining the pods, a place he considered his real home.

The apartment was bare, hosting only the essentials needed for a quick overnight stay or change of clothes. The view from the balcony looked out over most of Ipa. On a good day, the Professor could see everything from the MEW5 tower to the borders of Militia City.

But today, the Professor was lying on the couch,

half awake, half asleep, feeling the weight of the past few years hit him all at once, like a wrecking ball of espionage, plotting and fear. *We're so close now, please let Aurora be alright.*

He knew that the experiment must have gone well, or at least ok, as he hadn't heard anything from Lindar or the team back at the pods, however he couldn't switch his mind off. He had no doubts that first contact would be made, he just hoped it would be enough to awaken Aurora to her destiny. He was concerned about what lay ahead for the anomaly, and hoped they could keep her safe.

No sooner had that thought entered his head, a loud cracking started from his televised set. He'd had re-runs of The Goyan Show play on repeat since coming home last night, but his set was overtaken by a Breaking News edition.

The Professor removed the bowl of musenli bran that was balanced on his chest and moved it over to the table. He reached for his glasses and turned up the volume by tapping his thumb and forefinger together then swirling his index finger in a clockwise motion.

He looked at the screen, unable to process what he was witnessing. "Kilos helps us."

***

12th November, 6am Earth Time, Zaatta pod #3, Robertus, Higgins and Chloez sit around the monitoring station getting ready to watch Aurora's dreams on the gel monitor from the night before. Higgins looks tired, his heavy black-rimmed glasses feel like an anchor on his drawn face.

"Where's Zareb? Shouldn't he be here?"

"He's gone to Stoffenlaggen with Kara," replied Chloez, "checking in to see how the Professor and Lindar are."

"I've got a bad feeling in my gut." said Robertus. I travelled to the Indigan hills last night during dreamtime, don't ask me why, I didn't consciously decide to. Guess I felt drawn there. I observed some local vegetation and wildlife then dashed off to Havana, Earth."

Higgins logs in to the gel monitor, typing madly at the keyboard, retrieving Aurora's dream log for the night before.

"You love Havana, don't you?" smiled Chloez, "Or is it a particular dreaming subject there that you were monitoring?" Chloez' smile creases the scar on her cheek, she draws a short strand of red hair out of her golden eyes, sparkling bright through her freckled face.

"Very funny Chloez." Robertus' silvery white skin is tinged with blush now, his black eyes turn gold then aqua-marine. "Am I making you blush? The great Robertus?" Chloez jokingly nudges Robertus in the arm, toying with him.

"Carina is a very promising subject. She's on my watch list, you know, if the anomaly falls through."

"I bet she's on your watch list." jokes Chloez.

"Guys….you need to see this." Higgins' tone catches Robertus and Chloez attention in an instant.

Robertus puts his long, dark locks up into a ponytail and takes a look at the screen. He blinks, and his eyes turn black, the blackest shade Chloez had ever seen. Nudging in to see the screen, Chloez gasps.

"What time is it Higgins?" asks Robertus.

"What, now?" replies Higgins. Robertus nods.

"It's 6.04am Earth Time."

"And what time was the sighting logged."

"3.30am Earth Time."

Chloez, Higgins and Robertus stay frozen for a minute, their minds desperately trying to figure out what to do first.

"We need to alert the others," says Higgins, "emergency meeting, Operation Capsula."

"Operation Capsula." nods Chloez.

13

12th November, 3.30am Earth Time, Market Place, Planet Indigo

The day's suruprays were shining onto the cobbled hill where the market place stood, but it was the bright lights from every Indigan's flashing devices that were shining brighter than the suruprays that morning.

Aurora stood there, covering her eyes and looking around for an exit. She felt hot, very hot. She knew that something of immense proportion had just occurred, and not in a good way.

Aurora looked up to the sky for a sign, for help. Just then, she felt a tingling along her arm. It was the pirate with the goatee and stripey hat. It was Jasper. He had tried to touch her arm.

"Aurora, you must wake up, do you hear me?"

Next to Jasper stood the lady with the long blondey-orangey curls. "This is Hispanica, we're you're friends. You're on Indigo, but you must go now."

Hispanica touches the exterior of Aurora's hands. They spark. She can feel a surge around them. Aurora gets a closer look at the woman's eyes. They're a metallic sea of swirling brown, like velvet chocolate, and kind! These are knowing eyes, thought Aurora. They can see things.

"Wake up Aurora, wake up now dearest."

***

Three months later, 20th February 2003, Park bench, Barnsley, Earth

Aurora didn't want to go home yet. Her session with Doctor Fletcher finished around 2 hours ago, but Aurora was keen to stay out until dusk. Sam had texted her to see if she wanted to go to the cinema with her later that night. Aurora was considering it, but for now, she just wanted some alone time. The session had drained her, but she did feel marginally better for it. *Maybe I will get better, maybe this will end.* But Aurora knew that there was nothing wrong with her. She knew exactly what was going on. Something triggered it, the second night she dreamt of the little boy with the golden curls, the one she'd seen in Rome. It was faint, and she couldn't quite make out what he was trying to tell her, but she felt it. Aurora knew she was part of something bigger.

At night, when the visitors came, she'd occasionally spot some friendly faces, ones she would almost claim to recognise now. They usually had white lab coats on, or were holding certain devices, but they'd visit her too. It looked like they were in a jail cell, or a padded room, she couldn't quite make out, but they were friendly, she knew that much.

Aurora looked out over the cold, brazen park. The trees were bare and just one man and his dog were brave enough to venture out into the early evening of this cold November day. But Aurora liked the cold. It awakened her senses, senses that for far too long had felt numb, number than any icy wind could muster.

Her hands wander for something in her jacket pocket. She pulls out the pocket watch that Johan had given her, the present from Austria.

AURORA
December 15th 2002, 10.30pm, London, Earth

I wonder whether Johan will be back at a decent time tonight. Could really do with him here. Not sure what's going on, but I feel such a distance. It's like a chasm that's growing at an uncontrollable rate. Am so tired tonight. Sick of looking at this bedroom wall, anticipating the inevitable. Wine seems to help, but don't want to start going down that route. It's bad enough that I've been put on sick leave from work. Leaving the office last week was horrendous, but necessary. The teary breakdowns that started in the toilets but spilled out into the office. Turning up late, finding myself in a pool of tears in my own kitchen and not knowing why. It was true. I knew it, my boss knew it, Johan knew it and my GP knew it - I wasn't functioning properly. But then 4 weeks with no decent sleep will do that to a person.

Where is Johan? *Stay awake, you won't see them then*. Why hasn't he replied to my text message? *Hope I see the friendly ones, or at least end up on a desert island when I dream tonight, if I can sleep to dream.*

NARRATOR

After fighting sleep for what seems like hours, Aurora descended into hypnagogia. What followed rocked her soul, as it did every night.

AURORA

The tug, that tug. There it is, I can't stop, I have to open my eyes, I'm not even aware of it, my unconscious senses it first. There's something in the room. My eyes open. The outline of my room poses its usual normality, and, within micro seconds, they come. My conscious eyes are surprised, as they always are, at these dark apparitions that only my unconscious was aware of, until now.

And here they are. I look up to the ceiling and there are 4 men with long hair and beards, laughing and flashing knives at my face, I scramble around in bed, trying to move them on, praying for consciousness to set in.

But it doesn't. I know this, because to my left, a group of children are staring at me, pointing and laughing. They mock me. To my right, an elderly woman looks straight into my eyes, I know she feels sad for me, but did she really have to come see for herself?

Something's moving fast in the corner of the room, it's a woman in long robes, she has a hat on and is laughing an evil laugh. I can't quite hear it, but I know it's evil, I can see it in her eyes. Her eyes! She's above me now, a long machete to my throat. Those eyes! Go evil woman, go!

I'm sitting up. I'm fully conscious. I'm awake. The room is empty. I'm alone again. *So tired.*

If I knew that sleep would provide rest I'd take a bottle of night nurse to get me there. But sleep equals dreams, which equals being followed around like a prisoner inside my own head. I never felt that I had complete control of my dreams before. I knew that I was a participant, that I may have occasionally chosen the location or tried to manipulate the scenarios, but that I was never really controlling anything. I was an observer. But now, lucidity seems like a joke to me. Dreaming is a prison, and the only constant is that every night I know they'll come find me. The others. Unless I end up on a remote beach somewhere, which occasionally I do, but it doesn't take long for someone to find me. Always running, always hiding. What do they want from me?!

I hear the front door close. I hadn't heard it open. "Johan? Is that you?" No answer. I put the lamp on and grab a shoe from under the bed and walk towards the bedroom door. "Johan?"

The bedroom door opens. It is Johan. "Why didn't you answer me? You scared me half to death? Where have you been? I've been worried."

Johan walks further into the room, I can smell beer on his breath. His eyes are red. He's been crying.

"It's over Aurora. I can't do this anymore."

NARRATOR

Six days after their break up, Aurora left London to move in with her parents. She spent the first two days crying, unable to understand how Johan could have been so cold. How he was unable to help her through this 'periodic insomnia', as she called it. Periodic, because she was praying that it would stop soon and that she'd get her life back. But she knew there was nothing he could do, and deep down, she knew that this 'episode' was actually a pivotal turning point in her own journey, she just couldn't see how right now.

Aurora knew that she hadn't been the easiest to live with, especially of late, but she was still disappointed. Disappointed that Johan's love for her wasn't enough. That he couldn't find the strength to stick by her until she got through it. Disappointed that he wasn't made of the same stuff as her parents. *That* was true love, sticking by the person you love through all of life's ups and downs. Aurora dreamed of that, she would like it, one day, so that she could erase how easily Johan had just upped and left her that night, taking all his belongings in one go and not even offering her a hug on his way out the door. Aurora spent the third day messaging Johan, desperately seeking to speak with him to try and get him to change his mind. On the third day, Johan replied to her.

"I'm with someone else."

It was all Aurora needed to hear. On day four she packed up all of her belongings. On day five she went to visit all of her London friends for goodbye drinks. On day six, she helped fill the removal van, dropped her keys off at the landlords, forfeiting her deposit but not caring either way. From there, she headed to King's Cross and got a one way ticket to Barnsley.

NARRATOR
20th February 2003, Park bench, Barnsley, Earth

The sun had long disappeared over the distant hill caressing the town borders. From high up on this hill, Aurora could see the street lights come on across Barnsley, like little fairy lights across one of those toy replica towns used in architectural demonstrations. Aurora's pocket watch pendant felt cold in her hands, it never used to. She opens it and checks the time.

"So much for forever." Making a split decision, Aurora lifts the pendant above her head, getting ready to hurl it as far she could.

"Forever is now, and you're still here now, aren't you Aurora?"

Aurora spins around on the spot, spinning so fast that she almost tears the edge of her navy blue trench coat on the gap between the wooden slats of the bench.

As she turns, the pocket watch falls sharply in front of her, ricocheting off the ground like a small and bouncy hand grenade. It stops at the unknown person's feet. Who is this intruder who startled her, this unknown who changed her direction and trajectory so instantaneously?

She looks up, but needn't have looked up far. A small figure of no more than 3 feet, shrouded in a thick, dark grey woollen shawl is stood before her. The person is a woman, Aurora knows this from her voice, but she can't quite see her face. The grey blanket-like material covers it almost completely.

"Can I help you?" asks Aurora, unsure as to who this might be. She didn't recall knowing anybody of this size, either in Barnsley or London, but this person knew her name.

The woman picks up the watch pendant, walks in front of Aurora and places it in her hands. The woman's face is still covered up, but Aurora can smell lavender from her clothing and her hands send a warm ripple up Aurora's arms. "Keep this," says the woman, before coming round to Aurora's left and taking a seat next to her. "just for now. I know something we can do with this down the line."

The woman stares straight ahead, gazing at the flickers of evening light ahead of her. "My name is Stefania. I've come to help you."

Aurora turns round to face Stefania, who's still looking straight ahead.

"Well can I at least see the face of this kind person who's offering to help me?"

"Don't you want to know who I am? How I know you need help and how I found you?"

"I'm sure we'll come to that. But for now, I want to see your face please."

"Always about the eyes, our Aurora." Stefania removes her hood and turns to face her. Aurora sits in stunned silence. Stefania has the most beautiful angelic face she has ever seen. It almost reminds her of the cherub-faced boy she saw in her hotel room in Rome last year. Stefania's eyes are hazel brown, they're wise and knowing. Aurora never considered herself a spiritual person per se, but she could tell a lot by looking into someone's eyes. Stefania had seen things, things Aurora had seen. Other-worldly things, unexplainable things to the unknowing eye.

Aurora could barely see the soft blonde curls

sweeping off of Stefania's face for something was clouding her vision. Aurora touched her cheek and realized she was crying. But what a relief! For the first time ever, she was looking into the eyes of someone who knew her pain, knew about the figures she'd been seeing, and who knew that Aurora was not crazy. It overwhelmed her.

"So you know." said Stefania, brushing one of her silvery-blonde curls away from her eyes to reveal a small star tattoo by the corner of her left eye. She looked a lot younger than her crackly voice suggested.

"I can tell, by your way, your eyes – you've seen them too, haven't you?"

"You're not on your own Aurora. We are many, and at all different stages of our development."

"Development?"

"Yes, to hone the inherent abilities that already lie within us - in the world within us."

Suddenly aware that this woman knows a lot about her, Aurora starts to look around the now darkening park. "Who sent you?"

"Nobody sent me. Your friend Samantha, she Googled me."

"She *Googled* you?" Aurora is unable to retain a laugh between the tears.

Stefania pulls out a card. On it reads, *Stefania Greganof, Psychic, Spiritualist and Medium.* "I'm actually a full blown witch, but you know, society is *so* far behind when it comes to acceptable titles. My kind were still being persecuted and charged in the 1940s, go figure."

"What did Sam tell you?"

"That you haven't been sleeping. That you see people, that you travel when you eventually do get to sleep. I've known you minutes, and let me tell you, you are glowing with a green force so powerful you make radiation seem like a kid's glow stick."

Aurora looks down at her trench coat, unsure of what Stefania's referring to.

"Sam told me you might be up here, that you come here a lot, after your sessions at the Psychotherapy Unit. To be honest," Stefania pauses, as if choosing her words carefully, "she needn't have bothered giving me directions. I could have found you with my eyes closed."

"How can you help me Stefania?"

"We have our feet in both worlds, you and I. There are many who are so grounded in ego, this one reality, that they forget that their lives are a dangling array of thousands of possible realities. That's why we love stories so much; they explore all the different paradigms, they explore, they experience. People call it escapism, but it's far from it. We love stories, because it allows us to live out our every possible reality, without the restrictions of the physical dimension we are stuck in, currently speaking."

"Currently speaking?"

"We are made of such stuff as dreams are made on, young Aurora."

"That's Shakespeare."

"No dear, that's the truth. We are always here, we just keep bouncing back as different shapes."

"How can you help me Stefania?"

"Why don't I show you?"

***

20th February 2003, Stefania's Flat, Barnsley, Earth

Stefania lived on a quiet cul de sac in the Gawber district of Barnsley, not far from Aurora's parents' home. Aurora had texted Sam to decline her cinema offer and notified her that Stefania had made contact. She asked Sam if she would be her alibi for this evening whilst Aurora went to Stefania's house. Sam replied with a thumbs up emoji followed by the words *'Here's hoping she can conjure up something to help you get some *sleeping face emoji*'*. What a good friend Sam was, Aurora would be sure to treat her to very large bottle of wine for this incredibly good turn.

Aurora also spoke briefly to her mum, informing her that she was going out for an early supper with Sam at Victor's Diner, one of their favourite haunts. Josephine probed her daughter for some feedback on her therapy session. Aurora assured that it was going well, then pretended to greet Sam so she could come off the phone. Aurora hated holding things back from her parents. She was always honest with them, sometimes too honest. She could hear her mamman's voice telling her, as a teenager, that she needn't disclose *everything* that her and her friends were getting up to.

"Some things you can keep for you, ma petite. Always know that your mamman is here if you need her though."

Stefania's house was not what Aurora was expecting. It was modern, very modern, with grey laminate flooring, cream couches and a selection of black glossy furniture.

As though reading her thoughts, Stefania responds.

"What? Did you think it would be all incense, thick rugs and a bunch of cats?"

Aurora hesitated before answering, "Well, yes, kind of."

"I might dress like a hippy, but I like my home chic. Besides, we're not stopping here. We're going upstairs to my office. Can I grab you a drink before we start?"

As they ascended the clinical looking hallway, Aurora tried her best to not to spill the oversized mug of tea Stefania had prepared for her. Grey laminate and black glossy handrails continued up the stairs and Aurora couldn't fathom how someone so spiritual could decorate with such frostiness. Stefania was two steps ahead of her, and now at the top of the stairs. Aurora watched her disappear off to the right hand side, vanishing from view.

"Just this way Aurora."

It was dark at the top of the stairs, and Aurora could see a long corridor extending to the left and right. To the left were three doors and to the right were two. The place was a lot bigger than she'd imagined.

Stefania was outside one of the doors on the right hand side, a door with a solid red-amber glow coming out from around the door frame.

"We're in here Aurora."

For a split second it dawned on Aurora that she was about to enter a glowing room with a complete stranger that her best friend had found on the internet. There had better not be anything sordid on the other side of that door, thought Aurora. If there is, they're getting a large mug of tea thrown at them. Stefania smiles at her, and Aurora feels a tad guilty for not entirely trusting this woman whom she knows, deep down, is bona fide.

Stefania opens the door, and to Aurora's surprise, a completely different room bounces back before her. The room was head-to-toe covered in fabrics, silks and rugs. It stunk of incense. The windows were blackened out with thick heavy drapes, and possibly black out blinds behind that. A series of small lamps glow amber around the room. Stefania sets to and starts lighting some of the candles dotted around them.

"More what you had in mind?" asks Stefania, posing a cheeky grin.

"Yes, I'd say so." says Aurora, still scanning the room.

"Except I don't do cats," says Stefania, "Can't stand them. The devil's pet."

Aurora continues to look around the room. There are piles of books that touch the roof, like paper columns of power and knowledge. To her left, a deep purple cloak sits draped over a large cushion, presumably Stefania's seat. In front of that, and immediately in front of Aurora, sits a large deep dish on the floor. It looked like a giant wok. The inside was burnt to a charcoaled crisp and the lamp light reflected a metallic rainbow from its tinny interior. To the right of the wok sits a small beanbag, another cloak, black this time, and some

171

wicker-looking slippers. Beyond that, and in the deep of the room, lots of cushions, thick plush rugs and strange and wonderful looking objects lie sprawled. It reminded Aurora of an Egyptian tomb, pre-mummification. To the far right of the room, on the wall nearest the window, was a small gazebo-looking area. Like a Persian desert tent, deep red, orange and Aztec blue chiffon and textured materials lie draped over a wooden frame. There was a make-shift bed in there, with white cotton sheets and lots of lotions, potions and plants in little wicker baskets. Aurora raised her eyebrows. Just what did Stefania do in here?

"Please, take a seat." Stefania points at the beanbag. "Don't worry about the clothing, I'll explain all when we get started."

14

12th November, 10:10am Earth Time, Zaattan Monestry, Zaattan Mounties, Venezelu
It had been just over four hours since the scientists from MEW5 had heard the news about Aurora. Operation Capsula had been declared, one of a many planned scenarios on what to do should the anomaly's identity be compromised. Professor Sykes, Lindar, Zareb, Marcux, the pod scientists and Ray and his wife, Fran, were deep in the Andanuan forest. The group were sitting in a circle in one of the Zaattan monks' thinking shrine-rooms, part of the larger working temple. The only people missing were Gisella and Mia, both of whom were currently sitting in a café just by the Stoffenlagen point. This was an intrinsic part of the Capsula plan. Should the group get caught, at least two operatives would be on the outside, still able to help protect their work, maintain their cover and help them escape, if possible.

It seemed such a paradox. The monastery was one of the most beautiful vistas and tranquil settings in all of Venezelu, and here they were - planning and preparing against one of the most dangerous and unwanted situations they could ever imagine. The sky was a crystal blue with not a cloud in it. The shrine-room was open-ended, facing North West towards Ipa. But Ipa was long out of sight. All you could see was a sea of deep forest green, a million thick lush fern leaves that went on for miles. Each tree-top moved slowly in synch, waving gently back and forth. A metallic glow rippled across its treetops like an ocean surface rippling with petroleum. Below the trees, the forest animals were far from quiet today. Up on the hill, above the trees, the silence was tremendous.

The large square-shaped shrine-room was lined with wood, the finest wood in all of Venezelu. Even the fine wicker mats that the group were sitting on were made of it. Every move or shuffle upon the mats reverberated across the room's silence like a bunch of dry sticks being snapped in two. It was as if the noise was desperate to make its escape from the interior and out to the open balcony, just so that it could pass the Three Pillars of Hope that held up the temple's front facing balcony entrance.

It was a hot day, but a soothing breeze would occasionally swirl around the room, filling it with temporary relief. The group sat in silence, waiting for the Master Monk to join them. Zareb looks around at the crew. They look scared, but focused, as though they'd been preparing for this moment their whole lives.

The shrine-room door opens, and Lindar is quick on her feet. The Master Monk enters. The rest of the group follow suit, standing and bowing towards her.

"Please, please, be seated friends." says the

Master Monk. She is a girl who looks no more than 14, but is in fact an ancient soul in a young body. Her long red hair extends to her feet, and her face is dotted with golden markings. She is drowned in a red and gold robe. She removes her flip flops and joins the circle.

"I've spoken with the monks, and we wholeheartedly agree with your plan. As agreed in past meetings, you are welcome to stay here so as to protect the integrity of the pods." Professor Sykes stands up and places a large piece of paper in the centre of the circle.

"Thank you Kalista, Master Monk. We know from direct sources that Quern discovered evidence of our anomaly in the basement of MEW5 early this morning."

Zareb looks over at Lindar who appears to be in a trance. The Professor goes back to sit in his place.

"An operative discovered her at the site and has recorded evidence on their Quaz-device. This information has been held back, for now, whilst CERN officials investigate the bomb pack at the site, but something's for sure - we will be investigated, all of us still on the books and still on grid. CERN will start a thorough witch-hunt. The bombings will be blamed on pirates no doubt, but Aurora…"

Marcux takes a huge breath, fully grasping what's at stake.

"The Earth team at MEW5, well, CERN will want to know how someone like Aurora slipped by them for so long. And once they visit her, they'll see she has Feelers, they'll know we've gone rouge."

Zareb nods. "We have two choices. We declare the Revolution now and use everything we have against Quern, or," Lindar cuts Zareb off mid sentence,

"We're not going back there voluntarily. I say we stay and fight this out."

"What about your Supreme Court?" asks Kalista.

"We have with us the gel monitor and original recordings of Aurora's dream from last night, where she intercepts the pirates. Quern is mentioned, it's enough. We just need to get it to Gisella somehow, and quickly." Kara lifts the recording device to show the Master Monk. Higgins notices that Mikus B is looking out towards the balcony.

"What is it Mikus?" Mikus B looks down at the paper, a blueprint of CERN HQ and MEW5 tower. The group look down, they can see that the paper is trembling. They stand up and look out towards the opening. Kalista runs to its furthest point, a small pier deck that extends out from the balcony. For a moment Zareb thought she might jump off.

"They're here, destroy the map. Kara, run. Go now."

Mikus B torches the map with a strike-match. The map evaporates with a puff of black smoke. Kara hides the gel monitor in her rucksack and runs for the door.

From nowhere, six heli-choppers appear on the horizon. They look like giant scarab beetles scratching the blue sky.

"Quick," shouts Lindar, "to the sacred temple. Kara, we'll collect you when it's safe to do so."

Kara nods and goes for the door handle. She

barely had her fingers around the handle when the doors to the shrine-room fly open. Four men and three women dressed in CERN uniform walk into the room, closely followed by Quern and Griig Hawthorne. One of the officers grabs Kara, who struggles under their hold.

"Ah, so this is where all of my scientists are. On a retreat are we? Team building day?"

"Quern, be careful." warns Lindar.

Quern laughs in surprise. "Be careful? I'm not the one being arrested for treason."

"With what evidence?" asks Professor Sykes.

"Funny you should ask, *Justin*." says Quern, pulling something out of his pocket.

"I have here a list of every damaging item found at your apartment this morning. Bomb making materials, blueprints, plans. Looks like the pirates weren't behind this sabotage. Looks like you were, you and your band of merry scientists, and not to mention our glowing celebrity. You kept her quiet, didn't you Sykes?"

"No idea what you're talking about. And that stuff must have been planted at my place."

"Save it for the Supreme Court. Operatives, arrest them all. Stun anyone who resists."

The heli-choppers had landed on the grounds of the monastery. Out of them spilled another 10 stun-gun armed operatives who made their way to the shrine.

"Oh, and the monks are being detained until Zaattan police get here to take them into custody too, for aiding and abetting fugitives of the law."

Lindar couldn't hold her tongue. "You *really* want

to do this Quern? You have no idea what cards we hold."

"Just as well I'm not playing with you then, isn't it?"

Quern looks over at the Master Monk. "We'll take *that* one in our heli-chopper. She comes with us."

The group were arrested and placed in flexi-cables, a bright glowing figure of eight electronically charged chain that, once sealed, can only be unsealed by a CERN diffuser. Any attempt to wriggle or wrestle out of them would result in an electric shock to the nervous system. Once you'd been flexi-cabled, your best bet was to comply.

One of the officers alerts Quern to the gel monitor found in Kara's rucksack. Griig takes hold of it and has a look. "Sir, this could be it."

Quern goes over to Griig and whispers in his ear. "Destroy it. We don't want anything linked back to us."

"But Sir, we don't even know what.."

"Burn it!" Quern's eyes go red around the lids. It looked like sweat was burning his eyelids from the inside as fire brimmed out from his eyes. "Burn it *all* to the ground."

***

As the heli-choppers silently buzzed over the mile-high trees of the Andanuan forest, the group look back towards the monastery. The heli-chopper doors were open on one side. Wind bellowed in, bringing with it the faint smell of smoke from the burning temples below. Marcux watched as the ever increasing flames licked the wood, turning it black.

He starts crying. Kalista puts her arm around him.

"Don't cry wise Grentil, the Zaattan authorities will extinguish it. The forest is safe."

"But your home, everything you've crafted and worked towards."

"This," Kalista points to Marcux's heart, "and this," she points to his head, "are the only places that matter. They can't burn that down, not ever."

Marcux wipes his tears, Chloez gives him a hug from behind, stroking his hair.

"The Pendulum has swayed towards the dark, for now." says Kalista, tying her long red hair back into a bun. "But the gateway has opened, our time will come, it has begun."

15

Three Months Later, February 20th, Earth Time, Supreme Court, Ipa, Venezelu

The Supreme Court judges are made up of 10 women and 10 men, all from Venezelu with the exception of Duandarin Krespos from Jenar. Jenar is currently competing with Venezelu, but Duandarin Krespos acts as an ambassador from their planet. Their sole job is to give an outside perspective on things. Something every planet adheres to, something that came out of the enlightenment: that all democracies require an outsider's perspective too.

The judges are made up of people from all walks of life. They are chosen by the Koli Ceremony, a traditional choosing ceremony conducted by the Shamans of Fraz County. The Shamans use their prophetic journals and at least one Visionary from Li to assist. Everyone must be in accordance with the choices made. The group go on a long pilgrimage to find individuals for the Supreme Court selection. No-one can refuse their participation. The idea is that the ceremony will choose those of equal measure, those for whom the pendulum swings, but who can keep it predominantly stable. They are individuals gifted with patience, foresight and measured control of their duality. They seek justice, with a swing to the good, but they are not extreme in any direction. They remain impartial and balanced on all accounts. It's what helps make them such wise judges.

The Supreme Courthouse itself is one of the most spectacular buildings in all of Venezelu. Sitting at just over 600 Earth feet tall, the building is a large rectangular cube with a round dome at the very top. It's light grey in colour and made of stone from the Jorkey ruins, an old stone fixture deep beneath the Roko ocean.

Inside, the Supreme Court is magnificent. The ground floor hosts the main chamber which is towards the back of the structure. A series of smaller holding rooms sit out in front. Every inch of the interior is white-speckled marble, with silver glistening specks that shine and bounce like the inside of a massive prism. To the right hand side, before the main chamber entry is a wide spiral staircase, taking you 15 floors up, the 15th being the dome room. Thanks to their laws of physics and physiology, everyone on Venezelu's atmosphere is able to fly. The architects who designed the Supreme Court were asked, however, to install stairs, and for two reasons. Firstly, should they have anyone visit who is unable to fly, they can choose to walk or take the spiral chair-lift to where they need to go. And by anyone, that means Supreme Court staff officials or special invited guests. Secondly, it is widely believed that some of the best decisions ever made are done at walking pace. Flying through life cuts out that all important processing time. And Venezeluan's believe that the exact ideal pace for thought, or thinking, is that of a walking pace. It is for this reason that most judges walk upstairs to their offices. It literally helps them think. Each step brings them closer to an all important verdict.

In a Venezeluan Supreme Court, both parties are entitled to a prosecution team and a defence team. The idea is that both sides have to prove their innocence and prove the other party guilty. The charges made by Quern's side were numerable, but equally, the charges made by Professor Sykes and his company were also numerable. It took each prosecution and defence team the equivalent of 4 Earth weeks each to prepare for trial, collect evidence, build supporting statements and the like. After the collection period, there's a rehearsal period, which takes a further 4 weeks before either party is invited to court. Legal proceedings are a lengthy business in Venezelu, because if things need to be settled in court at all, then they're usually very complex cases to begin with. Enlightened ones usually resolve their own issues, and Militant Rebels are *so* far outside the legal framework that they are left to their own free will. Should some get caught by CERN or vigilantes, they are brought to court, but the game is so big, with so many spinning parts, that the court chooses its cases carefully. It does not want to waste time on matters they know won't have a definitive resolution. During preparation time, in the lead up to a trial, all parties have to stay in the Supreme Court's jailhouse. This is seen as a fair measure so that neither party can try to take the lead by manipulating the rules of the game. The Zaattan monks were transferred from the Zaattan cells to the Supreme Court Jailhouse just 4 weeks before the trial. There were a lot of bodies at the jailhouse that January. The officers could barely keep up with the food supply required to feed so many mouths.

It was the fifth day of trial. Zareb Fender, Lindar Tahelso and Robertus Zané had all testified for the defence. Griig Hawthorne and General Quern were awaiting questioning, followed by Professor Skyes, the main accused.

The morning's questions were for the monks of the monastery. The Prosecution for Quern's team were allowed a series of interrogators to question the group the cosmic press now referred to as the 'Dream Rebels'. The Dream Rebels prosecution was building a steady case against Quern and his crew, but decided to play slow, for they were also awaiting news of another potentially important witness to the stand.

On the stand at this morning's hearing was Zohali Lora, one the Zaattan monks. Marcux couldn't believe how cool and composed the monks had been whilst incarcerated. Zohali had explained to Marcux that bricks and metal were no boundary to them, they still felt free, and that the anomaly was coming. Marcux found it hard to believe that they could ever make contact with Aurora now. Her hypnagogic channels would be clogged up with unwelcome visitors and tormentors, all desperate for a look. Her dream travels would be worse. She would be recognised wherever she went, never left alone. She was an unrepresented soul. A tourist attraction. An abandoned one, for all to gawp at.

In the rear benches of the Supreme Court sat Marcux and the other scientists awaiting trial. Right behind them in the public docks sat Hispanica, Jasper and Gisella as well as a mountain of other Venezeluans who had been eagerly following the trial. Some of them had won registration tickets to attend the court session. Up in the balcony sat a flurry of other ticket winners. A group of shamanic women were among the crowd, women who happened to be Hispanica's older sisters. Mia Kranos, a retired operative and supporter of the Revolution, was disguised as one of them.

Marcux looked up. He noticed the women all staring at him. He spotted Mia first, then quickly looked away, still confused as to who the others might be.

A Supreme Court guard appointed to Marcux was fixated on the proceedings ahead. He was ordered to chaperone Marcux inside and outside of that court room and to never have him out of his sight.

As the court room listened to Zohali's testament, Hispanica saw that Marcux's guard was hypnotised by the trial. She took this opportunity to lean forward and whisper something into Marcux's ear. The guard spots this out of the corner of his eye and commands Hispanica to sit back in her seat immediately. Hispanica apologises and complies. To Hispanica's left hand side sits Gisella. Jasper is on Hispanica's right hand side. Hispanica looks up towards the balcony. Her sisters give her a nod. Hispanica squeezes Gisella's knee, prompting her to look over at Sykes who is up next. Sykes is sweating and looks pale.

"We don't have much time," says Hispanica. "The window, it's drawing close."

Zohali stands and bows to the judges, leaving Sykes to approach the stand.

***

Unbeknown to Gisella and the others, Marcux did hear what Hispanica said. Marcux turns to the Supreme Court guard and taps him on the arm.

"I need to go to the toilet."

"What, now?" asks the guard.

"Well, yes." replies Marcux.

As Professor Sykes gives his full name and job title to the court, Marcux and the guard quietly begin exiting the benches. They head towards the main chamber exit which folds out into the grand lobby. Professor Sykes sees Marcux leave. Momentarily distracted, he hesitates. The Prosecution ask him the question again.

"Mr Justin Frederick Sykes, are you the mastermind behind the Venezeluan bombings and did you plan to blow up MEW5 on the 564th of Krentas this last year?"

Professor Sykes returns his vision to the lead Prosecutor. With anger in his eyes and resolution in his voice, the Professor answers the question.

"No."

16

20th February 2003, Stefania's Flat, Barnsley, Earth

Stefania and Aurora are sitting face-to-face in Stefania's office. Both are cloaked in ceremonial robes. Stefania takes a drink of water before speaking. She motions Aurora to do the same.

"This *is* just water, right?"

Stefania laughs. "Last I checked."

Aurora takes a drink. The water tastes like fresh oxygen down her throat. She's surprised at how crisp and refreshing it is.

Stefania clears her throat, then looks Aurora straight in the eyes.

"Aurora, this room is a channel, it's a gateway. Many things come and go from here. That's why I keep my house, my *home*, as separate and as sterile as possible. I don't want anything following me out there."

Aurora nods, indicating that she understands.

"Please child, give me your hands."

Aurora places her hands over the wok-looking thing.

"Not that way my child, palms down please on the Mirror Bowl."

Aurora corrects herself, turning her hands face down. Stefania takes out a small red bottle from her inner cloak pocket. The bottle is no bigger than her pinkie finger. Stefania takes the cork lid off and pours the thick dark red contents over the back of Aurora's hands.

"That's not blood, is it?" asks Aurora, pulling a face that is less than enamoured with what's going on.

"Shh," says Stefania, slightly irritated, but not with Aurora.

"Is there someone else here?" asks Aurora.

"They're on the precipice. They're waiting for the channels to open."

Stefania rubs the thick red liquid into Aurora's hands. To Aurora's surprise, the consistency feels waxy, but it absorbs into her skin very quickly. There's a strong smell of Frankincense from the liquid. It's not Aurora's favourite scent, but given the potential gains this session could bring, she decides to embrace it.

"Are you going to help me get some sleep?"

"No Aurora, I'm going to help you make contact. First contact."

"What's that?" asks Aurora, feeling that somehow, she already knows the answer to her own question.

"Let's back-track a little," says Stefania, rubbing the excess liquid into her own hands.

"Have you been ignoring the predominus?"

"The what?" replies Aurora. This time she has no clue what Stefania's on about.

"Give me your hands again, just for a moment."

Aurora passes over her hands, Stefania examines them with her thumbs, moving in and out of all the little crevices and between the tendons on her dorsal side.

Despite Stefania's eyes staying closed throughout, Aurora can't take hers off what's going on.

"That time you dreamt about the castle in the sky, the one surrounded by clouds. You thought it was the Swiss Alps. You've been back many times since, but that first time...don't you remember? Your colleague showed you her holiday photographs the very next day. The ones where they'd taken a last minute detour to the Swiss Alps and gone to that castle up in the hills. The one that looks exactly like the one in your dream."

"Yes, but she had already made the impromptu journey long before I went there."

"True," replied Stefania, "but you had a conversation with her about it. In your dream. A conversation that would come to life, through no prompting of your own, the very next day."

All at once the dream came back to her. It was true. Aurora had not only visited that same place that her colleague Shirley had mentioned to her that day at work, but she remembered the whole conversation about the photographs. Shirley's husband, Phil, had accidently blown up their home printer by spilling a glass of white wine into it. Shirley had only been able to bring the photographs into work that day because Phil had gone to Boots the Chemist that morning to print them off especially. In fact, just hours after Shirley had shown the photographs to Aurora, they then slipped out of Shirley's bag on the tube. She would have to go back to Boots the following week to get them re-printed.

"Or that time you dreamt about that small brown bird flying into the freshly painted magnolia wall, only to see the exact same thing happen on your way to work the following morning. Or, the time you dreamt about the Indonesian Earthquake, in real time, even though it happened through the night whilst you were asleep and it wasn't on the news until the next morning."

"I always put that stuff down to coincidence."

"People use that word a lot, but with the frequency of your predominus, I'm surprised that you didn't pay more attention Aurora."

"You sound like my therapist." jokes Aurora.

"Please don't compare me to that intellectual gerbil with a ponytail."

Aurora flashes a surprised look. Stefania's either an amazing psychic or just a very good private investigator.

Stefania smiles. "Ok, enough messing about now. We have work to do."

Stefania puts a few sticks into the mirror bowl. White smoke starts to rise up, Stefania wafts it into the air above them. She takes Aurora's hands, one either side of the mirror bowl. Aurora finds it quite a stretch. Neither of them had been granted with particularly long arms.

"This is an initial assessment. We'll be moving over to the tent for the hypnagogic window."

Aurora nods, feeling a mix of fear and excitement build up inside her chest. For the first time in months, she feels safe in the hands of someone else. She had never imagined that this woman would be here, right now, trying to help her.

As if reading her thoughts, Stefania interjects.

"Try to relax, and trust that I was *meant* to find you. Trust that the prophecy sees to it."

"Out of all the psychics in Barnsley, and I can't imagine there are that many, how does Sam find you? A real one who actually gets it?"

"Sam doesn't know it, but she's descended from one of the most powerful witches that ever lived in Yorkshire. It was destiny that you two should become friends at such an early age, then re-unite, then have her find me. She has a good nose," Stefania pauses, "and doesn't even nose it." Stefania laughs at her own joke, making Aurora smile. For all her powers, Stefania knew how to ease the tension.

"Close your eyes with me please." asks Stefania. Aurora complies, then hears a slight humming sound. Is it coming from Stefania, or the bowl? She can't tell. She can feel Stefania's grip tighten around hers, then loosen, then tighten again. Aurora senses a shift or change in the lighting in the room. Through her closed eyelids she sees the room darkening, then growing lighter, then darkening, all in time with Stefania's grips. She can hear Stefania's breathing grow shorter and faster, as though she's taking in sharp little breaths. A clapping noise makes Aurora jump in her seat. Strange, she thinks, especially since Stefania's hands are still firmly closed around hers. Aurora feels a flash of heat rise up through her body. It's a warm and pleasant feeling, but her head feels a little light.

"Open your eyes Aurora."

Aurora opens her eyes, feeling a tad dazed and confused. Stefania's face looks serious.

"The window is opening soon, tonight, within the hour. We're going to need some help."

17

12th November 2002, 4:00am Earth Time, Sea Front, Indigo

Hispanica and Jasper are sitting on the pier at Vulcanus beach, facing out to sea. It had been thirty minutes since the anomaly was compromised, and neither had been able to speak a word about it since it happened. Hispanica notices a small flounder plant swimming up the surface of the water. Its bluey-green jelly skin makes it almost impossible to spot in the darker waters, but Hispanica has a good eye. She takes off her right boot and dips her foot in. The flounder plant, with its baby octopus shaped body and smiling face comes up to the surface and rubs itself against her toes. Hispanica smiles, unfolding little creases around her deep brown eyes, eyes barely visible through her mass of golden-orange curls. She tucks a couple of strands behind her right ear. Jasper spots a tear rolling down her cheek. She's trying not to cry, he thought. He extends a hand, placing it on hers.

"We tried our best."

Hispanica takes her foot out the water and sits crossed legged. She keeps a grip on Jasper's hand, and with her other hand, wipes her eyes. "We failed her."

"Doesn't the prophecy say that the protectors of the anomaly are compromised? That the great chamber is where her fate is chosen?"

"Yes. I'm just upset because I know the suffering that girl will go through now, it's not good."

"It isn't, but with every rebirth, darkness must precede. It's the way of things. It brought *us* together, didn't it?"

Hispanica looks at Jasper, wondering if he means what she thinks he means.

Jasper smiles. "We need to go to Ipa, find the ones who have been shielding her from Quern."
Hispanica nods in agreement.

"That's if they're not incarcerated already."
Hispanica puts her boot back on. "My sisters in Fraz county will need to be there, at the great chamber."

"How long have we got to pull this together?" asks Jasper, turning around to face Hispanica in one swift move without uncrossing his legs.

"I think we have 3 Earth months."

"Not much time for us then." replies Jasper, knowing that Hispanica cannot disclose any more with regards to the prophecy. Knowing too much can distort its outcome, which is why only the shamans have access to the full papyrus prophecy, which lies deep in the cavern of Herratta, nestled in the forests of Fraz County.

Hispanica spots something in the distance. A slow moving tsunami is brewing.

"The sea felt my woes."

"To Ipa then." says Jasper, standing up and putting out a hand to help Hispanica to her feet.

They both look out to sea, the mountain sized tsunami slowly edging forwards at a snail's pace. "To Ipa." she says, taking his hand.

***

12th November, 4.20am, East Wall, Militia City, Ipa, Venezelu

It's early in Ipa, but just 50 minutes since Aurora came flashing into the device of every living creature in the galaxy. The streets are filled with people chanting and singing. In Militia City, rebels are drinking and throwing furniture. Ipa's in uproar.

Lindar is dressed in a black cloak, her red wavy hair tied back in a bun which is poking out the back of her hood. She has glow-shades on, red reflective glasses that filter out excess light and that can be used as a heat sensor. She sits on a box by the tall stone wall and opens a can of wheat whisky. There's no free moment for privacy, the streets are dense and deep with people. She inserts her ear-call device and calls Professor Sykes.

She hears two pips before he answers.

"What took you so long?!" Professor Sykes voice sounds angry, it has a tremble in it.

"Stay calm now Justin. The streets have been packed, I barely made it here."

"I thought something had happened to you. I knew I had to stay here…my hands feel tied. I hate this."

"Wait, did you fry the apartment bugs?"

"Yes, of course."

"Well, even if you haven't, there's enough chaos

now that even Quern's men will be occupied."

"Are we going to Operation Capsula then?"

"Yes, now's our moment. Mia, Ray and Fran should be at your place in about 4 minutes. There's a dock shuttle ready to take you to our base. Just leave everything as it is. We deal with this once we've had our emergency meeting."

"It's happening Lindar, isn't it?"

"It has begun."

"Aren't you coming now?" asks the Professor, already knowing the answer.

"Mia and I have some intel to gather before we meet. Got a message early this morning that there was an intrusion alert in the basement at MEW5, it's gone straight to Quern's office but we're going to do some digging before we join you and the others."

"You better had join us, we can't move forward without you."

"I'll be there."

"Kilos speed."

"To you also." replies Lindar. She can hear a knock at Professor Sykes door. "That'll be Mia. She'll make sure you, Ray and Fran leave ok, then she's heading to my location. Go now, go."

Professor Sykes, now dressed and ready with his briefcase and black-rimmed glasses almost falling off his nose opens the door to see Mia standing before him. Mia Kranos is a five foot three woman with grey hair that swirls round her head in a series of buns. Her piercing, sharp black eyes peer out behind some slivery-blue pointed spectacles that sit on an otherwise, soft, plump and warm looking face. She is of medium build, stocky and wearing a red shirt buttoned up to the neck, black dungarees and sneakers.

"Where's Ray and his wife?"

"Sykes, you're 20 flights up, that's a long flight for *one* aging spy, never mind three of them. They're waiting in the dock shuttle."

"Oh," replies Sykes, as he rummages about in his pocket for his thumb pad to lock the door.

"Besides, we're trying to get you out of here before Quern puts two and two together about a supposedly Interceptor-free human who is not, in fact, Interceptor-free, but has been Cosmi-tagged and Feelered-up from the neck up. Not to mention that she has been monitored for some time without his knowledge." Mia takes a breath. "You're on the run now Sykes."

"Yes, I get, I get it. I was just disappointed not to see Ray and Fran when I opened the door is all."

"Oh, sorry to disappoint you with my old face. Nice to see you too. You'll get the meet and greet at the shuttle." Mia quickly cranes her neck into the room. "Have you cleared anything inconspicuous?"

"I don't have anything like that here, keep everything at the pods."

"Ok then, let's go."

As Professor Sykes and Mia leave the apartment, the Professor himself takes a final look around the flat. It's so sparsely furnished, he thought. *At least if I end up seeing jail time for this, my new decór will be a step up.*

***

12th November, 4:30am Earth Time, CERN Headquarters, General Quern's Office

Quern is sitting in his large wooden chair, tapping a small, pre-enlightenment hunting knife on the corner of his desk. His green eyes squint in the dark. Officer Griig is in another chair in the corner of the room. He has an equipad on his lap. He looks tense and uneasy.

"Sir, I know it's been a busy morning downstairs, but it's been an hour since the exposure. Do we have a plan to contain?"

"Silence Griig!" roars Quern. "I'm thinking." Quern stands and waves at his exterior windows. Suruplight spills inside like water bursting from a dam. He walks to the window and gazes out over Ipa and Militia City.

"You have our Operative in the questioning room still?" asks Quern, sliding a sweaty palm over his red head.

"Yes, as per procedure. We had no choice. He reported it to the other night guards in the first instance."

"And his device, they have it?"

""Unfortunately. By the time I got there they'd already hooked it up to our mainframe to download the recording."

"But it's contained for now?"

"Yes General."

"Beep the pirates for me, tell them to head to the base, now. I want a word with them."

Griig nods and scribbles something on his equipad.

"And retrieve anything you can find on Sykes, both at the office and at his home. The office bug is still operational, but he seems to have burnt all transmission devices we had in his apartment, probably used a slight radioactive charging device, the swat."

Quern walks back over to his desk. He picks up the knife and throws it at the back wall of his office, hitting an old-looking painting of the Supreme Court. "This girl, this...human," Quern puts his hand underneath the desk and presses the black button which loads the infra-red web-like net across his office.

"Before you ask, yes. She's definitely the same girl that's just flashed up on Breaking News." replies Griig.

"But we have no record of her, no signs of an Interceptor?"

"We can't inspect whether she has an interceptor until her next hypnagogic episode. It won't be easy, she's famous now, it'll be hard to access her alone."

Quern presses the dark gold button on his desk which opens the cupboard behind him. The monitor is activated. He looks over at Griig. "Make it happen."

Griig nods, stiffens his body and salutes.

"As for our busy scientists, we ought to track them down, starting with Justin Sykes. Gather our two on the inside and head over to his place. Take as much incriminating evidence as you can, including bomb materials from downstairs."

Griig continues scribbling things on the equipad.

"You're not writing this down, are you?"

"Of course not Sir, I, erm, had forgot to manually switch on the bug device in the questioning room. You know, to monitor what's been said. I've just enabled the remote setting now."

Quern rolls his eyes and sighs.

"I'll make the official visit to Sykes' apartment a little later on and then contact the Supreme Court asking for a warrant for his arrest. One for him, and ones for all of his no good friends that have been hiding this little glower from us."

"Is this the start of the prophecy Sir?"

"No, it's the end of it, and it ends with them in jail and us in the driving seat."

"But you know that by opening this can of worms, we too will be under investigation."

Quern's eyebrows rise. "You *think* I don't know that? We *are* the dark hand, Griig. For power to stay in our hands, we must play the game. Be confident, it's still our time. Our legal teams will crush those hippies. Plant the evidence, and find me all you can on the audio."

Quern motions for Griig to leave, looks at his watch and calls out, "Indigo."

The metallic screen starts to beep, followed by a visual of Frayaraz and Patró in front of the screen.

Griig is by the door, loitering. "Shall I?"

"Go, now, yes."

"Oh, ok General. Thank you General."

Quern turns to face Frayaraz and Patró. "I'll make this quick - the deal's off. The plot has been spoiled, you're not getting your final data deposit."

"You can't do that," says Frayaraz. She stands up, her long pink hair in a ponytail, Quern can see its green reflections sparkling bright through the monitor. She walks to the camera, her huge blue eyes cut through the screen like a Roko ocean desert shark.

"Listen, you filthy piece of Venezeluan,"

"No! You listen to me, you orphaned pirate scum. I've had enough of you thinking you call the shots. *I* have the footage I need. *You* have the zulan to prove it. As for the other deal, the bombing is off. I have other matters to deal with, you won't be getting your data, not now, and probably not ever."

Frayaraz is stunned by Quern's tone. She takes off her cloak and sits on the table.

"General Quern," she clears her throat, "I have no more than 70 different clients lined up, who are expecting this data transfer, data we were promised."

"I understand, but can't you see? With this green human on our radars, we have bigger fish to fry."

Frayaraz looks at Patró, who nods as though he's come to the exact same conclusion, in the exact same moment.

"You didn't know about her, did you? That's why you're being so cagey about the data, that and the fact that you're too much of a lost cause to set off a couple of pesky bombs in your own backyard, in the only place we actually need them to go off."

Patró joins Frayaraz on the table. "You have no historic data on this human, do you? We have nothing to give our clients now? Is that right?"

"Close your deals, it's a new deadline. It's open season for the human. Whoever can make meaningful first contact with her wins the game.

That's all there is to it. There is no extra data, there is no historic data."

"You will pay for this Quern, mark my Indigan words."

Frayaraz closes the transmission.

Quern bangs his desk in anger, bruising his fat fist.

"Kilos damn you Sykes! I will get that data from you."

***

12th November, 7:03am, Professor Sykes Apartment, Ipa, Venezelu

Quern and five officers, including Officer Hawthorne, arrived at Sykes 20th floor apartment block with fire under their tails. Two of Quern's inside men fry the entry thumb-pad, another kicks the door in. A Supreme Court officer is present with them.

"Was that *really* necessary General Quern? I thought this was an information finding visit?"

"Well, we know that the suspect, I mean the scientist, we're trying to locate isn't here, as he's supposed to be. He was on home arrest for breaching contract."

The officers pile into the small, empty flat. They start rummaging around, pulling off cushions from Professor Sykes' sofa and looking inside cupboards.

"I've found something!" shouts one of the officers, lifting out a pile of explosives from a kitchen cupboard. "Me too!" shouts another, pulling out several blueprints and boiler suits from the bedroom.

General Quern is by the window, looking out into the balcony. "Where are you Justin, where are you?" Quern moves his vision from outside the apartment to inside.

"Bag that stuff up, and keep searching for more, anything that might give us an indication as to where he is."

The Supreme Court official brings out an equipad. He frantically starts taking pictures and writing notes. "Well, this is shocking."

"I just follow my nose officer, just follow my nose."

Quern looks down at the floor. He kneels down. At his feet, is a large 3 x 4 Earth metre pale blue, silver, red and orange thick rug. It has tassels on the ends. The large knotted fabric feels smooth to the touch. "Officer Jenkins, do you recognise this material?"

Officer Jenkins from the Supreme Court looks down at the rug, his beady eyes and side parting as sharp as his geographical knowledge.

"It's a Zaattan rug, made by the monks there."

"The Andanuan forest."

"That's right."

"That *is* right." General Quern stands up and smiles. He nods at Officer Hawthorne.

"Get the heli-choppers ready, we leave in an hour."

18

11th November 2002 Earth Time, Zaattan, Andanuan Forest, Pod #3, Auditory Laboratory
Gisella is sitting in the centre of the room in front of a large desk full of screens, computers and audio equipment. The chair she sits in is an old, tan, tattered armchair. It has stuffing coming out of the armrests and one of the missing feet has been replaced, only just, by a small tin of potpots. The lab is dark, all but for a small lamp on Gisella's desk, sat in the far right hand side corner of the room.

Gisella's lab is high-tech, but littered with essential oils, old candles, different coloured fabrics on the floor and lots of other highly hazardous materials for an audio lab. The walls burst with painted colour on the rich polygrestav padding. Polygrestav soundproofing is grey. But not Gisella's, hers is rainbow-coloured. Gisella's lab has no windows, so she settles for a splash of paint on the walls and an array of traditional Li country music and Hermos ballads in her speakers. Not tonight though. Tonight, Gisella is sat upright in her tatty chair with a clipboard in front of her. She is plugged into her hypnopompic desk software, and has a huge pair of blue headphones over her head.

A red light flashes on the dashboard, indicating that a session is in progress.

"Every living being, on all planets, in all Universes, are restricted by their physical form – but there is a way in which all living beings, on all planets, in all Universes, *can* travel. Not all of them *know* that they're doing this, which can make it dangerous and humorous in equal proportion."

Gisella hears someone enter the room. She presses a few buttons on her dashboard and turns to see who it is.

"What are you doing?" asks Robertus.

Gisella says nothing and just smiles a coy, shy smile. The kind a naughty dog might pull after ripping up a household newspaper.

"I thought I'd reach out."

"But she's in Gamma by now Gisella." He takes off his top and changes into a t-shirt.

"Tonight's contact might not have worked Robertus, but I have to give this a try."

Robertus looks at her, confused. "Give what a try?"

"I think Marcux may have awoken something in her, enough for me to get through."

"But she's on the dreamland superhighway. It's like trying to communicate with a device that might as well be switched off."

"Babies can hear from the womb," Gisella replies "and a comatosed person can hear from their unconscious. I'm *sure* Aurora can hear me."

"I still say she's on the travel path. We need to wait for tomorrow's footage to see where she is."

Robertus starts combing his hair in Gisella's sink mirror, on the right hand side of the room. It has a pink spotlight on it. "Must all your personal belongings end up in my lab dear Robertus?" she laughs. "You have your own sink."

"I prefer yours, better lighting." Robertus stops combing his hair.

"If we make contact," says Robertus, opening the mirror cupboard to pull out some hair fixing gelatine, "then she'll inherit all this information. Her unconscious will soak it in during first contact download."

"But Marcux still has to transfer it, and it can take a while. Time and Quern are against us, I want to do all in my power to make this as easy as possible for Marcux next time around in case he doesn't have a proper opportunity to download."

"I admire what you're trying to do, I really do. You look after our wellbeing, and we'd like to look after yours too. Please, don't stay up all night."

"I have to try Robertus, you understand that, don't you?"

Robertus wipes his hands on a cloth by the sink and walks over to Gisella, placing a hand on her shoulder. "I guess I do." Gisella smiles.

"Besides," she says, shifting in her chair to make herself comfortable again, "I like speaking with her." Robertus nods.

Gisella goes back to her dashboard and flicks a few buttons on. The red light starts flashing again. Robertus smiles and leaves the room, quietly closing the door behind him.

"Now," says Gisella, holding up her clip board,

"where was I? Oh, yes." She takes a deep breath. "Universal enlightenment, as we sometimes call it, actually gives you, in time, the ability to understand how your own Universe works. It's the idea that something very far away can give you answers to something that's right in front of you, something *within* you even. It's the idea that this same thing that is so far away, has actually been accessible to you since the beginning of time itself."

Gisella smiles and takes a sip of cold gingero tea. Its sweet blaming touch soothes her throat and voice. A voice that was travelling the electrical waves. A voice which Gisella hoped was being heard by one Aurora Black of Earth.

19

"Two thousand miles I roam.
Just to make this dock my home."

Ottis Reading & Steve Cropper of Earth,
Musicians

20th February 2003, Earth Time, Supreme
Court, Ipa, Venezelu

It's quiet and warm in the lobby of the Supreme
Court. It's as though the activity in the main
chamber had manifested into a heat that couldn't
escape the stone building and which was now
making its way under every door and onto every
wall. The tall, normally chapel-cold white-speckled
marble walls in the lobby feel like hot plates today;
their normal glisten substituted for a dull murky tin
reflection.

In the centre of the lobby, between the wide spiral
staircase that sits to the right of the main chamber
doors and the outside doors, stands a Court guard.
It's Marcux's Court guard, and he's patiently
waiting outside the washrooms. He's facing the left
hand side of the lobby, in what looks like a stare out
with the marble walls. His short brown hair and

clean-shaven peach-coloured face look bland against his incredibly striking emerald eyes. They sparkle and swirl like hot metallic paint swirling in a glass of water, it's the only thing about him that is moving, the rest of him is stiff as a board. He sorts out his uniform, pulling down his top, then resorts back to his standing position. He stands rigid and tall, as though he's just been summoned by the supreme court judges in person.

The guard's attention is distracted by a loud noise coming from the front entrance. He looks towards the heavy wooden and glass panelled doors. Someone is coming in. It's Gisella.

Gisella holds the door open, letting in a fresh and comforting breeze. She could tell that the Guard was in deep appreciation of this. The sticky heat inside the lobby was intense. Lost in the relief of it, he smiled as the breeze blew into his face. The guard came back to his senses. His smile faded and he paces towards Gisella.

"Miss, close that door please. This is an official building, we have a large court case in session."

"I know," replied Gisella. "Doesn't everyone know that?"

The guard looked at Gisella inquisitively, trying to work her out.

"The door screen panel went yellow, indicating that you are registered to be here today. Why aren't you in the Chamber?"

Gisella hops along the large square floor tiles, made from the same white-marbling material as the walls. "Well, you know, it was getting a bit claustrophobic in there, it's very hot."

Gisella approaches the guard in a coy, playful manner. "What's your name?"

The guard looks taken aback. "I'm, erm, I'm Pholos."

"Hi Pholos, I'm Gisella Star. Nice to meet you." Gisella extends her hand to give a high three. The guard, on automatic, almost goes to return the greeting, then remembers why he's standing in the lobby and looks at his watch. He puts his head into the washrooms by the holding rooms. "Are you almost done in there? You might want to hear your friend's testimony."

Marcux's voice echoes back off the bathroom tiles. "Sorry, it's my stomach. Please bear with me."

The guard rolls his eyes and resumes his position in the lobby. To his surprise, Gisella is still standing there. "Please return to the chamber, Miss. The lobby is not for loitering."

"Isn't that exactly what lobbies are for?" says Gisella, dusting off a little fluff from the guard's left lapel. Gisella looks over the guard's shoulder and sees Hispanica and Jasper behind the pillar by the bottom of the staircase.

"Pholos, I want to raise something very important with you, something I noticed about the door when I came back in. I think the outer panel might be compromised. I'm no scientist, but if not dealt with, this could damage the inner electrics that help sustain a healthy working door screen panel. Won't you come take a look?"

Pholos looks over towards the front entrance. "I'll look at it later, I can't move from here right now."

"Come on Pholos, it won't take a second. Besides,

the fracture is hairline thin, you'll never find it. I wouldn't want an expensive door repair to be on your head and my taxes, especially if someone is making you aware of it in advance so as to prevent a bigger problem. Just one second, come with me," Gisella puts her arm on the guard's left forearm. Without knowing why, her touch sends a calming and centred feeling into his whole body. His previously contracted muscles relax. His legs feel soft and he can feel his heart start to beat a little faster. "Alright then," says Pholos, looking once more behind him towards the washroom. "I'll take a quick look."

Gisella slows her pace, trying to point out some interesting facts about the Jorkey stone and the history of the Court's architectural beginnings. Pholos doesn't change his pace, but every time his pace out walks hers, she tugs at his arm gently, sending those warm relaxed sensations through Pholos' entire nervous system. He looks back once more towards the washrooms, then surrenders to Gisella's charm and warmth. "How old did you say these lobby balconies are?"

At this moment, Jasper flies towards the washrooms. He lifts a scared looking Marcux from the corner of the first cubicle and flies back towards the door. Jasper, Marcux and Hispanica were already on the 5th floor of the building when the slow-release washroom door clunked back into its frame. The noise instantly caught Pholos attention, pulling him out of his dreamlike trance.

Gisella, sensing Pholos distraction, grabbed him close into her chest. "Pholos, you must take a look at this!" Gisella pulls out a small rectangular block from her daisy-patterned waistcoat and puts it in front of his face. Pholos, confused, looks at Gisella with surprise and annoyance. He goes to move away from her and towards the washrooms when Gisella puts the block right up to his eyes, "Sorry."

Gisella closes her eyes and presses the top of the block. A piercing bright phosphorous light flashes in front of Pholos' eyes.

***

Hispanica and Jasper enter the court's 15th floor's dome room. It's more grand chapel than room, thought Jasper. Its dimension must have been around 35 to 40 Earth yards, its full height, around the size of a small administrative building in Ipa.

As the three touched down into the room, their footsteps echoed across the shiny white-marble floor. The circular stone walls that surrounded them were of modest dark grey Jorkey stone, thick and cold, cemented together with thick layers of black Rokan salt-sand. The lower part of the dome, just above the wall, is made of thick glass, around 3 Earth metres high. The glass has a yellowy tinge through it, caused from the heating process used in the Hermosian desert. Prowlonium desert flowers are fused into the glass during production to give it its colour.

Above the glass, sits the remainder of the dome itself, made from a mixture of Ozro stone on the interior and dark black Li granite on the outside. The dome's interior is painted with a giant fresco of a young man, elevated from his bed, reaching out to touch the hand of an elderly woman, sat in a wicker chair and draped in purple robes that cover all but her face. They're both reaching out to each other, a bright spark of electricity appearing between their three middle fingers.

As Hispanica rushes to the centre of the room, Jasper stands guard at the door. Marcux follows behind Hispanica and notices a stone circle about a metre wide cutting through the marble floor's centre point. In the stone's inner circle lies a carving of the papyrus book. Hispanica rushes to it and takes off her thick white cloak, flicking it out onto the ground over the stone emblem. A sweet salty aroma comes off of the cloak's white leather outer lining. Marcux lays down on the multitude of soft colours that grace the cloak's inner lining. He can feel the softness of the material brush his hands, and the smell of Gojine plants fill his nose. Hispanica takes off a small purple shoulder cardigan and moulds it into a pillow, helping Marcux to get comfortable. Despite Hispanica's thick cloak, Marcux can still feel the floor's cold stony presence beneath him. It's not unpleasant, especially after all the hustle and heat of the main chamber. Marcux looks up. "Is that Jimus Krakovia from Freyal?"

"Yes," smiles Hispanica. "And that's Sister Pretya from Naboxulus in Universe 4."

"Wow," says Marcux. "I'd always heard about this fresco. Can't believe I'm staring at it."

Hispanica looks over at Jasper, then back at Marcux. She strokes his blonde curls away from his head.

"I need you to take some deep breaths now Marcux, you know what we need to do."

***

General Quern is shifting uncomfortably in his seat. Fat beads of sweat are rolling down his back and forehead, but it isn't the heat from the main chamber that's bothering him. Quern sits forward and looks over at Grigg, who is four seats away from him on the benches. The pair are separated by two Supreme Court custodians and a guard. Grigg looks back, then looks over to the benches in front and understands Quern's uneasiness. Marcux Grentil is missing, and no one seems to have noticed.

"And at that we shall break for recess. Back in 35 minutes." One of the Supreme Court judges bangs her gavel and the entire courtroom rises to its feet. They wait until the flock of judges leave the long rectangular mahogany podium, then slowly start to filter out into the lobby.

Grigg is accompanied by one of the custodians, whilst another one walks next to General Quern. They assemble out into the lobby to meet a frenzy of reporters, Venezeluan citizens there to watch the trial, lawyers, others on trial, as well as numerous guards and custodians who are never more than a metre away from those awaiting questioning. Supreme Court caterers walk around with refreshment trays around their necks, handing out ice-cold beverages and salta-snax. Only one major trial can run at any given time, for it requires all 10 judges to be present.

Grigg turns to the custodian stood next to him.

"Officer, the accused, Marcux Grentil, are you aware of his whereabouts? Didn't they exit the chamber some while ago? I didn't see him or your colleague return before recess."

The custodian, a small stalky woman with ginger hair and caramel brown skin calls over to a guard she'd been sitting next to.

"Oi, Flenander!" The room is so busy with people chatting and moving around that it was hard to get his attention.

"Flenander!"

The guard in question, a tall thin fellow with bright pink skin and turquoise eyes turns around.

"Check out the washrooms would you," says the stalky custodian, "I want eyes on Pholos and Sir Grentil."

Clearly slightly scared of the short ginger-set custodian, the guard salutes and proceeds to the washrooms without haste. He marches in.

Zareb, Lindar and the Professor are in the far back left corner of the lobby, the corner nearest the chamber entrance. They have their eyes fixed on Quern, Griig and the situation at the washrooms. Mia, disguised as a shamanic woman from Fraz, is lingering at the bottom of the stairwell, close to Ray and Fran on the right hand side of the chamber entrance. She keeps her distance so as not to arouse the attention of their guards.

The pod scientists are grouped together by the Supreme Courtroom's main entrance on the left hand side near the marble walls. They can barely see what's going on by the washrooms because of the sea of people swimming between them, but they know that something is unfolding.

The monks are nestled on the benches outside the holding rooms on the right hand side of the lobby. They are closest to the washrooms, sitting in between all the holding rooms. Kalista, the Master Monk is standing right in front of one of the holding rooms, counting square beads on her wrist, her eyes transfixed on the group of shamanic women from Fraz who are right in the centre of the room, in a huddle, humming a song.

"Aumm-ah-neah. Aumm-ah-neah." It's very faint and quiet but Kalista recognises its rhythm.

She smiles, then looks towards the stairwell.
She knows that the time is fast approaching.

20

"Am I awake or do I dream,
The strangest pictures I have seen
Night is day and twilight's gone away."

Jeff Lynne of Earth, Musician

20th February 2003, Stefania's Flat, Barnsley, Earth

"Thank you for joining us so quickly Sam."
Stefania re-enters the channel room with Sam at her heels.

"Of course! My pleasure." Before Sam has the chance to get a good look at the array of fabrics and silks draping the room, the smell of incense and Frankincense hit her square in the face.

"Wow, you guys been doing Aromatherapy shots in here, or what?" Sam spots Aurora lying down in a tented area in the far right hand corner of the room, near the front window. "Oh, hey Aurora, barely saw you there through all that chiffon."
Aurora smiles at Sam, but her smile seems strained.

"Hey," said Sam, "is she ok? I mean she looks a bit, drunk or something."

"She's fine, I've given her some relaxation

techniques to bring her heart rate down, that and some of my Tranquil Tea."

"You drugged her?"

"Of course not, it's all natural, but we don't have a lot of time, she has to be relaxed in order for First Contact to be made."

Sam raises her eyebrows.

"Remember how I asked you on the phone that you really had to keep an open-mind and that you could ask any question you wanted after this was over?"

Sam nods, "Understood Stefania. I'm here for Aurora, whatever she needs."

"A true healer. Our ancestors would have been good friends." Sam smiles, not quite sure what Stefania is referring to.

Aurora looks up the deep red, orange and Aztec blues around her head in the gazebo, she can feel her heart-rate slowing down, her muscles feel less contracted - she is definitely getting ready for sleep. Her make-shift bed feels like the most comfortable bed in the world right now, she craves rest. Her eyelids feel like dumbbells. Spotting her eyes rolling in her head, Stefania rushes over to the gazebo and holds Aurora's hand.

"Not quite yet my love, I need to come with you. I will be there, keeping the others out so that your contact can reach you. Sam here will be monitoring your breathing and making sure that you don't convulse too much or hit your head off anything. Once I'm the zone, I'll be of little use to you this side of our dimension."

Sam's eyes are wide in her head now. She senses

Stefania looking over at her, and just nods in agreement as though everything she's just said is perfectly normal and re-assures her that she fully understands her role in this.

The amber lamps around the room start to flicker. Stefania and Sam hear a buzzing sound. Sam looks down at Aurora, who is lying on her back, her chocolate coloured bob nestled around her head like an extra pillow.

"We don't have much time." says Stefania.

21

Supreme Court, Ipa, Venezelu

"Court back in session! Court back in session! Everybody please re-adjourn."

The small stalky custodian woman, called Jizobal, is standing on a box ringing a bell. Everybody assembles into the main chamber. Jizobal and a few other guards scan the room for Pholos and Marcux. "They're not in the lobby." reports Flenander.

"Keep looking," replies Jizobal. "We must re-start proceedings, take three guards with you and check the building." Flenander nods and goes to recruit a search party.

General Quern and Griig reluctantly go back into the chamber, Quern still outraged at Marcux's disappearance.

As everyone settles into their seats, the Judges return to the podium.

"This is an outrage!" says Quern to Griig. "They're up to something. How can you lose one of the most dangerous travellers in all of Venezelu?" Quern turns to his lawyers, three small women dressed in yellow who are preoccupied with equipads and sifting through large books. "Counsel, I demand that we stop court proceedings until

Marcux Grentil is back in the chamber."

"Mr. Quern, we have bigger issues at present. The Prosecution for team Dream Rebels have just announced a new witness to the stand. The judges want to proceed with the witness' testimony whilst guards continue to search the building."

"What new witness?" enquires Grigg.

There's a ruffle and some gasping from the benches. As the chamber door opens, people in the balcony are craning their necks over the edge to take a look. A guard walks forward. Behind him, dressed in iron-capped boots, long grey pantaloons and a dark purple cloak, is Frayaraz.

***

Supreme Court, Dome Room

Marcux begins his shallow breathing to induce relaxation. Hispanica rests her gaze on his.

"Marcux, there is something I must tell you before you go."

Marcux nods, his eyes sleepy and his body going limp. "I am not a good pirate." says Hispanica. Jasper hears this and looks over from the door entrance. Hispanica looks at Jasper and smiles.

"My name is Hispanica, that is true. But I am a shamanic witch from Fraz County. Only Jasper knew this, for it would be too dangerous for anyone else to know in case they tried to stop me being here today, with you, as the prophecy predicted."

Marcux's eyes begin to widen. "Please, stay calm, get ready to travel. I will tell you when Aurora is ready. She has help by her hand. Two Earthlings are present, just like the prophecy said. They will help us."

"Hispanica," says Marcux, his voice groggy, "what if I fail her again?"

Hispanica looks into Marcux's eyes and smiles into them. "Dear Marcux, you never failed her before. You were the one who woke her up."

***

Supreme Court, Main Chamber, Ipa, Venezelu
Quern and Griig are now sat side by side, with just one guard to Griig's right.

"Griig, this is ridiculous." says Quern. "They've put an Intolerant rebel on the stand to testify against me, meanwhile that little piece of scrap meat is Kilos knows where and with Kilos knows who. We *need* to do something."

Griig nods, "Yes General."

Griig looks up at the balcony. A man with a long black cloak is sitting at the far end of the chamber nearest the podium. Griig nods to the man, who pulls out a black leather book from his bag. He opens the book. The first page is blank, except for a fingerprint marking at the top right hand corner. He puts his index finger on it. It pulses red. The man nods down at Griig. Mia, undetected by Quern, Griig or the hooded man sees the whole silent operation play out. She leaves the chamber.

***

Yana's Heaven, Militia City, Ipa, Venezelu
Yana's Heaven is brimming this afternoon.

Apocalyptics are causing chaos in the drinking hole's main thoroughfare, clumsily bumping into card dealers and Yana's waiting staff. The thick red drapes that enclosed the stone-booth honeycomb's Western wall was being pelted by empty wheat whisky glasses and q-nuts. Each Apocalyptic was trying to aim at a particular booth and hit it. It appeared that they were placing bets on who could get closest. The staff were quick to descend on them, setting off their ankle alarms and prising out their stun-guns. It was probably in the Apocalyptics' best interests. Should a particularly nasty rebel come out from behind those red drapes, it would take more than Yana's highly trained staff to stop a full-on fight, something that had only ever happened twice before at Yana's. Once on the dawn of Henasoux's Eve, and the other was that time *everyone* knows about, but no one dares talk about.

Long wooden tables and benches haphazardly fill the main thoroughfare at Yana's. Round casino tables are dotted amongst the benches. At one of them, sits Dimetrius Kaniza. Dimetrius was a Jeopordiser. Not the pirate kind, but the nasty kind. The violent, unpredictable ticking time bomb kind. Loners, violent-hungry and weapons obsessed. Dimetrius was around 5 foot 11 inches in Earth measurements. A washed-out blue uniform sat on his muscular frame. The uniform looked similar to a formal CERN type, but theirs donned a black armband. Dimetrius' was wrapped tight around his chiselled right bicep. His weapons belt was shinier than a bristling waterfall cascade in the rocky hills of Li.

Dimetrius' hair was jet black, almost reflective black. His unshaved face looked spikey, not quite stubble and not quite beard. His eyes were a gunmetal grey, his skin a pale off-white. Slightly raised pink scars sat etched on his temple and around his cheekbones. He seemed untouched by the general chaos going on around him. He stared at the large televised circle above the main entrance at Yana's, the one that had been following the 'trial of the millennium' live and non-stop. Dimetrius had noticed Marcux's disappearance from the court room. He lifts a glass of hot wheat whisky and takes a drink. Its liquidy heat scorches his throat, a throat that boasts even more scars on it. He embraces the pain, then puts up his hand to order another. As he looks down at his playing cards, he notices that one of the many dull tin pin badges on his chest is flashing red. He puts his finger over it, presses it and it stops flashing. He folds his cards, stands up and places a bundle of zulan on the table. A thin snake-suited woman croupier with painted green skin and dyed gold hair looks at Dimetrius. "Have you stopped playing Ssssir?"

"No, I'm just off to find a bigger game." Dimetrius' contract had begun.

***

Lobby, Supreme Court, Ipa, Venezelu
Supreme Court guards Flenander, Kolo, Miso and Frapp are in the main lobby. "Ok, so we have one guard, Pholos, and one accused, Marcux Grentil, somewhere in this building. We know they must be somewhere in the building as the sensors body

count is still at 0." Flenander points to a large board on the left hand side of the main entrance. It shows a green '0' glowing brightly against some dimmed out words and numbers. "Kolo, for your benefit, any time the number is in positive or negative figures from the '0', it means we either have too many or too few people in the building. As it stands, we know that the missing are in the building and the doors have now been locked."

Kolo, a short dumpy man with a long grey beard and round hat puts three fingers up to Flenander, thanking him for the information.

"Miso, I'd like you and Kolo to do a thorough search of the lower annexes; that means all of these holding rooms, the washrooms, the kitchen beyond holding room 3 and the sub level library. Frapp and I will start to survey the stairwell and all of the adjoining offices. They can't be far." Miso salutes, her red hair tied back in a tight bun and her tall stature standing to attention. Her crisp navy blue uniform looks starched to within an inch of its life.

Frapp, an athletic looking young woman with a short brown bob and dark brown skin stands to attention, saluting the Guard and nodding to say she understands. Flenander pulls out a blueprint of the Supreme Court offices and shows it to Frapp. At the same time, Kolo and Miso discuss their strategy. "I'll start in the downstairs library," says Frapp, "you take the holding rooms. Once I'm done I'll come up to ground level, check in and we can take it from there."

"Affirmative." says Kolo, straightening out his beard and uniform jacket. He heads towards the first holding room door which is to the right of the washrooms. There's an obscured stained glass window. Behind it, the holding room is dark. Kolo opens the heavy walnut door, letting some fresh air and suruplight in from the main lobby. A large walnut desk sits at the back of the room, alongside two chairs and a bookshelf. Kolo squints his eyes. He can see something protruding from under the table. Is it a stick? An umbrella perhaps? He fumbles for the light switch. *Click.* Then comes the gasp.

Flenander hears it.

"What is it Kolo?"

Kolo is inside the room, holding the door open behind him with his left leg.

"I've found him." he shouts.

"Who?" asks Frapp, rushing up to the holding room.

"It's Pholos."

Frapp shouts down to the sub-level library by the Supreme Court front entrance, "Miso, come back up, Kolo has found Pholos!"

Miso pauses in her tracks, having just reached the bottom of the staircase. She flies back up. As she reaches the top she sees Flenander go inside the room to take a closer look at Pholos. He bends down and checks his pulse. "He's ok, just unconscious."

Frapp helps Flenander sit Pholos up into the desk chair, which is big enough to support his sleeping frame.

"What shall we do, the court is in full session."

Flenander pulls out a mini equipad and jots down

some notes. "Miso, double check the front door lock down. Frapp, put a message together for the Judges and pass it to them before next recess. Kolo, you come with me, we need to find Marcux Grentil, and whoever it was that sparked a flame-box at Pholos, making him pass out."

***

Dome Room, Supreme Court, Ipa, Venezelu

Marcux knew it was only a matter of minutes before he'd be in travel mode. Hispanica and Jasper were sat by Marcux's side. They saw him close his eyes. Just then, the dome door knocks three times. Jasper jumps up and runs towards it. "Wait!" shouts Hispanica. "It's ok, there's no one there. It's a message, from my clan, through Mia." She looks towards the arched door of the dome room. "Something…"

"What is it Hispanica?" Jasper puts his hands up against the door. "Are we in danger?"

"A Jeapordiser. The prophecy said this could happen, the knocks confirm it." Hispanica slaps Marcux gently on the face. "Marcux, do not go to sleep."

Marcux tries to sit up, a little startled by the slap. "What is it? What's wrong?"

"We can't put you under, not yet. We need your image to burn brighter than all the other visitors. And Aurora will get many during the hypnagogic window. Her healer may not be strong enough to ward them off."

"Why do we have to wait?"

"They're not ready, on Earth. There's been a hold

up. If you go under now, you'll be there waiting amongst all the others, she may not see you clearly, she may not reach out. We need your strength levels high, above those waiting. We need you to push forward and make that connection with her."

"What about the Jeapordiser?" asks Jasper. "How long do we have?"

"He'll be here soon, as will the Supreme Court guards. Gisella is on the 7th floor, she should ward them off for a while. The witches are on stand-by, as is Mia. They know what to do. I just hope that Aurora settles so that we can come through at the right moment."

***

Outside Supreme Court, Ipa, Venezelu
Dimetrius Kaniza approaches the Eastern side of the Supreme Court. He looks up at the never-ending wall of stone, tempted to fly to the top, but knowing that there was something he had to take care of first.

He looks down at his weaponry belt and removes a clench-hole dangle. He holds the silver implement up to his face, inspecting it as though it were a thing of beauty, as if he had all the time in the world to admire it.

Facing out towards the main road, with the Supreme Court to his right, he swiftly and sharply whacks the clench-hole dangle against the upper pane of the basement window, causing a crack that rippled around the small rectangular frame of the upper section. He pulls a suction cup from his pocket and removes the glass. He lifts the faded blue cuff of his uniform jacket, causing a crinkle up to his Jeapordiser black armband. Inserting his right arm into the window gap, Dimetrius could feel his extended bicep swell and stretch as he went for the twist lever. The twist lever tilted the bigger section of window underneath, just enough for Dimetrius to climb into the library basement.

With his first step inside the building, the main board detects his presence. The electronic tally goes up to +1.

The library is dark, all except for a pool of light gathered at the bottom of the staircase coming from the upstairs lobby. Demetrius heads for the power panel box, a small navy blue rectangular shaped metal container in the library basement's West wall. He pulls out a large hunting knife and tears open the container, prying its sides. Once inside, he cuts a green cord and attaches a small box to it. Upstairs, the main board goes back to '0'. Dimetrius hears someone coming down the stairs. He looks at the power panel box which is still prised open. He doesn't have enough time to fix it, so quickly hides behind a bookcase, hunting knife at chest height.

"Miso, come back up, Kolo has found Pholos!"

Dimetrius catches a glimpse of a tall woman at the bottom of the staircase. She pauses in her tracks just before reaching the last step. She turns and makes her way back up, flying this time.

Dimetrius pokes his head out from behind the bookcase, scanning the lower basement for any other possible guards. He wasn't expecting to hear so many voices upstairs whilst the Court was in session. They were probably looking for Marcux, he thought. Had they seen the sensor board change from +1 to '0'? They seemed pre-occupied with finding Grentil, he concluded probably not.

***

Supreme Court, Main Chamber, Ipa, Venezelu
Frayaraz sits in the dock, her legs crossed on the mahogany leaning post boxing her in. One of the judges spots it. "Even pirates must respect the Courtroom Mz Sommer." Frayaraz reluctantly removes her legs from the podium and sits back in her chair.

The Dream Rebels defence team continue with their questioning.

"Mz Sommer, before we show the Courtroom the evidence of your claim, can you repeat the allegation again, and may I remind you that you are under Oath."

Quern's defence team muster in. "Objection, the court has already heard the allegation."

One of the judges intercepts "Denied. Proceed please, but keep to the flow of your questioning if you please."

The Dream Rebel defence team look at Frayaraz, desperate for her to comply as per their brief and spontaneous rehearsal not long before she took to the stand.

Frayaraz sits up in her chair. "I told you already, Quern has been making deals with pirates across the galaxy. He's been selling them data from MEW5. He's also been spying on pretty much everyone he can afford to spy on, then using any material he has to blackmail people into doing what he wants. On top of that, he's been violating his dream travel

229

rights, entering bed chambers and homes of women across neighbouring planets, and then deleting any recorded footage afterwards. On one occasion, he got caught in the wrong house at the wrong time. We captured that, and have been blackmailing him ever since."

The court sits stunned. Even the judges look taken aback.

"Please, court official, play the evidence."

***

7th Floor, Lawyer's Study, Supreme Court

Gisella is lying on the floor, belly down, fixing a thin metallic wire to the base of a bookshelf. The opposing end of the wire is attached to a sofa leg on the other side of the room. She pings the wire to test its resistance, then double checks that the front door to the study opens clear of it. It's at ankle height - the perfect trip wire.

She closes the three tall deep red velvety drapes, unleashing a tonne of dust which floats up into the suruplight. The small mahogany study has tall windows and is sparsely furnished; just a large desk, chair, bookshelf and sofa. Most of the studies look the same, no particular grandeur, just the essentials.

Main Lobby, Supreme Court

After the voice recordings presented by Frayaraz and the Dream Rebels team had been heard by the courtroom, flutter and commotion ensued. The shamanic witches and Mia see this as their opportunity to discreetly leave the courtroom. They stand up from their seats in the balcony and head towards the stairwell. Coming down it, they see something move past the small oval windows ahead of them. It's Dimetrius. He flies past them and up towards the dome. One of the witches stamps her knobbly and twisted Fraz County Oak walking stick three times in the stairwell.

The Dome, Supreme Court

The large door in the dome room bangs three times. Jasper jumps up and runs towards it. "Wait!" shouts Hispanica. "It's ok, there's no one there. It's a message, from my shaman clan." She looks towards the arched door of the dome room. "Something…"

"What is it Hispanica?" Jasper puts his hands up against the door. "Are we in danger?"

Stairwell, Supreme Court

As Pholos rests in the ground floor holding room he was found in, Flenander, Miso, Frapp and Kolo start to fly up the stairs. "We stay in pairs and take a floor at a time, there's nowhere else he could be now." Flenander and Kolo fly ahead to the 2nd floor, whilst Frapp and Miso take the 1st.

7th floor Lawyer's Study Room, Supreme Court

Gisella peers out the window. She looks worried. She opens the study door to its fullest then sits in the desk chair. It's positioned in front of the desk and directly in line with the study room door. Feeling settled in the body of leather around her, she waits.

22

*"Acceptance of oneself is the essence
of the moral problem and the acid test of one's
whole outlook on life."*

C. G. Jung of Earth, Psychoanalyst

1 Earth month prior to the trial, Venezelu Jailhouse

The jailhouse was a five-sided one storey building that sat 10 miles North of Ipa. It was dark grey on the outside and clinical white on the inside. It looked scary and threatening to anyone who wasn't from Venezelu, but once inside, it was actually pretty bright and comfortable. Many things had changed since the Enlightenment, including the reintroduction of the swinging pendulum between light and dark, and with that, came people wanting to disturb the peace again. But on Venezelu, they had learnt something about the values of change, forgiveness and reform and understood that if you ended up in the jailhouse, then much darkness must have crossed your path for you to get there. Jails were always considered temporary holding pens after the Enlightenment. Should an individual be a danger to others or themselves, there were other facilities for those individuals, but all tailored according to their mental illness or inner excess darkness. Nobody committed atrocities against children anymore, it was one of the greatest achievements of the awakening, but violence, anger and greed still ran strong in the blood of living beings across all universes. Like a dormant gene, most people had learned to identify its presence, accept it as part of their make-up, learn to control the urges and temptations and yet not be ashamed of who they were. That they were light and dark combined. Problems often started when people professed to being just one or the other. Those who claimed to be greater than great, good to their cores, honest and sound and with no darkness in them – these were the ones who often offended in the worst ways. For they buried their dark side, they pretended it didn't exist, and as such, they made it angry. Their dark side felt abandoned, and so it rebelled. But not just a little rebellion, one with the force of a volcano that had been quietly bubbling and brewing underneath a false smile or insincere kindness. One which, eventually, would explode with a venom and hatred that burnt all those in its way.

At least the ones who revelled in darkness alone were easier to identify. Some were damaged, some were sick, some had never seen the light (or its power). Others were just very, very insecure. It was always easier to shine some light into the darkness than it was to make someone see their own darkness. That stuff was usually hid way down, and it was a journey only they could make.

Jasper and Hispanica were dressed in olive green all-in-ones as they entered the Jailhouse main gates. They had ordered their suits from the courthouse a week before making their application for a visit. The suits changed colour all the time, so you always had to pre-order before arriving. Visitors had to wear the same, so as not to indicate their identity to anyone on the inside.

When news of the arrests became public knowledge, Jasper and Hispanica had made an appointment to go to the Jailhouse straight away to speak with Professor Sykes, Zareb Fender, Marcux Grentil, Lindar and the others. The group had been branded 'The Dream Rebels' by the cosmic press, and it kind of stuck.

The Dream Rebels weren't sure what to make of two strangers turning up to see them, and they almost didn't accept the visit. The previous week had been hectic with lawyers and preparing for the case. Jasper had sent Lindar a letter saying '*the Aurora over Indigo looked lovely last evening.*' This caught Lindar's attention as no one knew the anomalies name yet. Further letters followed, and it was made clear that Jasper and Hispanica knew of the anomaly and that the group had allies on the outside. In one of Lindar's letters back to Jasper and Hispanica was a poem by Jimus Krakovia. Embedded within it were Mia and Gisella's locations as coordinates. Lindar was directing them to work together ahead of the trial date.

It was early morning when the pair arrived at the jailhouse to make their rounds. They visited everyone in the group, including every single monk. They tried their best to keep spirits up before the trial, used code to communicate on how Aurora was doing and kept them informed of what the general sense was on the outside. Other than the chunky and rather uncomfortable ankle tags they all had to wear, the group eat and slept well whilst on the inside. You could say they were all ok in body, but perhaps not always in mind. One of the punishments at the jailhouse was a travel ban microchip. Every inmate is injected with one. It limits your dreamtime travelling rights to just one flight per week.

After their 5th visit to the jailhouse, Jasper and Hispanica had an idea of what might be able to help the team during the trial.

Jasper and Hispanica leave the jailhouse with their visitor's outfits folded up in their hands. Jasper motions for Hispanica to pass him her outfit. "I think I know how we can help them." "How?"

Jasper walks over to a large transparent dustbin in the clearing. He dumps the two outfits inside. The dustbin starts to whirr. The waterless washer-dryer spins the outfits around before evaporating them. Two slices of melon sweet-o-chew pop out of the base in return. Jasper passes Hispanica a sweet treat before unwrapping and eating his own. Its juicy and refreshing flavours soothe his throat. "We need to go to Indigo, tonight."

Later that evening, Indigo

The last of the suruplight casts a dark orange and yellow shadow over the black-looking sea. Jasper and Hispanica sit on an old rum barrel tipped on its side. The beach is quiet, but the street procession and its parties murmur quietly in the distance. The delicately warm wind moves in and out of Hispanica's hair, whirling and swirling it around. Jasper looks at Hispanica with love in his eyes. "Hispanica,"

Hispanica breaks her gaze from the soothing sea breeze and looks at Jasper. "when can we tell the others, you know, about you?" asks Jasper.

"We can't. It's too risky. We can't tempt anything to sway us in a different direction from the prophesised route. The shamanic book says that out of all the hundreds of millions of galaxies crossing paths right now, and out of all of the billions of life bearing planets at play and within touching distance of each other, if an opportunity came to Venezelu, then it would be a shamanic witch, a pirate, an ex-spy and whisperer who would come together in the end. I'm not even sure if I was supposed to tell you that, I didn't seek the advice of the coven first."

Hispanica looks back out to sea, lost in a deep sea of her own thoughts. Jasper puts his hand on her leg. She turns to him and smiles. "And us," he says, moving his body closer to hers. He can smell sweet Gojine berries from her cloak, and another smell in her hair, one he can only describe as home. "Could you see *this* coming?"

Hispanica smiles and pulls Jasper in towards her, kissing him on the lips with fervour. Their lips separate after some time. Jasper sits back, pleased and wide-eyed. "I bet you didn't see *that* coming." she laughs.

There's a noise behind them in the bushes at street level. Hispanica and Jasper stand and turn. Frayaraz emerges from the bushes, picking bush leaves out of her cloak and hair. As she walks towards them, music from the procession is getting louder.

"This better be important." says Frayaraz. She looks Hispanica up and down, then over at Jasper. "Deserter." The night was warm and the sea breeze warmer, but Frayaraz's cold gaze could have turned the sea to ice, and that gaze was directed straight at Hispanica.

***

"I won't do it Jasper, no way."

"But Fray, Quern needs to be stopped. Who knows what lies and deception he's been cooking up in the jailhouse. The soles on his lawyers' shoes are probably burnt out after all the false testimonies they've been gathering."

"Why do you care anyway? Is it her?" Frayaraz points at Hispanica.

Hispanica, still sitting on the barrel, looks straight at Frayaraz, indicating that she has no fear of her.

"Of course not Fray, this thing – it's bigger than all of us. The Dream Rebels case goes to court within the month. You could stop the case in its tracks with what we have on Quern. Where are the tapes anyway?"

"As if I'm going to tell you, deserter. You made your choice when you left us to shack up with golden locks. Putting forward that evidence would only implicate me and the others. I hate Quern, have more reason to hate him than anyone, especially after what he did to us, but I'm not stepping foot inside that Supreme Court. I'm a pirate, something you seem to have forgotten how to be."

"He knows who he is Frayaraz," says Hispanica. She stands up and puts her hands on her hips, indicating a growing boredom for Frayaraz's tone and games.

"Let's go Jasper. This one is too far gone into the darkness, it's affected her ability to see the bigger picture."

"Excuse me?" says Frayaraz.

"You heard me." replies Hispanica. Jasper senses a change in Hispanica's tone. He knows she has restraint, but isn't keen to see her shamanic powers tested. Frayaraz's vile and violent temper is volatile. Jasper knows she is less measured.

"What sort of a pirate are you anyways? For all I know you could be working for Quern."

"Fray that's ridiculous." says Jasper. "You're right Hispanica, this was a waste of time. Only someone with a conscience would get it."

Frayaraz spits at Jasper's feet. "Well at least I'm not a traitor. What are you now anyways? Part of the Revolution?"

"More than you know." says Hispanica, turning her back on Frayaraz. Jasper follows her. They walk along the beach front, the sea to their right and the night street parties, now in full swing, to their left.

Frayaraz watches them go, and kicks the wooden barrel, smashing her iron-clad boot right through it. Whilst the noise catches Jasper's attention, Hispanica ignores it. Jasper turns anyway and takes one last look back at Frayaraz. She quickly looks the other way, scared that her old friend might catch that one emotion she never wanted him to see. Sadness. But she couldn't hide it from the evelight.

***

20th February 2003, Stefania's Flat, Barnsley, Earth

Sam watched as Stefania's body rocked back and forth. "Keep her awake Sammie," says Stefania, "squeeze her hand, don't let her sleep just yet." Sam nods and gently squeezes Aurora's hand. Aurora smiles and gently squeezes it back.

Stefania is seated in the lotus position. Her rocking becomes more aggressive. She starts to chant something under her breath. Sam can feel Aurora's grip start to loosen in her hand. She grips her hand again, squeezing it gently. There's no squeeze back.

"Aurora, don't go yet, Stefania hasn't said it's time yet."

"Chicken dinner." replies Aurora, "I need to make a list."

Sam looks down at Aurora, puzzled. Stefania, despite having her eyes closed, rocking back and forth like a mad woman and in mid chant is quick to jump in, "Don't worry Sammie, it's just her brain preparing for sleep, she's replying to things she thinks she's been asked." Sam gets a fit of giggles. "Quiet please Sammie," says Stefania, "I need to have a clear head to pick up the signals. The ones we're trying to make contact with, they're in position."

Sam's phone starts to ring. "Oh blimey, I'm so sorry Stefania, I'm sorry Aurora." Aurora stirs and opens her eyes whilst Stefania keeps rocking, "It's ok, please turn it off completely."

"Yes, of course, I'm sorry." Sam fumbles to turn her phone off with her left hand so as not to let go of Aurora's. "Done."

"They're waiting for us," says Stefania, her rocking motion slows down to a gentle sway. "Ok Aurora, you can go now." Sam feels Aurora's grip go again. The room becomes pitch black, all candles and lamps go out simultaneously. Sam is startled and looks over to Stefania for comfort, but can't quite find her. She waits until her eyes readjust to the dark. She can now see Stefania look up towards the ceiling. Sam looks at Aurora, who is breathing deeply. Not quite sure what to do with herself, Sam just sits, watching Aurora as instructed.

"Aumm-ah-neah. Aumm-ah-neah." It's Stefania, she's chanting something very quietly under her breath. Aurora twitches, just enough to cause a ruffle in her cloak.

"Aumm-ah-neah. Aumm-ah-neah." Sam's eyes have now completely adapted to the dark. She can see Stefania's outline and she's started rocking again. Aurora starts moving too. Sam notices that Aurora has turned onto her side and is now facing Sam and the inside of the room. Stefania stops rocking and becomes still. Her movements were jerky, like she'd just picked up a noise or a new presence in the room. Sam is terrified, but sits on, dutifully. Out of nowhere, Aurora sits up and jumps out of her skin so quickly that she hits her head on an overhanging shelf with small towels on it.

"Argh. Wait, where are…" Aurora's heart race beats in her chest like a set of pistons going off. "Help, I can't…..I can't breathe."

"You can Aurora, look at me, look at me." Stefania has quickly moved from her seat and is now on the make-shift bed with Aurora. Much to Sam's bewilderment, at some point in the last few seconds, three lamps have come on.

"Let me see your head." asks Sam, kneeling over her friend. Aurora's temple is red on the right hand side, but the skin isn't broken. "That will be a beauty Arry, good job pal." says Sam, trying to lighten the mood.

Aurora is awake, but looks sleepy, her eyes are having trouble re-adjusting to the light. She touches her head. "Ouch, I proper smacked it, didn't I?"

"It's ok," says Stefania, "due to your severe lack of restful sleep, your body stalled a bit there. You skipped Theta and went straight into Delta before your body had a chance to come with you. It's like going from sixth to first gear without changing speed. That sleepy tea must have been too strong." Sam looks at Stefania with disbelief.

"So you *did* drug her? That wasn't our deal Mrs."

"We need to bring her back to the Alpha-Theta gate. She needs to hit the right frequency so that contact can be made. Am not sure how long the others can wait."

Sam holds Aurora's hand and helps her to lie down and settle. The lights begin to dim. "Come on Arry, whatever it is you need to do to get through this, let's do it. I'm right here." Aurora smiles and kisses her friend's hand. "Thank you Sam. Thank you Stefania. I'm ready, let's try again."

***

Main Dome, Supreme Court, Ipa, Venezelu

"They're not ready, on Earth. There's been a hold up. If you go under now, you'll be there waiting amongst all the others, she may not even see you clearly, she may not reach out. We need your strength levels high, above those waiting. We need you to push forward and make that connection with her."

"What about the Jeapordiser?" asks Jasper. "How long do we have?"

"He'll be here soon, as will the Supreme Court guards. Gisella is on the 7th floor, she should ward them off for a while. The witches are on stand-by, as is Mia. They know what to do. I just hope that Aurora settles so that we can come through at the right moment."

"I think we should just go, I'll have the strength to shine through. I don't want to risk losing her at the Alpha-Theta gate."

"Are you sure?" asks Hispanica, aware that Marcux's presence at hypnagogia could set off another chain of attack from those also waiting at the gate.

"We're running out of time, this is it."

"I can hear people coming up the stairs, are we on?" Jasper closes the door behind him, his eyes full of anticipation.

"We're on." replies Marcux, taking a full deep breath to induce relaxation.

Hispanica brushes his blonde locks away from his forehead. "Marcux, whatever you hear or sense, do not come back until you reach her."

Marcux looks at Hispanica. Understanding her intent, he nods and closes his eyes.

23

"I sent a note across another plane,
Maybe it's all a game, but this
I just can't conceive."

Jeff Lynne of Earth, Musician

Televised screens are flashing across the competing planets with breaking news of Frayaraz's evidence against Quern. Raucous laughter and celebration at Yana's Heaven sees tables upturned and drunk rebels fighting each other in the booths.

Meanwhile, in Militia City, Apocalyptics are in full celebration mode, rolling in the muddy waters of the jade cobbled streets and passing out over wheat whisky barrels.

At the Supreme Court, Dimetrius is wasting no time, now at the top of the dome, looking in, knowing what he must do. He pulls out a large copper stick from his armoury and squeezes it. A solid orange-blue light exits the stick, a perfect right-angle of flame. Dimetrius starts to apply it to the robust dome glass. It cuts through like butter, but the glass is so thick that Dimetrius has to put some force into it. Inside the dome, Jasper senses someone above them and flies up to take a closer look.

Jasper glares at Dimetrius through the thick smoky glass. Dimetrius stops, giving Jasper a deadly stare from his stone-cold grey eyes before continuing with his work. Dimetrius had etched a square block into the glass. Just a few more passes and he would be through.

Marcux was already past Alpha state and entering Theta. Once in a deep sleep, Marcux would make his way to Aurora on Earth. Jasper and Hispanica knew the danger that lay ahead for them should the Jeapordiser get through. Jeopardisers were assassins, cold-blooded killers and very tactical. Hispanica may be able to beat him on a normal day, but this was no normal day. Marcux needed her protection, so Jasper knew it was up to him to stop the Jeapordiser from getting in.

7ᵗʰ Floor, Lawyer's Study, Supreme Court

Gisella sits in an arm chair facing the front door. She can hear footsteps approaching. Two women charge into the room. Initially, they seem more surprised to find someone in there than they do at the fact that they are now hurtling through the air. Gisella's booby trap worked.

Both women land at Gisella's feet with a thud. The tall sterner looking woman with red hair tied back in a bun clambers to her feet immediately, the smaller one with a brown bob seems a little more stunned after her fall.

Miso grabs her stun gun and points it at Gisella. "Who are you? Where is the accused?"

Gisella stands and goes over to the window. Miso,

flabbergasted at this response, probes her further.

"I will stun you. Who are you?"

Frapp is on her feet, and she looks towards the door. She can hear Flenander and Kolo's nearing. The two men almost run past the study, keen to take flight again and get to the 8th floor.

"We're in here!" shouts Gisella. The two guards screech to a halt and run back towards the room. "Watch the wire for Kilos'…"

It was too late. Both Flenander and Kolo were in a pile next to Miso and Frapp. "…sake." says Miso.

"Who is this? Why haven't you stunned her yet?" asks Flenander.

Miso walks over to Gisella tentatively. "I will ask you one more time, and if you don't comply, my colleagues here will grab you and I *will* stun you. We can start this here or at the Jailhouse."

Gisella walks towards the guards and puts her arms up in the air. "You got me."

"Where is Marcux Grentil? What have you done with him?" asks Kolo.

Gisella looks over at the door. Everyone turns to look. As they do, it slams shut by itself.

"How did she…" Frapp barely has time to finish her question before noticing that Gisella has a Flame-Box in her hand. "Quick, flame-box!"

Miso shuts her eyes but makes the jump to stun Gisella, catching her on the arm and stunning her instantly. Gisella already had her finger on the button, and managed to take out Flenander, Kolo and Miso, with only Frapp noticing in time to close her eyes. Seconds later, and knowing that the flame-box would need another 20 minutes to reset its charge again, Frapp opens her eyes to see her three guard comrades and Gisella passed out on the floor.

"That's it, flame-box woman, you're in big trouble now."

Frapp hears the door behind her open and close again. She turns to discover that the study is now full of women in shamanic dress.

Mia walks out from the huddle. "Based on what we've just seen, I think the others may need our help up there. Half of us must go help them, half stay here. You,"

Mia points to Frapp. "Why don't you sit tight with us a little while."

Frapp looks at the group then back at Mia, who just smiles and taps the seat in front of her.

Main Dome, Supreme Court

"Jasper, he's in travel mode, he's found Aurora. She's just about to enter the Alpha-Theta gate. It's busy there, he's barging through. Someone is helping him by trying to shield out the others. We just need a few more minutes."

Jasper is pushing his body weight against the large glass block which Dimetrius is trying to push inside the dome. "Give up Pirate, this block will kill you in worse ways than I."

Jasper saves his breath and puts all of his energy into edging the block back into position. Its weight is crushing Jasper's arm and spine. His face is as red as the stripes on his hat.

"Be careful Jasper!" shouts Hispanica.

Dimetrius flies away from the block, letting go of its tension and almost causing Jasper to push it out himself from the inside. Jasper holds the block in place. Its enormous weight feels like it's crushing his insides. Jasper's not sure how much longer he can hold it in place.

Main Court Room, Supreme Court

In the courtroom, it's Kalista who is up on the stand to make her statement. The judges were overwhelmed by the evidence against Quern, but in light of fairness of trial, they sped up the individual investigation's statements, pleas or anything that either side wanted to add to the proceedings.

Lindar, Zareb and the Professor are desperate to leave the court room, knowing that something is at play. Lindar turns to Zareb, "The witches should have been back by now, First Contact should have been made." The Professor leans over, "That was the plan, but where is everyone? Trust my dear. Trust."

Kalista begins her statement.

"A wise man on Earth once said "The meeting of two personalities is like the contact of two chemical substances: if there is any reaction, both are transformed."

Quern rolls his eyes, his legs tapping and his fingers twitching. He looks over at his lawyers, still a babble of yellow trying desperately to come back from Frayaraz's statement, but struggling to turn his case around.

Stefania's flat, Barnsley, Earth

For Marcux, the worst part of the descent into Stefania's flat started around a mile above her house. It was at this point that Marcux was struggling to get past the other travellers, all pushing to catch a glimpse of Aurora at hypnagogia. Occasionally, he would see a bright flashing light, which seemed to affect the travellers around him, stunning them out of the way, pushing them behind a cloak-type black wall and giving him a chance to push ahead. He took these opportunities to fly towards Aurora at full speed. Eventually, he descended into the house.

Marcux is metres away from Aurora now. Around him, hundreds of travellers are pushing through the wall, trying to stop him.

In the flat, Aurora lies on her back, still in the darkness.

Stefania is still chanting and occasionally snapping her hands into the air. Sam is sitting by Aurora's side, tears rolling down her cheeks. Marcux can tell this girl really cares for Aurora.

Aurora opens her eyes. Stefania uses all of her energy to push the other travellers away.

Marcux pushes through.

Aurora opens her eyes as wide as she can. She sees Marcux super-imposed in front of the four walls of Stefania's room. To Aurora, the boy looked as beautiful now as he did the first time she ever saw him.

Her body remained still, but her heart rate accelerated. Aurora knew she had to remain calm so as not to lose sight of Marcux.

Sam sees Aurora look up at the empty ceiling. She notices a tear roll down Aurora's cheek.

Marcux starts his descent from the top of the

room. He flies down gently, conscious not to stir her consciousness too much. Marcux can see Aurora's eyes follow his descent.

He smiles at her, just like he did that night in Rome almost four months to the day. The night Aurora's life changed forever.

***

Dome Room, Supreme Court

Dimetrius is about 30 Earth yards away from the dome. He can see Jasper struggling to hold the block, but knows that time is running short before the boy makes First Contact. Dimetrius prepares himself for descent into the dome. He charges, head down, gaining speed and momentum.

"Jasper!" shouts Hispanica, cautious not to wake Marcux from his sleep.

Jasper cranes his neck to see Dimetrius charge towards him. He looks like a speck in the burnt orange glass, a pin-like projectile getting gradually bigger.

Just before reaching the dome, Dimetrius spins his body round so that his heavy iron-clad boots are out in front of him. He straightens out his legs and gets ready to kick the glass block inside the dome.

Jasper braces himself for impact.

Main Court Room, Supreme Court

Kalista comes down from the stand and calmly walks back to her seat on the benches.

Quern looks ready to burst. Without notice, he stands and charges out of the court room, Griig runs after him. The judges notice their exit.

The Professor, Lindar and Zareb come to their feet. "He knows how the prophecy ends, he must do." The Professor runs after Quern who has already started making his way up the stairs. Suddenly, the entire courtroom descends into complete chaos, and everyone spills out and heads to the staircase.

Jizobal quickly stands on her podium. "Complete lock-down! Complete lock-down! Code Red!"

Lawyer's Study, 7th floor

The witches had lined the guards up on the floor and wrapped them in a carpet, just for fun. Gisella was also on the floor, sleeping off the stun-gun.

"What's that noise?" asks one of the witches.

Mia cranes her neck out to listen.

"Sounds like a stampede." says another witch.

"This wasn't in the prophecy." says another witch.

Mia clicks. "They're heading to the dome – *everyone* is heading to the dome."

Dome Room

Dimetrius blasts into the glass block, causing shards of glass to fly from the outer lining. The block was solid, like a giant ice cube, and it wasn't going to shatter under any amount of pressure. That said, Dimetrius' momentum was enough to break two of Jasper's ribs and shatter some of his left arm bones.

"Argh!!!" shouts Jasper, grasping his chest. He falls towards the ground, the glass block falling steadily behind his back. Despite the glass block's weight, Venezelu's gravitational law means that things fall much slower than they would on Earth. Dimetrius is behind the block, using its momentum to help push it on its way.

"Jasper!" shouts Hispanica. She looks down at Marcux who is still in deep travel mode.

Four witches run into the dome room and quickly scan the room. Two of them run towards Marcux whilst Hispanica runs towards Jasper, catching him just in time. She looks up to see the block still headed South and straight for Marcux's body.

"No!" she shouts, running back towards Marcux.

One of the witches flies up to the block and tries to steer it off course, the other grabs Dimetrius by the jacket, trying to pull him away from Marcux's direction. Dimetrius pulls out a long swoard and slashes her hand away from him, cutting off the tops of her fingers.

The witch screams. One of the other witches by Marcux's side flies up to attack Dimetrius. He is too fast, and escapes her grasp. She tries shooting bolts at him, but they miss him right and left as he swerves away.

Hispanica makes a bee-line for him, but Dimetrius side flies towards her, kicking her hard in the stomach. She flies into the stone wall. Jasper lies paralysed near the front door, on his side, blood on his lips, feeling powerless. Only the venom in Jasper's eyes tells Dimetrius what he would like to do to him right now. The block picks up speed in its final descent. It crashes to the ground, missing Marcux by a metre. The witch who deflected it comes crashing into the wall after it.

Stefania's room, Barnsley, Earth

Marcux stops in his descent. A loud noise makes him aware of something happening back in the dome. He hears Hispanica's voice in his head. *"Whatever you hear or sense, do not come back until you reach her."*

Marcux sees Aurora in perfect vision. Of the two other women in the room, he knows one can sense him. She is the one who is helping him keep the others away. The other has great potential, but isn't tapped in. He feels happy that Aurora has two such powerful people by her side.

The cloak walls start to give way, Marcux can see that the connected woman is trying her best to hold them back. He must go for it.

He puts his hand out towards Aurora. She smiles and looks up towards his hand. She extends her too. Everything in Marcux's body, mind and soul is melting with a euphoric feeling. He tries to focus. First contact. Don't startle her, don't scare her. Keep her attention but remember - she hasn't got long in this state.

Dome Room, Supreme Court

As the two remaining conscious witches scramble over Marcux body to protect him, Dimetrius slowly strides over. Marcux has his hand stretched out above his head. He is smiling.

"All this over a *boy*? I can end this with a whip of my swoard."

The witches look up at him, daring him to make a move and willing to sacrifice their lives to stop him. Dimetrius pulls his swoard out of his belt.

"Goodnight, dreamer."

The dome room doors fly open. It's Mia and the remaining witches. The witches band together and eject a blanket of piercing lightning bolts from their hands and wrists. The force looks like electricity in motion. The light combines as one and goes straight into the back of Dimetrius, right through his heart. He drops on the spot.

Quern and Griig run into the room, pushing the witches out of the way. "No! Stop this!"

Mia puts out her foot, tripping up Quern. He flies across the floor, hitting his jaw off the stony marble and smashing out all of his front teeth.

Quern and Griig are followed by the rest of the courtroom, including the judges who followed the commotion.

The two witches sit back onto their heels, revealing Marcux who is slightly elevated from the ground. A buzzing electricity sound makes its way across the dome room. Lights flicker. Marcux's hand is fully outstretched. Quern can barely lift his bloody jaw to take a look.

Stefania's flat, Barnsley, Earth

Aurora is slightly elevated from Stefania's make-shift bed. Her arm and hand reached out above her.

Marcux can see her index finger extended. He mirrors the gesture, and extends his.

She reaches out. Sam can see a spark of electricity coming from Aurora's index finger. "What the…?" It's at this point that she notices Aurora's elevation from the bed. Aurora is smiling like someone whose heart couldn't be more full of love and happiness.

Dome Room, Supreme Court, Venezelu

Electricity is piercing out of Marcux' index finger. The entire room is silent. They wait.

Between two dimensions, two souls connect - their index fingers touch.

24

"What questions I asked, and how little I know
Of all the vast show, and how eagerly,
Tremulously hopeful of some day knowing
More, learning the meaning of these divine
symbols
Crowded together on this wondrous page."

John Muir of Earth, Explorer

For the first time in Aurora's life, time stopped. She feels a vibration through her body.

No sooner had she asked herself, *'Where am I?'* Aurora found herself suspended above the Earth. She could see Stefania's wicker slippers on her feet. Her black cloak was still on her back, floating in the air like charcoal ribbon in a sea wave.

Aurora looked down at Earth below her. Through her mind flash a thousand revelations. Space, time, oneness. *"This is so beautiful."* Aurora knows she is in space, but she's not cold or scared. She looks down at Earth with an overwhelming feeling of euphoria.

She looks above her head, and sees a super-imposed image of two dimensions, like slices of bread, starting to pass over each other. There's a

tiny dot in one dimension, which she knows to be
Earth, and another tiny dot in the dimension above
it, which she knows is Venezelu. Venezelu. Sounds
like Venezuela. What a lovely name.

Galaxies and stars and planets appear before her.
She is travelling at a ridiculous speed now.
Suspended, hovering over all different looking
planets, with all different looking people. Some she
recognises, almost feels a familiarity with. "Have I
been here before?"

"Yes." says a voice. It's Marcux's voice.

She can't see him, she's still suspended in space,
but she knows he's there. "How do I know so much
about your planet already, having only this glimpse
at the bigger picture?"

"That'll be Gisella. She's been talking to you for a
long time, just in case we didn't get good first
contact."

"Gisella. Yes, her voice."

"You'll meet her soon, you'll meet everyone
soon."

"I know what I must do, Marcux. I need to tell the
others, on Earth. I need to let them know about all
the other planets and living beings, about our
dimensional neighbours."

"That's right. Work begins in your universe,
galaxy by galaxy until all the billions of galaxies are
connected, on the same page. You won't reach them
all, but planets that do find each other, and the
travellers who dare to travel there, it's the beginning
of your revolution. To make contact with the next."

"Will I know what to do?"

"It's within you, all the evidence you need to

make your case to your people. It's in your head. You must present it to them. Your planet, more than most, needs to come together again, before you destroy each other and your home. This will give you a common goal, until the Duality Pendulum decides to swing again. This will give you peace for some time. A chance to recover and repair."

"Marcux," Aurora feels like her heart is bursting out of her chest.

"I'm ready to go back now."

"Ok. We'll see you soon. One, two…"

Stefania's flat, Barnsley, Earth

"Oh my God Aurora!! Oh my God!" Sam is bent double over Aurora's body. Aurora sits bolt upright and opens her eyes, almost knocking heads with Sam.

"You stopped breathing darling, I…." Sam descends into tears. Stefania puts her arm around her. "It was a bit hairy for a moment there Aurora, wherever you were, you stopped breathing for about 3 minutes."

"I got back in time then." smiles Aurora.

"The one time you didn't seem in a hurry to be somewhere, when we *really* needed you back!" laughs Stefania.

"Did you see it? The final piece of the jigsaw?"

Aurora sits up and makes herself comfortable on the make-shift bed. She looks exhausted and drained. "Let's just say it's time for a new pocket watch Stefania. We have lots to do."

Stefania smiles.

"Did we do it?" asks Sam. "Did we help Aurora

beat her insomnia?"

Aurora and Stefania look at Sam, then each other, then start to laugh until Stefania has tears rolling down her cheeks.

"My dear, wonderful, loving, gifted friend Sam - yes, we did it." Aurora hugs Sam tightly.

"Aw, that's great." says Sam. "You're definitely getting a good review online."

Stefania strokes Aurora's hair. "We're going to help tip the scale for good again."

Sam smiles, not quite understanding what's just happened, but happy to see her friend smiling again.

25

"Time is a child – playing like a child – playing a board game – the kingdom of the child. This is Telesphoros, who roams through the dark regions of the cosmos and glows like a star out of the depths. He points the way to the gates of the sun and to the land of dreams."

Carl Gustav Jung of Earth, Pioneer

2 weeks later, Ipa, Militia City, Venezelu
It's early dawnlight and Militia City looks like a ghost town. Most of the rebels from other planets have gone in search of new 'business ventures', knowing that their previous trades and endeavours had all but dried up. Yana's Heaven closed its doors soon after First Contact, deciding that the aftermath wouldn't be worth the repair costs caused by disgruntled rebels and vagabonds.

The trial had been televised live across the neighbouring galaxies from the Supreme Court's Main Chamber, but they also managed to catch footage of First Contact in the dome room. Footage that the Revolutionaries made sure to play on repeat so that the message would be picked up far and wide.

Quern's sentence was made soon after First Contact. Quern and Griig were taken to the Jailhouse with immediate effect. They were sentenced to 3 weeks in prison, followed by mandatory community service for 10 Venezeluan years.

Dimetrius had been put into a body freeze, which had stunned his inner electrical circuit so as to stop him dead in his tracks. He received the same sentence as Quern and Griig, but with three weeks additional solitary. Associates of Quern who helped Griig plant evidence at Professor Sykes' apartment were also sentenced, but got off much more lightly.

Back at MEW5 tower, Professor Sykes, Zareb and Lindar are in Sykes old office packing boxes. The Professor is busy packing items on his desk, including little ornaments and trinkets from his academic days. Zareb is by the filing cabinet, evaporating documents and files they no longer need. Lindar is by the electricals, unplugging and tidying up wires and attachments.

"Zareb, pass me a hunket-clench please."

Zareb throws Lindar the hunket-clench, a long twisted metal implement that looks half spanner, half drill bit. "Fancy a drink after we clear this up?" asks Sykes. "I could do with a stiff one."

"I thought you didn't drink?" said Zareb.

"Well, today marks the end of another era. It's worth celebrating."

"I'll drink to that." says Lindar, busy unscrewing something at the back of the televised set.

Zareb lifts another shiny plastic looking document from the filing cabinet and drops it into the evaporation bin. "Have you decided what you're going to do with yourself now Justin?"

The Professor takes a seat in his chair, savouring its leather crevices and soft touch. "I've accepted a position at the University. We all have, except Robertus and Gisella."

"What will they be up to?" asks Lindar.

"Gisella has decided to join Ipa's Rebuilding Project, led by Mia. They are going to turn Militia City into a top training facility for travellers. It will help our travellers go on meaningful journeys, gathering information about other planets in other Universes. Robertus, well, he's taken an undisclosed sabbatical."

"Sounds good." says Zareb.

"What about you two?" asks Sykes.

Lindar puts down the hunket-clench and sits up with her back against the wall.

"Zareb and I have spent a good deal of time watching the rebels drown their sorrows,"

The Professor looks at Zareb. "It's a hobby I never knew she'd love so much." says Zareb.

"Then we're going to start our own Dream Travel Academy, where we'll offer training and guidance to newly individualised and awakened ones from Earth, and any other planets that join in thereafter. A kind of 'introduction to travelling'."

"That sounds wonderful!" says the Professor.

Lindar stands and walks over to Zareb. She pulls in him tight and kisses him.

"And we have something else to tell you Professor."

"What's that?"

"Shanna Delti is getting betrothed. Down by the old tree of enlightenment at dusklight this eve."

"That's doubly wonderful!" says the Professor, doing a little dance around them.

***

Back in Zaatta, some of the scientists are packing up their pods, laughing, drinking and having a good time. Some monks are there too, having fun rolling up rugs and packing up boxes.

Over at the Monestry, Kalista, the remaining monks and the remaining scientists are sweeping up ashes, constructing new timber frameworks and rebuilding the monastery.

***

Frayaraz and her crew are out at sea, sailing the Indigan waves, laughing and joking around. Patró has got his beard stuck inside a barrel and the other pirates on deck can't stop laughing. Frayaraz has a bottle of rumgin in one hand and is hanging on to a rope with the other. She looks out to sea, unafraid to mask the slight sadness in her eyes now, quietly content.

Indigan beach, Indigo

Jasper and Hispanica are standing by some rocks facing out to sea. "Watch this," says Hispanica. She picks up some sand, adds a little sprinkling of pink powder from her pocket and mixes it together in her hand. She counts the waves coming in and out. On an outgoing wave, she throws the mixture into the sea. Jasper looks at her with admiration. He thinks she suits the newly formed scar above her right eyebrow. Jasper's arm is still in a sling and his face bruised and cut. They were thankful for the medical attention received after First Contact. It saved all their lives.

"What is that for?" asks Jasper, confused as to why nothing has happened with the sand.

"Just wait my dear." replies Hispanica.

Jasper can see what looks like an army of ripples coming straight for them and towards the rocks. "What?" enquires Jasper, squinting in the early suruplight to get a better look.

He bends down and a flounder plant appears, spitting water straight into Jasper's face. It makes him step back, confused. He opens his eyes and sees hundreds of flounder plants scaling the surface edge of the water. Their bluey-green jelly skin creates a massive colourful blanket in the shallow waters.

"You called in a friend to soak me in water?"

Hispanica is almost on the ground with laughter. "Your face!" she exclaims.

A hundred smiling octopuses look up towards the couple as they stand on the edge of the rock face. "Jasper Nomix, will you take me as your betrothed?"

Jasper smiles and goes to hug Hispanica, almost forgetting about his crushed ribs, bruised spine and broken arm, "Argh, yes!! Yes, I do."

Hispanica gently pulls him in and kisses him tenderly on the lips. Without hesitation, the hundred flounder plants jump into the air and spit sea water out at the couple, completely drenching them. They laugh and dance in the waterfall. Jasper takes his stripey hat off and throws it in the air.

Havana, Earth

Robertus sits on a porch watching a young woman asleep in a hammock. She is a raven beauty, with cappuccino skin and charcoal black hair. Her cheeks are rosy and her button nose has freckles on it.

"Ah, Carina," says Robertus, mesmerised by the sleeping subject.

"It won't be long before Aurora presents the truths of the universe to your world. I know that if it hadn't been Aurora of Earth to make First Contact, it would have been you. But no matter. What's important is that you'll be able to see me, for longer than our few Earth minutes at a time. You can come visit me too, any time. I will look after you. We can never be together dimensionally, but you are closer to me now than you could ever imagine."

***

Ipa, Venezelu

Marcux is sitting under the old tree of enlightenment. It's just under an hour before the betrothment of his uncle Zareb and Shanna. The seats are out, the welcoming drinks are poured and his parents are getting some final things ready in the marquee.

The tree sits high on a hill on the border of Militia City's Southern wall. It used to be the Jeapordiser's camp, but they left around 10 days ago and

Venezeluans were busy rebuilding and remodelling all of the old Militia territory.

Marcux's parents exit the marquee and head over to some tables in search of ribbon. Marcux's mother, Harria Fender is medium height with blondish-brown straight hair and luminous black skin that looks like early nightfall. Marcux's father, Joshu Grentil, is also medium height with a mass of curls on his head and pale peach skin that looks like cream against his chocolate brown hair.

"Marcux, thanks for putting those chairs out darling. They look divine!"

Marcux goes to put three fingers up, then stops himself and puts one index finger up to his temple instead. "You look beautiful mother. And looking sharp dad."

Joshu and Harria smile and go back into the marquee.

The air was warm and the early eve suruprays were casting a perfect light across the hill and the marquee. "Tonight will be perfect." said Marcux. Just enough time to go visit an old friend, he thought. Marcux closed his eyes and descended into a deep, sleepy snooze.

26

"We is in Dream Country…This is where all dreams is beginning."

Roald Dahl of Earth, Writer

2 weeks after First Contact, The Civic Arts Hub, Barnsley, Earth

Aurora is sitting in the café bar of The Civic on a pleasantly bright, yet nippy, March evening. She's in one of the booths at the back of the café which is lined with red faux leather plastic. The walls behind her are bare stone and the bar spreads out to her left-hand side. In front of her, tables and chairs pepper the open floor space, but all sit empty. No one is there, just Aurora and the barmaid.

On her table, Aurora is sat amongst bundles of paper, a calculator and a small laptop. She sits transfixed to the screen with eager fervour in her eyes. The barmaid approaches.

"Another cup of tea?"

Aurora looks up from her laptop. It takes her a second to register what she's just been asked. Her head is full of equations and words and emotions. "Yes, that would be lovely. Thank you so much."

Aurora's face is brimming with joy. The barmaid can't quite make sense of Aurora's overly elated smile, but she just smiles back and returns to the bar area.

It's a Thursday night and Aurora's at The Civic to see a comedy show with her parents, Grandpa Tom, Sam and Stefania. The show starts at 8pm. Aurora had been at the library that day and when the library doors closed at 5pm, she made her way straight to The Civic so that she could sit in the café a while to make some finishing touches to her work.

It was 6.30pm. The barmaid brings over the tea. Aurora looks at its soothing steam rising from the ceramic cup. "Thank you." she says, with a sincerity that the barmaid was not too used to receiving. "You're welcome." she replies, before walking back towards the bar.

As Aurora takes a sip, she can feel the warm liquid kiss her throat on its way down. She looks up over the cup to see a man sitting at the other end of the café. *How long has he been there?* Aurora blushes. Not because she's just stared over at a perfect stranger, or because the tea's vapours are warming up her cheeks – she blushes, because it feels as though this man is looking right into her soul, and she wasn't ready for it.

The man smiles, stands and makes his way towards her. The barmaid is busy cleaning wine glasses, but her eyes are glued on the man's approach, intrigued to see what might happen next.

She wasn't the only one. With each step, Aurora could feel her heart beating faster and faster. *This is worse than any hypnagogic vision!* She jokes, knowing that she is fully conscious and that this is actually happening in her reality.

"Hello," says the man, "I'm Paul. You look very busy, but would you mind if I came and sat with you whilst you have your tea?"

Normally Aurora would give her excuses as to why she had to carry on working, it happened often enough at the library when strangers would playfully want to talk or find out what she was doing with such speed and focus. Aurora knew she was only 2 pages away from finishing her presentation, but she saved her work on the laptop and closed the screen. Aurora had always been in a hurry to do things, but this was an opportunity that she simply couldn't miss. The presentation could wait.

"I have time for tea and a chat if you like."

The barmaid comes over, as if on cue. "Another tea?" she smiles.

"Yes please." replies Paul.

"Shall I put it on your tab Mr White?" asks the barmaid.

"That would be grand." smiles Paul.

"What's your name?" asks Paul.

"Aurora. Are you a regular here?" asks Aurora.

"Wow, that's a beautiful name. And yes, you could say that." replies Paul. "I'm one of the comedians in the comedy show tonight. We've just finished tech rehearsal."

"The show that starts at 8pm?" asks Aurora.

"The very one."

"Oh fabulous, my family and friends are coming to see you this evening." Aurora suddenly becomes very aware of herself. She tucks her hair behind her ears, feeling her cheeks blush even further.

"I'll be kind and not pick on you then, if you promise not to heckle me."

"I can't promise that," jokes Aurora, "but I'll try my best."

Paul laughs. His short caramel hair catches the light. The barmaid arrives with his tea. "Thank you Kirsty."

Aurora looks at Paul. There's something kind and loving in those green eyes, it radiates when he smiles. He is a sincere type, she can tell.

"You a comedy fan then?" asks Paul.

"Oh yes, I love it. I used to go to the Covent Garden New Talent Night all the time, and The Strand New Talent night. I love how comedians' minds work, so observant and inappropriate at the same time."

Paul smiles at Aurora, gazing upon her just enough to make Aurora's face burn. She removes her shawl.

"Well I hope you're not disappointed tonight. All my material is positively clean."

Aurora laughs. The smiling barmaid is now chopping up lemons, eyes and ears glued to the conversation.

"I actually used to perform there, at The Covent Garden New Talent night."

"You did?" asks Aurora, "Well there's a chance I've caught your act. I thought you looked familiar to be honest."

"I had the same feeling about you funnily enough." Aurora's cheeks feel like they can't get any hotter. She takes a sip of tea. "Did you live in London then?" she asks Paul.

"No, I live in Sheffield, but I used to kip on friends' sofas and the like whenever I was down for a string of gigs. You lived there I take it?"

"Yes, for a while. It's a beautiful city, isn't it?"

"It is."

There's a bit of a pause. Paul is smiling at Aurora, and Aurora smiles back.

"Erm, I'm not normally this forward," Paul goes to grab a piece of paper from his pocket, "but would it be ok if I gave you my number? We have a small after-party with comedians and friends backstage. Why don't you and your family and friends come join us for a drink? I promise we're not the drunken reprobates we're painted to be. Not after a Thursday night show anyway."

Aurora laughs. "I'd like that. *We'd* like that, I'll ask them. Thank you." She lends Paul her pen. He jots down his number.

"My Grandpa Tom will be there, can he come too?"

"We're not ageist, of course! As long as he stays away from my gin slammers." Paul winks and goes to leave.

"Lovely to meet you, Aurora."

"Lovely to meet you Paul. We'll possibly see you after the show."

"Come! It would make my night."

Aurora blushes a final time, surprised that her hair hadn't caught fire or been singed by the heat radiating from her face.

***

It's 7.30pm. Sam, Aurora's parents and Grandpa
Tom all arrive at The Civic Arts Centre. Aurora
gives them a big hug in turn. Josephine and Victor
Black were positively brimming with joy. They
were so happy to have their daughter back. The last
couple of weeks had been wonderful. Aurora was
sleeping again and her health was coming back in
abundance. Victor puts his arms around Josephine,
watching Aurora as she fixes Grandpa Tom's tie.
"Do you think our little one has finally found that
thing she was so desperately in a hurry to find?"

"Oui," replies Josephine with tears glistening in
her eyes. "She is happy again, our bebe."

Sam is at the bar getting in a round of drinks.
Grandpa Tom goes over to help and the two get into
an argument over who is going to pay. "I'll get it
Tommy," says Sam.

"Let the gentleman pay, or are you saying I'm not
a gent?" teases Grandpa Tom.

Sam smiles and nudges Grandpa Tom playfully in
the arm.

A while later, Stefania arrives. She walks straight
over to Aurora and her parents. "Good evening you
fine folk. Am I right in thinking that it's time to
start taking our seats?"

The bell rings a second after the words leave
Stefania's mouth. "You're good, I'll give you that."
says Victor.

"Well, my watch says 7.50pm, so it was a rough
guess really."

"And here's me thinking you were a proper
psychic!" jokes Victor. Josephine rolls her eyes and
pulls Victor by the arm. "Very funny darling, come,

let's help Sam and dad with the drinks and take our seats."

Stefania smiles and takes Aurora by the arm. "How is the presentation going?"

"Two pages left."

Stefania's eyes light up. "That's great! Well done."

"I sent the proposal away last week and they want to meet me next week to go over the rest of the presentation."

"You'll need to speak to your parents, and soon."

"I know." Aurora sighs. "Getting this down was easier than I thought it would be. Trying to explain it to the world doesn't phase me either. But telling two people I love most in the world, well, am not sure how it will go down."

"You're scared that they will worry for you, going forward."

Aurora nods. "We both know the impact this will have once it's presented. It challenges lots of things. We've fought wars and lost lives over less. The team want 6 months preparation time."

"Preparation of global proportions," says Stefania, understanding the impact Aurora is referring to.

"Are you ready for this Aurora?"

"We're all born ready. It could have been one of the other planets, but it was us. We don't have a choice now. It begins."

Stefania pulls a square mass of green tissue paper out of her patchwork bag. "I got you something."

"What is it?"

"A gift, go on, open it."

Aurora starts to unfold the green tissue paper.

Inside sits a brand new bronze pocket watch on a pendant. The clock is about the size of a 50 pence piece. It has a pendulum etched on the back.

"I really enjoyed burning that old watch together," winks Stefania, "a very cleansing experience. Felt bad for leaving you timeless, though."

"Very nice," says Aurora, smiling. "Thank you Stefania, for, well, you know."

Stefania smiles. "New beginnings call for a new watch. We'll *all* be there for you - you won't go through this on your own."

Aurora hugs Stefania. "Let's go and have a good giggle."

Aurora and Stefania walk into the auditorium. Josephine is waving frantically from their almost front row seats. "There's mum." smiles Aurora. "Oh, almost forgot. I just met a guy in the bar, he's invited us for a drink afterwards."

"That's a quick date." jokes Stefania.

"It's not a date!" laughs Aurora. "He's invited *all* of us. I hope he's good."

"I'm sure he's more than good." winks Stefania.

***

6 months later, NASA Headquarters, Washington D.C, USA, Earth

Aurora and Paul are standing in a corridor next to a set of steps that lead up onto a stage. The stage is shrouded by a huge black curtain. The corridor is stone grey. In the background are 4 security guards and 5 advisors, all with clipboards and ear pieces in. Aurora is dressed in a white dress. Her hair is up in a tall bun. Paul is in black trousers and a green shirt.

Paul notices Aurora twiddling her pocket-watch pendant necklace between her fingers, something he knows she only does when feeling nervous. He pulls her into his arms and kisses her, warmly. The security guards look away. The advisors don't even notice, they're too busy talking into their walkie talkies, getting the last little details ready for the presentation.

Aurora glances down lovingly at her wedding ring. She takes a deep breath.

"Sure you don't want me to go out there and warm them up for you? Tell a few opening jokes? It's no problem."

Aurora laughs, her nerves escape her momentarily.

"Honestly, I'll never have a crowd this big, it would be an honour."

Aurora kisses Paul again. "Thank you. For making me the happiest girl in all dimensions."

An advisor comes up to Aurora and Paul. "We're ready when you are Aurora."

Paul holds Aurora's hands and looks deep into her eyes. "I'm so proud of you. Go get them, Mrs White."

Paul kisses Aurora on the head and she smiles. Aurora walks up the steps and stands behind the large black curtain. She can hear clicking and the chatter of people in the room in front of her.

The curtains open, side to side, and Aurora walks out. She receives a round of applause. Paul looks on from the side of the stage with tears in his eyes. He looks into the audience and finds Stefania, Sam, Josephine, Victor and Grandad Tom, all sitting proudly in the front row.

In front of Aurora is a huge press room, packed to the rafters with photographers, camera operators, journalists and scientists. Flashing lights probe into Aurora's eyes, and it takes her a minute to focus on the audience in front of her.

In the front row, sit representatives from NASA, the UN, world governments and the press. The flashes reduce, the crowd quietens down.

Aurora steps onto the podium, her heart echoing in her ears.

"Thank you for joining us." Aurora takes a look into the audience and freezes. She turns to look at Paul in the side curtain who is silently fist-pumping his arm into the air, mouthing 'You've got this!' Aurora smiles, takes a breath, and continues. She *has* got this.

"As you know, we are here today to discuss some exciting new evidence which will illuminate our place in the Universe." Some flashing resumes, momentarily blinding Aurora.

I've got this.

Aurora smiles, then resumes focus. She breathes in.

"Every living being," she continues, "on all planets, in all Universes, are restricted by their physical form – but there is a way in which all living beings, on all planets, in all Universes, *can* travel."

THE END

THE LETTER

TECTONIC PLATE THEORY – THE PARALLELS WITH INTERNAL/EXTERNAL SPACE STRUCTURES OF ELECTROMAGNETISM.

Dear Dr. Masters,

In these last years, I've noticed many parallels in the behaviour and relationships between mantle dynamics and plate tectonics on Burov with those of internal/external space structures of electromagnetism.

It seems as though there are many elements of tectonic plate behaviour, convection currents and the visible dimensions that occur as a result of the above that follow a similar pattern to the laws of particle relationships in our Universe.

A very simplified comparison, sure, but my mathematical investigations have added some weight to the matter, especially when looking at how the process is working.

For example, within Burov, irregular convection cells within the mantle transfer heat from the core to the surface of the planet. This mechanism is the driving force behind both heat transfer and the global processes of plate tectonics. The key here is the irregular convection cells – I've found parallels in the behaviour of these irregular cells linked to the behaviour of photons.

i.e., the irregular cells are spreading heat without getting directly involved, in the same way it does on planet Burov.

Similarities I noticed:

1) When tectonic plates meet, there is a tension. The behaviour of the plates determines the way in which things will move. What we see on the surface is a result of things going on underneath.

For example, if you look at the sea sediment on ridges, Burovians used to think that the planet was expanding. It isn't, the sediment is going somewhere else, it's going underneath the sea bed. It's all down to perspective and where you're standing when you observe these things. Remember when Burovians used to think that our planet was flat! Haha

Earthquakes, tsunamis, mountains - we can't see the cause from surface level, but we can work out what's happening by observing the kind of movement that occurs - through the way it *moves*.

But what causes this specific movement if it isn't gravity?

A superforce does. Ultimately the external space is only made visible from this origin. Therefore, in the plate analogy, I look at the various components.

Superforce = power and energy that is generated from the core and mantle of planet Burov.

This energy is then spread via convection currents which make the tectonic plates move, which then create VISIBLE dimensions to us, up here on the surface.

And to use another analogy, I'd say that magma lava is the conduit between these dimensions (it acts like gravity does) and that the number of dimensions reflects the same number of ways in which internal spaces collide or move.

I think it would be interesting to further investigate the following areas:-
1) If we look at the history of Burov's geological movements, will we see any kinds of patterns in relation to the behaviour of the Universe over relative / comparable timescales?

The cycle of a Supercontinent works like this:

Continents move through time, they collide with each other (over and over) and they form supercontinents. The majority of the rocks that compose continents are insulators, they don't want to transfer thermal energy, thus building up heat beneath the continent.

Continental crust operates in a repetitive way. It swells, it stretches, and eventually, it ruptures. New ocean floor starts to build up inside the rupture zones. Bits of the supercontinent start to spread as the ocean plate grows along a new seafloor.

Because Burov is a sphere, the moving continental fragments inevitably reassemble about every 500 million years. The birth and death of mega continents has played a huge part in geologic history.

What if our Universe is just like one of these continents, on a sphere that inhabits all the other Universes?

This supercontinent cycle – the assembly, rupture, breakup, spreading and reassembly - is a pattern followed by the continents. Isn't it possible that our Universe is one piece of a much larger spherical game of superuniversal tectonics?

Was the Big Bang the separation of our Universe from the superuniverse? The break-up part?

From where we're standing, it looks like the Universe is expanding - is it? Or is it just subsiding and spreading underneath another Universe?

2) Plates can move side to side and on top of each

other. They can:

Transform: where they grind past each other with no subduction.

Converge: where plates collide.

Diverge: where plates move apart.

Maybe we only see three of the extra dimensions because these are the ones that live on the surface, on the crust, on the fault lines.

That's where they are *seen*. Three - because it's related to the three different ways in which internal spaces move around.

We can't feel tectonic plates move, but we can experience an earthquake.

People ask the question: what is the precise structure of internal space?

Well, in this analogy, it functions like a tectonic plate does, so I'd say that the structure itself is not as important as asking what it *does*.

After all, in plate movement the interaction areas are called boundaries, and that's where stuff is happening.

I think that things can appear flat, but they are not, in fact, flat. They are curved and operating in a flat-looking way.

So in this analogy I'd say that the weak forces are the equivalent of subduction (and what's going on underneath) and that the structure is determined by the movement, which is influenced by the opposing forces / tension of the plates, which is influenced by magnetism, heat from the core and energy from the core.

I think by looking closer at the functionality of convection currents we may find some similarities in the behaviour of electromagnetic forces.

Yours sincerely,

Dr. Rushton

Quarta Office, Planet Burov

APPENDIX

THE AUDIO FILES

**FOR THE ATTENTION OF:
AURORA BLACK OF EARTH**

FIRST CONTACT DOWNLOAD MESSAGES

**SENDER:
GISELLA STAR, PLANET VENEZELU**

AUDIO FILES INDEX:

1. **INTRO**

2. **UNIVERSE 4**

3. **NABOXULUS, Universe 4**

4. **UNIVERSE 5 - Our Competitors**

5. **VENEZELU:**
   - **MEW5**
   - **CERN**
   - **REVOLUTIONARIES**
   - **IDOLISERS**
   - **REBELS: INTOLERANTS, APOCALYTICS, JEAPORDISERS, PIRATES**

6.   **YOUR UNIVERSE, UNIVERSE 6, and the planets we monitor therein: IZIM, FERNDO & EARTH**

7. **HOW WE TRAVEL**

8. **DREAMING**

9. **THE GAME**

10. **DUALITY PENDULUM: NEGATIVE & POSITIVE FORCES**

11.   **THE EGO**

12.   **FAITH**

13.   **HOW WE MAKE CONTACT**

14.   **FREEDOM OF MOVEMENT**

15.   **PASSPORT OF THE SOUL**

START OF TRANSCRIPT

1. INTRO

We are in a galaxy that is within a patch, or edge of Universe, that is currently gliding close to a patch of your Universe, which just so happens to have your galaxy amongst it! Like two bits of sandwich bread whose crusts are a slither away from the other.

Right now, there are 543 life bearing planets in your Universe that are in the vicinity of our gravitational patch. Just 3 of those planets are within our current bandwidth. These are: Earth, Ferndo and Izim.

2. UNIVERSE 4

A long, long time ago on our 'soccer ball', Universe 1 made contact with 2. A while after that, Universe 2 then made contact with 3. More eons of time passed before Universe 3 made contact with 4, until, eventually Universe 4 made contact with us. Simple enough, yes?

However up until this point, no existing 'awoken' Universe has ever had to pass the baton twice. These tectonic 'hexagons' move and interact in a seemingly random way, but no two Universes have ever met twice. We find this interesting.

As it happens, Universe 4 didn't glide over us, they *crashed* into us. The gateway was open. We were the next receivers, and as such, the next messengers. Game on.

Universe 4 had to wait patiently until they could find someone with an open mind, someone they could start work with. You see, Aurora, it always starts with one person.

3. NABOXULUS, Universe 4

Naboxulus, in the Grogodamine galaxy, was the first planet in Universe 4 to make inter-dimensional contact with planet Freyal in Universe 5. (Freyal happens to be within the same galaxy as Venezelu. Venezeluans are very proud of that.)

It was through the eyes, mind and determination of a young man called Jimus Krakovia from Freyal that contact was made between our Universes. But that's a different story for another time.

4. UNIVERSE 5 - Our Competitors:

At present, the 'edge'of Universe 5 that is gliding over your Universe has five inhabited planets in the boundary zone. They come from three different galaxies.

5. VENEZELU

Planet Venezelu is in the Bromindine galaxy, Universe 5. Our planet has one continent, Roka. Roka has 5 countries which all share a border. They would do, being one continent and all. These countries are called: Li; Hermos, Fraz County; Zaatta and Ozro. Ozro is our largest country and holds our planet's administrative capital, Ipa. In other words, Ipa controls pretty much everything on Venezelu.

There's also Indigo, a volcanic planet full of pirates, Crystalis, Hydros and Jenar.

All five of us are competing to be the first planet to make contact with someone on Earth, our only shot for a while before our Universe starts to glide further across yours, expanding the surface area and opening up the game to more galaxies and more inhabited planets. Remember, every living thing in our Universe *knows* about the game, but not all planets are within the boundary zones just yet.

Humans can technically travel to all Universes, but none have mastered multi-verse travelling. They have been visiting the competing planets because they are currently sucked in by them, in a mind-magnet gravitational way. In fact, humans tend to pay more visits to our competing planets in their neighbouring Universe, than they do to planets in their own Universe. That's because the draw towards us is strong right now. The short cut makes it speedier to visit us than it does to travel along one's own Universal highway.

When two Universal plates are in contact like this, gateways, or possibilities for connecting, increase. Imagine a router and a PC trying to connect remotely. Right now, we're in close enough proximity to do just that. And right now, you, Aurora of Earth, despite your lack of understanding of your own electrical brainwaves, are picking up the signals, travelling between dimensions (like surfing on a radio wave) and might possibly start the Revolution we need to happen in Universe 6.

It wasn't just time and introspection that allowed us, here on Universe 5, to develop the technology and tools needed to see, communicate and enter into inter-dimensional travel. Before we could develop ourselves, we had to learn how to see that which defied all logic. That which defied the laws of our own Universe.

MEW5

Stands for **Multi Existential Window.** The 5 represents our Universe's position of discovery. It is interesting that on Earth (Universe 6), mew is a falconry term. It refers to the cage hawks are placed in when moulting. Scientists work at MEW5 and they, alongside our Government officials based at CERN, believe that the success of our project is dependent on the metaphorical moulting of ego: exposing the cage and showing it not as a limitation but as the seat of answers. The word also means a secret hiding place, a hideaway, to confine or conceal. What we're trying to say is that the answers were concealed within us all along and it reminds us to keep our mind's eye open.

CERN

Stands for **Consciousness Evolution Review Nest**. CERN has three jobs:
1) to monitor MEW5's work;
2) to provide and monitor inter-galactic communication within Universe 6 and
3) the small business of managing every aspect of Venezelu.

THE THREE GROUP TYPES ON PLANET VENEZELU

REVOLUTIONARIES

Workers at MEW5 and CERN form the **REVOLUTION**. What are they revolting against? Some say pirates, competing planets, corruption and greed, but our biggest competitor is time. The one thing that controls us all. Our aim is to win the game before time is up, or before one of the other planets in our 'gravitational zone' gets there first.

IDOLISERS

Yes, there are those who idolise you.
Literally idolise you. Earthlings are
celebrities and you don't even know it.
Some of the most idolised are those who
are either incredibly lucid and even
though they don't fully understand where
they are or what they are engaging in, they
know that they can take control of their
behaviour whilst they are here. We also
know who these people are through their
Interceptor Device reports and the fact
that they glow greener than the caves of
Fraz County. Younger Venezeluans chat
about some of the crazier dreamers, the
ones who do things in our dimension that
we didn't even consider possible. Like a
child, you have no fear when you dream.
Your ignorance allows you to express
yourself freely and without limits. You
cannot hurt yourself in our world as your
physical self is your own. There are some
possible exceptions, which you'll discover
later.

With one hand we invite all kinds of
living beings into our dimension and yet
when they get here, they are often faced
with resentment or toyed with. You would
call these nightmares, we call it the less
favourable beings in our societies. These
are the rebels.

REBELS

The Rebels live in Militia City, an historic part of Ipa, rich in culture and Bohemian fare.
In Venezelu we've conquered most physical diseases, but the one area still open to attack is disease of the mind and brain. Such diseases are affecting a large number of our people. It afflicts them with the worst attributes of all living beings, and the result is The Rebels. Certain Revolutionaries' would argue that Rebels are not sick, that they have made a pact with negative matter and are on a path to self-destruction and destruction of others and everything in their path. Others would argue that they are sick and that if we cannot succeed to help them back onto the right path, that we at least have a duty to be merciful. It's sad really, that even with so much enlightenment, time can erode just about anything.

THERE ARE FOUR KINDS OF REBEL:

INTOLERANTS

The Intolerants are regressing. Time and influence has led this group to forget what we learned during the awakening. Their lack of self-acceptance and self-awareness results in an arrogance quite potent.

Worse than any egotistical arrogance known on other living planets. At least humans live in ignorance. Venezeluans know the deal, but unfortunately their weakness and the lure for personal gratification, greed and intolerance is too strong.

<u>APOCALYPTICS</u>

Through the disease of fear, Apocalyptics actually believe that our purpose is to leave well alone. That the sooner we make contact with Universe 6 and then 7, the sooner we destroy everything. The Revolution is true to the fundamentals of continuation, so in a sense we're with the Apocalyptics on that point. We just disagree about how to get there. We see it as our purpose in life, they think our purpose is purely to enjoy ourselves and think only of ourselves, on our planet, with no consideration for helping others - to enjoy the wisdom we got from the enlightenment and leave the rest alone. Better said than done when the majority of your clan is high on powerful hallucinogens that turns that fear into the most unsavoury behaviour. Apocalyptics preach a good game, but their actions against dream travellers here on Venezelu is most cruel. They're the worst teasers of them all.

JEAPORDISERS

Jeopardisers are a group of violent bullies, dressed in washed-out CERN uniforms complete with black band around their right arm and a weapons belt so shiny that it would make your eyes blink. They have manifested every dark and violent behaviour that they had previously made peace with, and enhanced it for 'the cause'. Despite being a group, they tend to work alone and spend a lot of time enhancing and modifying their weaponry. So obsessed are they with war weaponry that they often miss out on the actual action of any fights taking place. Don't be fooled though, you wouldn't want to bump into a Jeapordiser on a dark night. They are violent for violence sake and what makes them more reckless and dangerous than any other rebel is that they are unpredictable. The fear nothing, and therefore have nothing to lose.

PIRATES

Pirates are living beings from other planets, coin hungry entrepreneurs working with the Militia to jeopardise our progress so that they can gain advantage and be the first planet to make contact with Universe 6. For them everything is a game, they're ruthless gamblers, motivated by envy and greed. Pirates are not permitted on Venezelu, but many hide and reside within Militia City. They tend to work in small groups and are a dangerous force to be reckoned with, but they are more about business than they are brutes. Everything they do is motivated by zulan and winning. Despite their natures, pirates are very serious about their deal making. They keep to their word on any transactions engaged with, and do not take well to broken deals. As with all groups, sometimes an individual who has lost their way ends up joining the wrong kind of group, the wrong side of the Pendulum. And sometimes it is that one individual who will make the greatest change. In our story, that individual is one Jasper Nomix, look out for him.

As well as planning regular attacks on CERN and MEW5, the Rebels also torment dreamers. Every nightmare you have ever had is actually a disgruntled rebel, from a planet you are visiting within your tectonic plate zone, having some fun at your expense. And the worst of it is, the more lucid and inquisitive the dreamer, the more fun it is for the rebel, for they know that these dreamers feel everything so much more intensely.

6. YOUR UNIVERSE, UNIVERSE 6, and the planets we monitor therein: IZIM, FERNDO & EARTH

Izim is mostly ice, but their living creatures show promise. They work well together as a species, but since Izim is rich in Merjo plants, their connectivity levels are close to zapped. Merjo is an hallucinogen that stunts the mind, and Izimites *love* Merjo.

Ferndo showed promise, but they were recently hit by a massive asteroid, killing off everything except basic Ferndo organisms. So we may have some wait on our hands before the exchange of conscious communication is possible with that lot. That leaves Earth.

When information was shared across Venezelu and the competing planets that Earth was now our best bet, people were more than disappointed. Your planet has idolisers (more on them later), but not many *real* fans. Many feel that most humans aren't very good at seeing what is right in front of them, so what chance do they have of acknowledging their dimensional neighbours?

7. HOW WE TRAVEL

Communicating and travelling are very different things. The first requires a specific set of scientific conditions, the other knows no bounds other than the physical body.

The act of inter-dimensional travel knows no bounds and doesn't involve space crafts or phone boxes (a popular time travelling symbol in most planets within your Universe). Everyone calls it something different, but, with our current focus being on you, one Aurora Black of Earth, let's call it *dreaming*.

Earth travellers, all asleep, behave in the most ridiculous ways when they're in travel mode. I'm not saying us Venezeluan's are morally superior - we're not. Even after our enlightenment we've gone back to primitive ways ourselves, swayed by the great Dualism Pendulum that is 'The Game', or the battle between negative and positive forces as we know it, but we were always good travellers. Well, in the beginning anyway.

We can see you when you roam our Universe. With your Universe being largely unawake, only a small percentage of living things in your Universe can see us in return, even if they don't know what they are witnessing. Earth animals and children can see us very well, but adults, not so much.

Aurora, you were one of the first humans to be aware of your presence on Indigo. You asked locals all sorts of questions in an attempt to 'locate yourself'. These kind of fact finding missions are really only synonymous with 'awakened' ones who, for whatever reason, lose their bearings. When human's ask too many questions, it can make the people in your 'dreams' become rather suspicious of you.

Humans, Izimites, Ferndonites and Burovians (before their complete extinction) have been making inter-dimensional visits for some time – they just have absolutely no awareness that this is what they've been doing.

On Earth, for example, you have many reported sightings of 'ghosts' or 'apparitions. They aren't ghosts - they're your inter-dimensional neighbours. Most of them can see you, so you can imagine their amazement when a largely 'unenlightened' planet gives the impression of being able to see them too. It's pretty cool for them.

Through dreams, life sources travel. They travel to planets in their own and neighbouring Universes and the only reason that they think their dreams are the fabrication of stuff up in their heads is because they have no way of knowing about the existence of inter-dimensional travel to parallel Universes. Think about it, how often have you woken up and told someone "You were in my dream last night. You were there, as was my aunt, my uncle and George Clooney [of Earth]." You think that said person is in your dream because you've either been spending a lot of time with them recently or you've seen them on TV. This isn't the case. For a start, the person you're dreaming about is not that person. It is someone *like* them, they may even look the same or have the same name. A parallel them.

Have you ever noticed that even though the people you know in dreams resemble people you know, there's always something a little different about them? They way they look, the way they act, or the fact that they don't recognise you? The reason you dreamt about them is because, having seen said person in *your* reality, your mind's contact list is activated, and it decides to go looking for them. It makes connections. The reality *triggers* a memory of a place or a person you actually already know of, but don't know you know.

You do know them, because we're all connected, throughout all Universes - we're all from the same origin, that one clump of stuff, and we're linked, in ways you'd never believe.

So how do you find George Clooney of Agatha in the Hosmiat galaxy, having never been there? Well, simply put, you find them in the same way a mobile phone can find another mobile phone across the other side of the world. The number is already programmed into your unconscious. A kind of old-as-the-big-bang phone book. All you have to do is dial, the rest is wireless connectivity.

So how can humans travel to parallel

Universes in their sleep but know nothing about other life-bearing planets in their own Universe?

Living things are restricted by their physical bodies, but not by their minds. Living things on Earth can't visit every planet in their own Universe. The amount of time it would take to get there outnumbers their organic life span. Space is dangerous (though that doesn't stop them exploring their own back yard.) The laws of physics are too different for their bodies and they don't yet have the technology to get them there. But other planets in our own Universe are not an ethereal concept. Just because they aren't currently touchable within our physical dimension, doesn't mean that they don't exist. They are there, and when you dream, you are in a place out with your physical world and out with your conscious world. When you dream, you often don't even know you're dreaming (unless lucid) and that everything you experienced wasn't in your dimension, until you wake up. Just because we are physically trapped within the walls of our own dimension, doesn't mean we can't be free in the mind. With time you'll figure out how to communicate with other planets in your own galaxy and further out still, but I'm not going to tell you right now, and you wouldn't be able to comprehend at present anyway. We didn't, until Universe 4 made contact with us. Even then it took us a long time to decode the answers.

There are downsides to being awake. Once we gained insight, we started seeing living beings everywhere.

Unawakened ones don't know they are travelling. We do though. They appear like ghosts or holograms of themselves. They have a glow around them which show us their lucidity levels. The more lucid the traveller, the more green their glow.

8. DREAMING

Certain humans on Earth have always felt very connected with this process they call dreaming, others do not. The more 'rational' person, firmly founded in 'fact' and what they know about what they know in their small patch of land in an expansive Universe, may explain dreaming as a fabrication of thoughts, memories and events being organised and then re-played into a narrative text. Its purpose? As a way of breaking down information, a brain exercise.

More open-minded people have listed a whole number of explanations for this process, which include titles such as Astral Projection, Lucid Dreaming and Out Of Body Experiences. Knowing what we know, we don't label it any of those things and find it interesting how living beings in your Universe can have so much conviction over things they know nothing of. Ironically, this is one of the best things about your species – the ability to take such a leap of faith with no way of being able to see out with your own dimensionality, your own cage. In short, the awareness of 'something', and human refusal to ignore that 'something', is the key to our eventual success in the Revolution.

To refer to one of your famous Earth human astronomers, Carl Sagan, imagine this: living beings in your Universe are squares. We are the apple that crosses through your dimension. You live in Flatland. We live in Up. When you hear a voice from within, it's us you hear.

Dreaming, for all life beings, takes up a big part of life, and there *is* meaning in that. Not just from a biological point of view, so that proteins or vremtoxins or swygratins can repair whilst you sleep, but so that we can connect. We connect so that we may praise the fundamentals – to create, to play and to survive. But not everyone connects so well. Burovians could do it, but they weren't particularly great at it. And now they're extinct, so it doesn't really matter.

■■

9. THE GAME

Why do we want to make contact? Revolutionaries will tell you that it's because it's in all of our interests to connect with beings in the next dimension, that it's or purpose and that somehow, through making contact and passing on our knowledge to you, we may find some deep rooted answer to all our Universes. They'd also tell you that it's because it will awaken an inter-dimensional consciousness that will lead to a period of happiness for all living beings in your Universe, for as long as they desire it. And finally, that it will allow us to connect with Universe 7 – a further piece in the jigsaw puzzle. We've visited Universe 7 through our dreams, but we can't locate its position. Finding it could mean we delay the big 're-set'. The 're-set' is when all of the floating universal plates come together again to make one big plate – or superuniversal continent. Once we're one, it's only a matter of time before we split up again – and the big bang repeats itself over and over. We know we can't avoid it completely, it's the way things are, like Earth Global Warming. You can't stop it, but if you work together you can slow it down and exist longer. Some humans are great at working together, but others want to destroy things as quickly as possible for financial gain. The irony and short-sightedness of that is this: what use is gold with no planet to spend it on?

The strive for survival is there, it's still part of our programming, and knowing where the pieces lie means an extended game for us. Extra time is granted

Time is the prize and we race against it. Like the beauty of genetics and natural selection, it appears to be our turn to have the advantage.

At first, there will be great peace and excitement at the discovery of your place in the Universes. Over time, a galactic war will break out amongst all the life bearing planets in Universe 6. You'll become aware of one other. And this war will be about trying to be the first to make contact with a planet in Universe 7, if, when and how it decides to cross your path. Game on, again.

If I were a human, and if you'd told me that the meaning of life is that everything is really for the joy of play, connection, competition and survival, I wouldn't have believed you. But look closely at your life Aurora, wherever you are, and you'll see that all the clues are there. To play, to enjoy, to create connections and to continue are the basic fundamental guiding principles of everything across our known Universes.

But not everyone here wants to connect with you. Just because we have awoken doesn't mean we stay compliant. It takes a certain amount of strength, dedication and hard work to stay committed to the Revolution and over time Venezeluans, amongst other living beings in Universe 5, have found their excuses to opt-out. They've negated their new found knowledge and chosen a different path. In a multi-verse which is also based on the principle of opposites and duality, a dark side is always a choice. We call it the Duality Pendulum. The battle between light and dark, Positive and Negative forces. The very building blocks of everything we know and the very game we all play, whether we choose it or not. What we *can* control is *how* we choose to play.

10. DUALITY PENDULUM: NEGATIVE & POSITIVE FORCES

We worked harmoniously for a long time, as harmoniously as the components of a human cell. Each person doing their job. But then, the Dualism Pendulum kicked in again, and parts started going haywire, because that's what happens with all organisms, with all things. A shake up occurs.

Humans are good connectors. They

connect through facets such as love and teamwork and creativity. They build, but much to our bewilderment, they are the quickest to ruin and destroy things they've spent a long time building. There no pause button for some humans. No reflection period. At one point that would have made no sense to us, but their entirely paradoxical nature makes them who they are and it highlights the Duality Pendulum, the game, the battle between Negative and Positive, in its most primitive essence.

11. THE EGO

Humans love to prove stuff all the time. Their planet is 3 billion years old, their modern species but a fraction of that, 200,000 years old at best. Like children, they still fight over possessions. Like animals, they continue to kill and harm one another. They are grounded in the Ego and consumed by Narcissism, and all too often they look outward for answers, not inwards. Every problem on Earth stems from a lack of three fundamentals: knowledge of oneself, acceptance of oneself and, finally, perspective. From here, greater knowledge can be obtained, including the knowledge and acceptance of others, empathy towards others and a new perspective on life - what we know and more importantly, what we don't know. As soon as we looked inwards and realised that our knowledge would always be limited by our dimensionality, it was then that we could actually see outwards, toward a new dimension. It was then that we understood how to look down upon ourselves and see what others see. It took us a long time.

Things like 'faith' and 'money' have been the scapegoat for many a human out of kilter with their inner world. They abuse these things to mask their inner issues, but you'll often see an external manifestation or compensation as a result. For example, there was a particularly damaged individual on planet Freyal who not only stole and cheated his way through life by taking advantage of others, but he used to build enormous golden towers, as high as the clouds. These towers are an example of external manifestation, a visual representation of the equally enormous void or insecurity that this individual felt about themselves. He thought it solidified his success status to the outside world, whereas in fact, he was hanging out his weaknesses on the washing line for everyone to see.

12. FAITH

Your progress is going the way we

expected. Your developmental stages are on track. Your analysis of Earth and your Universe is getting there, and your interpretations on the meaning of life diversely wonderful. Knowing what we know, we respect what you call faith - because you're all right. There is an all-encompassing energy, and we're grateful for it too. It's why we're all here. It gave birth to us, it generates and propels us. It kills us, then re-cycles us so that we can re-awaken, time and time again. We find it strange that Earthlings fight and kill each other over definition. Arguing over what the 'correct' interpretation is of the exact same thing, but then when humans go haywire, some of them really go haywire. Earth is still a very young life-bearing planet. There are many on Earth who make good choices, led from an inner guidance not reliant on reward but pushed by a genuine empathetic and altruistic angle. These are the ones who, no matter what their faith or even faithless, try to keep your balance tipped for good.

■■

So now you know about our Universes, the monitored and competing planets, dream-travel between Universes, the awoken and the sleeping, how we work and how you work. You also know the Revolutionaries' main aim is to be the first to make contact with you - but how does this inter-dimensional communication actually happen?

***

At the moment, travel mode is only one way. We can visit you anytime we sleep and we can see you when you visit us (you are also in sleep mode, just not conscious that you're travelling). The Revolutionaries *want* you to know that you're travelling. They want you to know that a window of communication exists. But before any of this can happen, we need an exchange to occur. We need *you* to know we are here. We need one of you to see us. How do we monitor this? As mentioned, Venezelu has two viable planets in their remit: Izim and Earth. Each one is different, and so we use different language when reaching out to them as individual planets. What *is* consistent, is the way in which we make contact. We use three very similar experiments.

- -

13. HOW WE MAKE CONTACT

The first is one we use to say hello. On Earth, we do this by sending in Feelers.

Feelers are inter-dimensional drone travellers, built to withstand most hazards. They have the ability to travel quickly, really quickly. To the human eye, Feelers look like spiders. We had to make it something recognisable to the human species, something even a child would know. There's a network of electronic pathways and in-ways around your planet, kind of like a web, so spiders seemed quite fitting. We also wanted an image of something that could appear in your bedroom and not seem too out of place, but equally something large enough that would catch you attention. Essentially, Feelers replicate what we do when we travel to see you. They are machines, controlled by us, manipulated by us, and at the mercy of electricity.

It's amazing how many living beings have reported seeing what we call Uni-drones. On Earth, for example, Feelers have been reported millions of times, on web pages, sleep chat forums, medical help sites and so on. What saddens us is the automatic response to things humans can't explain – that there is something physically wrong with the subject at hand. If they're not ridiculed, they are judged, or sent to a specialist or drugged. Others, who know how inexplicable their Feeler visits seem, keep their experiences to themselves, ashamed to feel different from their fellow race. But a change is coming. On Earth, dream research is largely unfunded, so its progress is slow and steady, but it's progress nonetheless. One of the most promising collaborations is the International Association For The Study Of Dreams. It's a society made up of some of the world's most creative thinkers, a large number of individuals whose life work and interests are based on looking beyond, to the not so measureable. Psychiatrists, neurologists, neurosurgeons, psychologists, artists, healers and many others come together to discuss and examine the human brain without restriction. We look at them as pioneers of the evolutionary Revolution of consciousness. Their determination to stay on this path, despite attempts to debunk their investigations is a testament to your species' most admirable traits: curiosity and courage.

Back to Feelers. The aim of them, is to try and visit every single human on Earth, and at regular intervals if they show promise. We're also doing this for two other planets at the same time, so it's a large project. For humans, we use the hypnagogic stage as a window into your mind. This stage is imperative. We can only speak to you through your unconscious mind, so in order for you to make any sense of our visits, you need to be unconscious but slightly conscious at the same time. Asleep but partially awake. It's all stemmed around two things: brain hard-wiring and an open mind. The best subjects are those whose brains have the right chemistry and physical structure to support our visits during hypnagogia. Good eyesight helps too, as a lot of our imagery is related to photon activity in the brain. The dark acts as our canvass. The human eye can see things without light being present via photons, electrical impulses in the brain that act as a scanning or radar devise. They can see images that bounce off of things, a kind of intrinsic laser beam that's motivated by movement or electrical impulses. It's one of those things that's both quite phenomenal and boring to explain. I'll read you some short notes from MEW5 official documentation:-

- DOCUMENT START -
SECURITY CLEARANCE LEVEL 6:
GRANTED
Earth electrical frequencies:
  Human Body = 62-68 MHz
  Human Brain = 72-90 MHz
  Recordings: Vibration, Electricity, Zines, Shadowman, Night Terrors, Chameleon, Spider, Narcolepsy, REM sleep.
Primitive part of the brain:

Spectator – hypnagogic
Participant – dreams
Default Networks / Visual Cortex (Right Hemisphere)
From Alpha to Theta:
Gate opens at frequency 8 infinity, contact with other dimensions possible.
VISIONS:
PHOTONS
ELECTRONS

- Light goes into the eye – focused by cornea & lens onto retina.
- Thin layer of neural tissue at back of the eye has photoreceptors on it.
- These photoreceptors transduce light into neural signals and pass these signals on to the brain.

+ photon – negative electron
DIALOGUE

- Light filling darkness - to do its job, darkness must be present.
- Light is a wave & a particle.
- Smallest unit of light – photon.

When negative electrons jump about, photons have their chance to come out – the gateway is open.
PHOTONS travel about 300,000km p/second
WAVELENGTH – distance between two peaks of a sinusoidal wave

- DOCUMENT END -

Every Feeler has a recording device within it, and so, when we load the Feeler into dream state so it can visit you, we can tell whether or not you can see the Feelers by your reaction to it as your eyes open during hypnagogia.

We had an employee who lost their job because they'd made a mash-up of all of the funniest reactions to Feelers from all three monitored planets, and then posted it anonymously on the Scatternet. The Venezeluan Government, ruled by General Quern, saw it as insensitive to the cause and potential treason as the employee was leaking sensitive information about our best visionaries to other competing planets. The man was sacked and jailed. The Supreme Court, Venezelu's independent ruling body, revoked the sentence, much to General Quern's dismay.

If you can't see the Feeler, which around 94% of Earthlings presently can't, we just make a note of it and re-visit you later in your life. If you can, which around 500 million Earth people can, then we re-format the Feeler to re-visit you and do some fine tuning via electricity so that we can piggy back onto your visions. This doesn't mean that we can see through your eyes 24 hours a day, nor would we want to quite frankly. But it does mean that we can tune in, like a radio, during hypnagogia, so that we can momentarily see what you are seeing. We can also record your dreams.

The only way we can begin any humanoid monitoring programme is through Feelers, who impregnate an electrical charge through the human eye that is then triggered by the activity in your brain during hypnagogia. It has to do with synapses and what happens in your brain as it shuts down for sleep, we basically add a hot wire in there, not physically of course because we cannot exist physically in your dimension, but through the channels of electricity, electrical impulses, particle frequencies and light, things we can attach onto remotely.

So why is an open-mind important? Well, without it, none of this could happen. It's about believing what you see when there is no rational explanation for it, or at least being interested enough to pay more attention and not just write it off as 'dreaming'. We have a *long* list of living beings who can see us during hypnagogia. But that does not mean that every one of those beings pays attention to it. Those who do try to talk about it are often labelled with a sleeping disorder. But many know that there is something more at play. If there really was something wrong with them, why are their visions so predictable? Why does this phenomenon only happen to them whilst they are in this dream-like state? Why does it only last seconds? In our world, an open-mind means Feelers, it means phase-two and eventually, shadow people. And the point of it all? To grant you high level access to our Universe. Ironically, every human with a pineal gland has the ability to join in, but most are too involved in their conscious world to care or comprehend it.

After making contact, after we know you are on board, your dreams will no longer be a random assimilation of places, people or stories. Your dreams will become the channel on which we speak, the paths on which you travel and the road on which the Revolution begins.

14. FREEDOM OF MOVEMENT

When we dream, we have no travel ban. We have no restrictions to free movement. The awakening opened our eyes to the fact that it all belongs to us all, it's just a case of learning how to fly long distance.

That said, we can only send Feelers to neighbouring or touching dimensional planes. Minds are restricted by nothing, nothing at all. Electrical manipulation, gateway jumping and time / space travel isn't always straight forward, but we're learning all the time. Funnily enough, the way we, and Feelers, gateway jump between Universes acts very similarly to the way Nodes of Ranvier operate in nerves of the human body.

Nodes of Ranvier, also known as myelin sheath gaps in a nerve cell, are a clever little 'short-cut' idea. These gaps allow us and Feelers to communicate faster, in the same way that the gaps in the insulating myelin sheaths of myelinated axons where the axonal membrane is exposed to extracellular space. That's why we call it gateway jumping.

When you visit us in dream state, you're more than a little excited by the differing realities, the experience that everything you're doing feels as real as your own reality. It was terrifying for us at first, but we're used to your visits now.

Not everyone on Venezelu likes Earthlings. Imagine having what *appears* to be a really drunk person just turn up whenever they want, uninvited, elated at testing out different laws of physics, trying to sleep with just about everybody they can - basically living out their fantasies in our worlds. That's what less shy dreamers do. It's not their fault, we know this, but they can be annoying.

15. PASSPORT OF THE SOUL
Acknowledgement of the worlds you are visiting grants you, with time, different levels of connectivity with those worlds. After all, it is difficult to gain the upmost benefit from something if you don't even

believe in its existence.

Let me put it this way, hypnosis only works if the subject is willing to believe the suggestion. Dream travel is the same, but here's the difference - it's not the puppet mastery of a hypnotist controlling the wheel and all that you do, where you go and what you see - it's you. In dreamland, each individual controls their own flight path, builds their own package holiday.

It's the inner self that decides the itinerary and it's the mind that takes you there. Yes, there are physical boundaries set by the contours of space and time, but who knows, maybe one day we'll find the tools to allow us to travel further out.

We know how difficult it is, living in your world, to be consumed by everything in it; to be distracted by the day to day business of *living*.

You have an amazing planet, filled with beautiful and interesting things. You are at a stage in your development where progression is accelerating quickly in comparison to your life span.

Your every day is filled with love, emotion, creativity, science, religion, information, music, tenderness, pain, loss, horror, death, life, fear, joy, separation and connection.

Why, when you have all that, and a planet that is good enough to provide you with light and warmth and water and

nourishment would you pay any attention
to your dreams?
Yes, life is hard for many living things,
(humans sometimes forget that they're not
the only living things in their galaxy or
universe) and it is through developing a
sense of good and bad, of pain and joy
that you are able to then distinguish
between the two and take enjoyment when
it comes.

How else would you be able to appreciate
things if you were not aware of an
alternative? How sweet is the human
weekend, for it is only appreciated quite so
because of the human working week that
contrasts it, making you grateful for rest
and time for yourself and your loved ones.
But for some reason, awareness of the
alternative isn't always enough for
humans. They still engage in exposing
themselves and others to the darker side
of their natures, the 'not-so-nice' side.

We believe in acknowledging that darker
side, in utilising it and not being ashamed
of it, but there are beings in other
Universes, much wiser than ours, who'll
never understand man's desire to hurt
others.

We know that life is harsh, fascinating
and beautiful in equal measure. We know
that from the moment that alarm clock
goes off, so too does your day and
everything in it. Like a flurry of sounds,

smells, tastes, feelings and conscious thought.

Unconscious sleep is a welcome resting time for the conscious soul. But it is those who cannot rest, who do not want to rest, who are in a hurry to experience everything and experience it now - these are the ones who live a parallel existence.

Those that do not rest, who listen and watch, after all others have switched off, they are the ones who, in the end, will see behind the curtain. They are the ones who will make our Revolution begin.

At one time, humans were very good at spotting and interpreting the signs, but as their physical world accelerated into a technological era, they drifted further and further away from their subconscious mind, from their internal voice and the treasures therein.

So many Earth tribes, such as the Aborigines and American Indians, are losing that connection with younger generations who are lured by the beating drum of modern day. It's a drum that is so alluring. It's a drum that connects humans to each other, and I can understand its appeal. However, the deeper humans go into that day-to-day search for acceptance, the further they float from their own internal drum, the only one that guides them in this world and the next.

Awareness and acceptance of themselves – these are the paths to answers. And here's the funny thing. In taking this step 'back' into the self, rejecting the lures of modernity, we actually managed to move forward technologically and all the rest. It was the strangest awakening ever. By having this knowledge, we gained perspective, we learned about the joys of play.

Things don't always work out the way we want them to though, this is also true in Universe 5. And that's where the agencies step in. MEW5 and CERN are there to monitor and protect every living thing engaged in the Revolution, or at least try their best to. Oh wait, is that the time? I have to go Aurora, the others will be wondering where I am. Speak to you soon.

END OF TRANSCRIPT

– THE AUDIO FILES –

GISELLA STAR, PLANET VENEZELU

ABOUT THE AUTHOR

Hypnagogia is a real night-time phenomenon. The main character's journey starts with an unexpected night-time visitor. This experience happened to me whilst on a work trip in Rome, aged 22. How I describe the encounter in the book is exactly how it happened.

Unable to logically explain the strange dreams and twilight apparitions that followed, I felt compelled to write this book in an attempt to express it.

The World Within is a culmination of some actual life events and real dreams that followed after that first hypnagogic experience, mixed with a heavy dose of fiction, science-fiction and pure imagination.

I am 38 years old and currently working as a venue manager for an indoor archery centre. The World Within is my first novel.

In 2002 I graduated from Edinburgh University with a MA Hons in European Union Studies and European Languages. I've worked everywhere from Starbucks to No.10 Downing Street.

In 2009 I started my own self-funded community production company, Stay Curious Productions. Working with artists in Glasgow, I helped bring their films, photography and music to a wider audience. I produced 14 successful projects in 7 years.

30292505R00184

Printed in Poland
by Amazon Fulfillment
Poland Sp. z o.o., Wrocław